Deadly Lies

ANGUS BRODIE AND MIKAELA FORSYTHE MURDER MYSTERY
BOOK TEN

CARLA SIMPSON

OLIVERHEBERBOOKS

Prologue

EARLY DECEMBER, 1891, OXFORD STREET, LONDON

HE WATCHED...

From the shadows as streetlights slowly glowed to life along the sidewalk, mist wrapping around the golden light...

As icy rain began to fall...

As a young woman crossed the street and entered the print shop.

He watched. Then crossed the street, and waited.

There was no sense of time, only the waiting.

Then, the sound of the merchant's bell above the door, a printer by trade. And she was there, a package tucked under her arm as she paused and drew the collar of her jacket up against the damp and cold, then turned.

The waiting was over. He saw the surprise in her soft blue eyes, a question she might have asked.

Then, after all this time, it was quickly done.

He gently lowered her to the sidewalk, her expression startled, her lips moving as the last breath left her, the contents of the package scattered to the pavement stones. Ink on the invitations ran like blood.

"Forgive me," he whispered as he laid a single red rose across her body, then disappeared into the night.

One

I HAD BEEN STRUGGLING over the next chapter in my latest Emma Fortescue novel since Brodie and I had returned from Scotland.

In my two previous novels, she had ventured into the nasty business of murder, stumbling upon one during her adventure in Budapest, then being drawn into another one by a character of dubious reputation who coincidentally had a dark gaze, was most proficient with a firearm, and had rescued her from a very dangerous situation.

True to her nature, Emma Fortescue, promptly left Budapest when the murderer was caught, only to find the man of *dubious character* on the same train as it barreled toward Paris.

I had ended that particular novel there. Let the reader think what they might, with Emma's next adventure to be taken up in the book I was presently laboring over at the behest of my publisher, James Warren.

That previous novel had, he had informed me, quite literally flown off the sales table at Hatchards. It did seem that my readers had an appetite not only for adventure, but murder with a little romantic mystery thrown in.

"We are receiving letters daily," he had informed me in the

weeks after it was released. "Readers are demanding to know when the next book will be released and who, precisely, the dark-eyed man of questionable reputation might be."

And then his most recent reminder when we last met.

"You simply must have the book ready before Linnie and I leave for the south of France after the wedding."

I stared at the blank page in my typewriting machine. Said wedding was three weeks away and they were planning to leave the month following for an extended stay in France, then possibly to Italy.

For whatever the reason, the words did not magically appear on the page before me. I did wonder if Mr. Dickens had the same issue when starting a new book.

Of course, it could have been due to the recent change, said the *dark-eyed character* who had finally taken up residence for the most part at the townhouse after I pointed out that it was quite acceptable for people who were married to live together.

The winning aspect for my argument had actually been two things. Brodie was particularly fond of my housekeeper's cooking skills, which I had few of—some would argue none—and which I made absolutely no claim to.

And then there was the shower compartment in the bathing room at the town house, which was far more convenient than the one down the hall from the office, and it did have other... *attributes* which I appreciated as well.

Of course, he insisted that it was Mrs. Ryan's skill in the kitchen and the promise of her Irish stew that had lured him back to the town house the previous evening after another long day at the office on the Strand.

A handful of inquiries awaited our return from Scotland, either by way of a note sent round, or through Mr. Cavendish, who always had his 'ear to the street' when it came to such things. It did seem there was no end to crimes across the East End and even into greater London.

Brodie had been following up on the potential cases that

included a missing payroll at a local mill, along with another from a man, somewhat older, who wanted him to make inquiries about his much-younger wife, whom he suspected was having an affair.

A third potential case had come from an acquaintance of my great-aunt, Lady Eugenia Davenport, a most dire situation. Little Bitsy had gone missing.

Bitsy? I didn't ask.

"She provided his jumper along with his favorite toys when I met with her," Brodie had exclaimed the previous evening. "Along with the last meal on the finest bone china before he disappeared."

He was quite beside himself, and only another dram of whisky eventually smoothed the edges of that temper. Somewhat.

"A dog!" he had then exclaimed. "A black pug, that eats off of fine dishes and has his own servant. The woman talks on and on about the animal as if it's a child."

"I would imagine that she's quite lonely, since Sir Lionel's death," I ventured in an attempt to soothe the raging beast.

"It's verra possible she talked him to death."

"What of the man with the much younger wife. A few years younger? And there is difficulty between them?"

"He's over seventy, and she is quite a bit younger." he replied. "It seems that the woman married him for his money, and the affair is not the first. Hers, that is. Apparently, the list is long."

"Oh my," I replied.

"I suppose ye have no objections to such things, with yer modern woman's ways."

I did sense a bit of temper.

"It would be interesting to know how the husband might have carried on in his younger years," I pointed out, merely for the sake of argument, which brought a glare.

"Ye approve such behavior?"

"I'm merely pointing out that in this case, what's good for the gander is good for the goose."

"What the devil is that supposed to mean?"

I was very possibly poking the bear, but he was so very attractive when he was glaring at me.

"The usual saying is, 'What is good for the goose is good for the gander.' However, this is a bit turned around. It does seem that perhaps he has gotten some of his own, and the shoe does not fit particularly well. You might remember that."

"She warned me."

"Warned?" I replied. "About what?"

"Her ladyship warned me that ye can have a quarrelsome spirit and an odd way of looking at things."

So, my great-aunt had a hand in this.

"Not at all," I replied. I have simply come to believe that what is acceptable for a man, should also be acceptable for a woman—travel, their own money so that they don't have to go begging to their husband, and the vote."

"Vote?"

"I consider myself as well informed on any of the issues confronting Britain as any man, more so than many," I pointed out.

"Her ladyship and yerself are the exceptions," he replied. "Ye do not take yerself off worrying whether or not Bitsy has a jumper to wear when it gets cold."

I did suppose that was a compliment. While I was contemplating that he was plotting his escape from the conversation at hand.

"Is that Mrs. Ryan's fine cooking I smell?" he asked.

I let him escape for the time being.

Her roast chicken had 'soothed the beast' somewhat, as they say, and we had retired afterward to the parlor, where we shared a dram of whisky.

After complimenting Mrs. Ryan on the most excellent supper, he had retreated into himself, sitting before the fire at the hearth unusually quiet, as he had since our return from Scotland. At least he was not of a mood to return to our previous conversation, which he could not win.

The thought *'brooding Scot'* came to mind. I had discovered they were inclined to brood over just about anything—the weather, which no one could control in spite of a fist shaken toward the darkened sky as a downpour set in. It was usually Mr. Hutton, who managed Old Lodge for my great-aunt, with complaints about his rheumatism as he set off through the snow from the main lodge to the distillery.

Or it might have been an affront over some past issue—Munro, his good friend was inclined to this. Or possibly someone's late arrival for an appointment—usually mine, however always with a good excuse.

Yet, this was different and I knew the cause. Knowing him quite well and not one to pry, I let him have his thoughts. Eventually he had shared them.

It was about Rory, a young boy caught in the middle of that previous murder case.

Brodie and the boy's mother had been together for a time, years before, and he had reason to think the boy might be his own son.

He had spoken of Rory, how fine he was, how smart and good, in spite of everything he'd been through. How proud he was of him, as any father might be, and he had been spending a good deal of time with the boy.

"There's somethin' I want to tell ye," he finally said.

I listened as he explained, even as I felt a tightness at my throat, knowing what the boy meant to him.

It seemed that Rory had a distinctive mark on the back of his left shoulder. He had been born with it, and it was identical to a mark his father had.

"It would seem that Stephen Matthews was his father."

I could only imagine the effort it took to say those words, knowing how he had hoped that Rory might be his son.

I took a deep breath against the pain I felt for him, and saw it in the expression on his face. I knew about loss.

"When our great-aunt took Linnie and me to live with her, I

couldn't see how an old woman who had never had children and had never married could possibly know anything about what a family was," I began, drawing on those old memories as he took another swallow of whisky.

"I was angry, and hurt, and scared, I suppose," I added. "She would have none of it, of course."

I thought I caught the slightest softening of his mouth surrounded by that dark beard at the mention of my great-aunt and her stubborn determination. He was quite fond of her.

"Of course," he replied.

"During a particularly difficult period, we had an argument," I continued to explain. "I told her that she had no right to order me to study harder or inquire where I had taken myself off to, that she was not my family."

At the time, I had taken myself out the second story window at Sussex Square and was gone for hours.

"I canna imagine," Brodie sarcastically replied. He could, of course, as he knew me quite well.

I then told him that my great-aunt had not sent the servants out to search all of Sussex Square. Instead, she had left me to myself, even as a storm set in. Cold to the bone, soaked through, I had eventually sneaked back into my room the same way I had left, and lay there cold and hungry through the night, certain her wrath would come crashing down on me the next day.

"The next morning, she explained to me how she was raised, for the most part by her governess," I told him then. "Her father was often away on some matter or another, and quite simply didn't know what to do with a headstrong young girl.

"She considered her governess to be her family, the person who was always there to guide and love her, patched up her scraped knees, cared for her when she had a fever, summoned the physician when she fell from a tree and broke her arm."

I caught his slightly bemused expression. It had been said more than once that my great-aunt and I were very much alike.

"The woman quite bravely stood between her and her father

over some matter when he thought she needed to be reprimand-ed," I continued.

"There is a point to this?" Brodie had replied.

I had joined him before the hearth.

"She explained to me that family is not always those who share one's blood, but those who love and care about you, share your life, the good moments, the difficult ones. Those who are there for you, as she was for Linnie and me.

"I've seen how you care for Rory, and his affection in return," I told him then. "I think that it does not matter who sired him. He will need a strong, good man to be there for him, to guide him, to love him... to be a part of his family, and I know that Mrs. Matthews feels the same."

His expression was sad, wounded, and should have been a warning. Or possibly I didn't want to see it, so badly had I wanted to ease his pain.

He grabbed me as if he wanted to shake me, anger there along with the pain, then crushed me against him with a strength that drove the air from my lungs.

There were no words. There was no need for them as I wrapped my arms around him and took the anger and the pain because I understood all of it.

"Mikaela...!"

The sound of my name, as if it came from some place deep inside him.

"I'm here," I whispered.

Two

THE NEXT MORNING

BRODIE HAD LEFT EARLIER for the office on the Strand, while I chose to remain at Mayfair, staring at the blank page in my typewriter. Several more pieces of paper wadded up in my attempts at the first chapter in that new book lay scattered about the carpet under my desk.

I looked up to find Mrs. Ryan glancing about the sea of crumpled paper, a bemused expression on her face, and a tray with yet another pot of coffee—the third that morning—held before her. It wasn't as if she hadn't seen it all before.

"Going well, is it?" she asked.

She had been my housekeeper for several years, and in my great-aunt's employ before that. She was Irish through and through, most usually with a twinkle in her eyes, dimmed two years before at the tragic murder of her daughter.

Brodie and I had eventually solved that first case together after the failures of the police. And as I had told him the night before, family wasn't always defined by blood relations.

From my own experience I believed that it was defined by the people in one's life who mattered. One of the persons who mattered now stood looking at me with a curious expression.

"It does seem as if we will have enough paper to start the afternoon fire," she commented as she set the tray on the desk.

And that other Irish quality, the comment with just a bit of humor as well as a tart opinion. I was quite use to it. She did, after all, have red hair, although a bit lighter with the hint of gray.

"And the morning paper as well," she added as she removed it from the tray and handed it to me. "Along with the morning post."

She poured more coffee for me as I opened the paper.

"I will be going to the grocers today," she announced as she began picking up wadded pieces of paper.

"Is there anything special that Mr. Brodie might like for supper tonight?"

I didn't hear the last part as I set my cup back down rather sharply. It clattered on the saucer.

"Is here something wrong?"

I stared at the glaring headline at the front page, then scanned the accompanying article by Theodolphus Burke of the Times.

I was somewhat acquainted with Mr. Burke. In spite of the fact that he had a habit of sensationalizing a story for his own glorification, he had been with the Times for several years and enjoyed a certain notoriety as well as a considerable readership. I ignored his disdain over my novels.

He had written extensively about the murder of Rory's mother, in that previous inquiry case. He had also written extensively about the Whitechapel murders in the East End of London a handful of years earlier, the killer never found.

Now, I stared at his article with the glaring headline:

HAS THE WHITECHAPEL KILLER RETURNED?

A young woman had been found stabbed to death. Accompanying that horrific headline was the victim's name that seemed to leap off the page at me.

The body of Miss Charlotte Mallory of Knightsbridge was found outside an establishment near Oxford Street...

"Is something wrong, miss?" Mrs. Ryan inquired.

I collected myself and quickly folded the paper, not wanting to cause her any distress. We had eventually found the one responsible for her daughter's murder, but I was mindful that the pain of such things never went away.

I tucked the paper into my bag that usually held my writing pen, notebook, and the revolver Brodie had given me.

It wasn't that she wouldn't find out about it. The London gossip mill was most proficient in spreading stories, and the ones about the Whitechapel murders had kept the city filled with terror and almost morbid curiosity years before. Mr. Burke had built quite a reputation on those unsolved murders.

"I will be going to the office. I will need a driver," I decided as I crossed the parlor, then ran up the stairs to change my clothes. Emma Fortescue would have to wait!

THE STRAND

"I read about it earlier," Brodie commented as I paced the office. "My thought is that it's not the same as the Whitechapel murders. Those victims were all found in the East End, and known to solicit customers from time to time. This young woman... do ye know her?" He looked at me with a thoughtful expression.

"In a manner of speaking. She gave Lily music lessons after Mr. Finch was dismissed."

That had not been entirely unexpected after the somewhat colorful performance Lily gave at Sussex Square with a bawdy song she'd learned on the street. I had commended her on her skill at the piano—most creative.

"Music?" Brodie replied.

I nodded. "After that previous performance at Sussex Square, it was determined that perhaps he was not best suited for her. It was thought that someone else might be better suited. Charlotte

Mallory was Lily's instructor for the past several months. They got along quite well. This will go very hard for Lily."

Lily had once lived in a brothel in Edinburgh. We met during a previous case. Point of fact, she had saved my life.

She was street-wise beyond her years and might well have spent the rest of her life in that brothel rather than merely as the young lady's maid there when Brodie and I encountered her.

I was quite fond of her and couldn't bear the thought that was all her life would be. I had spoken with Brodie on the matter since it affected us both. In the end, I had brought her to London as my ward with the promise of an education other than the street education she had acquired, along with the opportunity for a better life.

She was intelligent, had a mind for numbers and codes, and had also proven herself quite accomplished with clues we uncovered in a previous case.

Our inquiries often took both Brodie and me far afield at odd times of the day or night, and it was therefore decided that it was best for her to live with my great-aunt. Or I should say that my great-aunt decided it.

Not that the arrangement was without some concern, as my great-aunt was eighty-six years old, somewhat of a free spirit, as my friend Templeton described her, and at the time was planning to go on safari to Africa, a trip that eventually included Lily and myself.

We were gone for almost four months. During that time, I took the place of her academic tutor, more or less, as academics were never a favorite pastime. But we both survived the arrangement.

Charlotte Mallory had been her music teacher before our departure some months before, and Lily had recently resumed those lessons with her.

She was only a handful of years older than Lily, and they were soon thick as thieves, as the saying goes, with a friendship that went beyond student and teacher. Miss Mallory hadn't blinked an eye when Lily acquainted her with that particular song learned on the streets. It had reduced Charlotte Mallory to laughter until she could hardly breathe.

And now? I could only imagine that the news would be devastating for Lily.

"Will you see what you can learn about it from the police?" I asked.

Brodie still had a close relationship with a handful of officers at the MET and relied on them from time to time as needed, along with his old friend Mr. Conner, who was now retired but shared drinks with some of his fellow police at the local taverns. And then there was Mr. Dooley, who had recently been promoted to inspector.

"I'll see what can be learned. Hopefully the lads have more information than Mr. Burke has been able to learn."

As I knew all too well from past encounters with Mr. Burke, it was not unusual for him to hold back information, to be written about in subsequent articles, hooking the readership in like fish.

"What about Lily?" he asked.

"I need to go to Sussex Square...she needs to be told," I replied. "She will have questions. I hope she hasn't read about it in the daily. Mr. Burke is particularly known for his somewhat graphic and gruesome details. I wouldn't want her to read about it first."

"I'll put a telephone call in to Mr. Dooley." That dark gaze met mine. "Then I'll go with ye. No need to do this alone."

"Thank you." I appreciated that very much. Both were Scots and somewhat given to shutting things away inside until they festered, much like a boil. He had a way with her, an under-standing that came from a shared background, even though he had shared more than once that we were quite alike.

"She is a lot like ye, even though there's no blood between ye. She has a temper, and will want justice for her friend."

There it was. I had no idea where he came by that.

I put through a telephone call to Sussex Square. It was picked up by the house steward. I asked to speak with my great-aunt and explained what we had learned.

"Oh, dear," she replied. "Yes, of course. I do understand. Mr. Symons has not yet brought in the daily. I will see that she is not aware until your arrival. Such dreadful business."

～

We arrived at Sussex Square, no more than an hour later. Mr. Symons, my great-aunt's head footman greeting us at the door.

"Good day, Mr. Brodie, Miss Mikaela," he greeted us, the use of my name a habit of many years, no disrespect toward Brodie. He leaned slightly closer.

"I intercepted the daily at her ladyship's request," he assured us. "Miss Lily finished her writing exercise some time ago, and is presently in the sword room, practicing, I believe."

It was then my great-aunt swept into the main entrance to greet us. I say *swept,* as that was usually the way of titled ladies. She had re-defined the word over the years. It was more of a marching, take-charge gait, an authoritative style that immediately put anyone in a room on notice that here was a woman of title, presence, and no small amount of power. I adored her.

"Mr. Symons has informed you?" she inquired. I nodded.

"The sword room is possibly not the preferable location to deliver such news. She will be most upset. She and Charlotte Mallory did get on so well, more like dear friends than instructor and pupil."

Lily was the sort who kept things inside herself, I had learned. The bravado and stubbornness were often a shield she kept firmly in place around her emotions. It was something I understood.

I handed Mr. Symons my umbrella and hat. When I would have headed for the staircase that led to the second floor and the sword room, Brodie laid a hand on my arm.

"I'll see to the lass. I wouldna want her to take yer head off in a

15

fit of temper when she hears the news. I prefer it right where it is on yer shoulders."

When I would have protested, he shook his head.

"It would be best if it comes from someone who has experienced this sort of thing before."

We waited in the solar where my great-aunt had previously installed a miniature jungle in anticipation of the safari we had recently embarked upon.

The plants were still there and added an exotic atmosphere to the large room that opened out onto the pavilion in warmer weather.

There was also the Egyptian sailboat with sail unfurled, as part of the replica of the Nile River, merely a shallow stream of water that flowed through the solar, another of my great-aunt's eccentricities as the gossip pages often reported. Everyone who had been invited to that particular celebration had marveled at it.

Not that she gave a fig what other people thought.

"Whisky, my dear?" she inquired now as we sat at a nearby table.

I nodded. I had a feeling we were all going to need it, once Brodie was able to persuade Lily to join us. And it was after the noon hour, after all.

I was encouraged as an hour passed and there was no clamor from the second floor, or wild dash of servants fleeing for their lives, including Mr. Munro, who had appeared with said whisky.

He and Brodie came from the streets to London together as boys, both orphans who escaped the poverty of Edinburgh. Munro was now manager of my great-aunt's estates, that included Old Lodge in the north of Scotland and her properties in France, as well as Sussex Square.

"It will be all right, miss," he assured me as I held out my glass for a second portion.

I did hope he was right. I had just taken a sip when Brodie and Lily appeared at the entrance to the solar. There was no sight of blood; Brodie's hand lay on Lily's arm where it looped through his.

It did seem as if there might have been a few tears when Brodie told her of Charlotte Mallory's death. Yet the gaze that met mine now, a very striking shade of blue, was quite composed.

We remained at Sussex Square, and then took supper later that evening with my great-aunt and Lily, who remained unusually quiet rather than her usual boisterous comments over something or another.

After supper she asked to read the newspaper with the article Theodolphus Burke had written.

My first instinct was to protect her from that. But my great-aunt pointed out the obvious, that it would be all over London and Lily would see it sooner or later, or undoubtedly hear some overly dramatic and colorful version of it. Brodie was in agreement.

She frowned as she read the article, there was then the obvious question from those glaring headlines.

"Could it be the same man who killed those other women?"

"It is always possible," Brodie replied. "Or it might be someone entirely different."

"The article says that the police will be investigating. If it is the same one, they have not been successful in the past."

For a girl who once could only read numbers in the amounts the prostitutes charged their customers and a handful of words when they gave her a note, her reading skills had substantially improved since arriving in London.

It occurred to me that Lily had changed in other ways as well, that included the sad news that day. A little bit more of the young girl was gone, replaced with that sad, solemn expression.

"Aye," Brodie replied. "A most difficult case. Perhaps this one will be quickly resolved."

Lily nodded as she stared down at that glaring headline of the newspaper on her lap with a frown. Then she looked up, the expression on her face now quite determined.

"I want to hire you to find who did this."

To say there was a moment of surprised silence is an understatement. I looked over at Brodie. Of all the things I might have imagined when she learned about Charlotte Mallory's murder, this was not it.

Hire us to find the young woman's murderer?

"A marvelous idea!" my great-aunt announced, lifting her whisky glass. "You will begin immediately of course."

Three

THE NEXT MORNING...

"YOU DON'T APPROVE," I commented as our driver arrived at the office on the Strand and we stepped down from the cab.

The building did look substantially improved, with better signage, the sagging wood steps near the alcove replaced, and fresh paint over the old stones on the walls.

I did wonder if Brodie had made any inquiries about another location for the office. He was convinced that he would not be able to afford the rents for the new improvements once the new owner contacted him.

He had been unusually quiet, even for Brodie, since supper the previous evening with Lily's announcement and my great-aunt's enthusiastic support.

"It appears that it doesna matter whether I approve or disapprove. The decision has been made by Lily, yerself, and her ladyship," he snapped somewhat peevishly as Rupert the hound emerged from the alcove to greet me, followed by the keeper of the alcove, who rolled out on his platform.

Mr. Cavendish had lost both legs in an accident years before, and the platform provided a means for him to get around.

I chose to ignore Brodie for the moment as Rupert nudged

my hand, looking for his usual morning treat compliments of Mrs. Ryan, usually sponge cake or possibly a honeyed biscuit. I handed Mr. Cavendish the wrapped package that included a piece for Rupert.

"You have a new platform," I complimented him. The old one was a precarious contraption. It was held together with strips of leather, and few random bolts that frequently loosened and disappeared on his forays about the Strand. He did seem to prefer high speeds, diving in and about carriages and coaches on the street.

"The old one was a bit worn. I was informed this one is more reliable, made of good stout hickory and stained with paint against the weather with metal bolts that lock to hold the bloody thing together." His eyes sparkled. "It corners like the devil, full speed."

Oh, dear.

"Most impressive," I complimented him.

I suspected who might have suggested the new platform. He did seem to have a stalwart friend in Miss Effie at the public house down the Strand, and she had commented more than once that the old platform would be the death of him. It did seem of late that their friendship might have progressed.

It also appeared that Miss Effie might have suggested the woolen trousers that had replaced the previous ones that were more a collection of patches, badly stained with whatever came up off the street as he paddled about. And there was a homespun shirt under the woolen vest. Altogether, he looked quite dapper. I complimented him.

"Mr. Dooley is up in the office," he informed us. "He arrived some time ago in the matter of inquiries you made?"

Indeed, I thought with a glance over at Brodie. He had been adamantly opposed to taking on the case of Charlotte Mallory's murder. Or rather *silently* adamant against it after supper the previous evening with Lily and my great-aunt. And then still silent in the matter this morning, except for that one comment.

I had decided to let him grumble a bit over it. As I knew only too well, he would eventually voice his objections and then come around to my way of thinking with a little persuasion.

"Best go up and see what he knows about the matter," he replied now.

I caught the look in that dark gaze, the glower there that only made him more handsome. Nothing like a brooding, cantankerous Scot, as he waited for me at the bottom of the stairs.

"Have ye exchanged all yer morning pleasantries?"

"Almost," I replied as I glanced over at Mr. Cavendish. We were both quite accustomed to Brodie's grumblings. I called to the hound as I joined Brodie on the stairs.

"I made a call to Dooley this morning while ye were still upstairs getting ready for the day," he explained. "It canna hurt to ask a few questions."

Brodie had worked with Mr. Dooley during his previous time with the MET, and a bond of mutual trust and respect remained between them.

After Brodie left the MET, Mr. Dooley had been a source for information from time to time. He had recently been promoted from constable to inspector after several years' service, but remained a stalwart friend and confidant.

He had let himself into the office and, good man that he was, had a pot of coffee simmering at the stove on this cold morning that had a hint of snow in the air.

"Nasty business, murder of that poor young woman," Mr. Dooley commented as he sat across from Brodie at the desk while I removed my hat and coat.

"Music teacher, she was?" Then with a look over at me.

"She provided lessons for my ward," I explained. "They became good friends as well."

He nodded. "And more's the pity, she had just left the print office where she apparently had picked up invitations. It seems that she was to be wed in a few weeks."

"What else can you tell us?" I inquired while Brodie listened from across the desk, coffee cup in hand.

"The fiancé's name is Daniel Eddington, according to the invitations that were found on the sidewalk, and the information the printer was able to provide."

"What about her family?" I then asked. "I understand they live in Knightsbridge."

He nodded with a look over at Brodie. "Her father is Edward Mallory, a barrister of some reputation. You might remember him from before with the MET."

Some reputation? I did wonder what that might mean.

Brodie nodded. "I gave evidence in two cases brought before the magistrate regarding persons he represented."

Mr. Dooley nodded. "Made quite a name for himself over the years. The fiancé is a member of his office. I would suppose that is how he and the young woman met."

"Have you spoken with the family?" Brodie inquired.

Mr. Dooley nodded. "Contact was made the night of the murder, and then yesterday as well, for any information the family might have. Sad affair, such a pretty young thing."

"What about any connection to the Whitechapel murders?" I asked, since Mr. Burke had asked the same question in his article for the daily.

Mr. Dooley shook his head. "I pulled up the old files. There are most definitely differences between the two. Miss Mallory was from a well-placed family, the murder took place in the West End, and there was no..." He hesitated before continuing.

"It's quite all right, Mr. Dooley. I read the articles about the Whitechapel murders when they took place."

He nodded, still a bit uncomfortable. "There was just the one wound with a sharp instrument, most likely a knife, and there was no sign of any other disturbance of the body."

I knew quite well what he spoke of. According to the articles at the time of those other murders that had terrified all of London, two of the women had been sexually assaulted before they were murdered.

However, whether or not it had been committed by the

murderer was never established, as both women had worked as prostitutes.

"What information was the printer able to provide?" Brodie asked. "Did the man see anything?"

Mr. Dooley shook his head. "He only became aware of what had happened when a couple, a man and woman, found the poor thing, apparently right afterward, and put up the alarm. He wasn't able to provide any information other than Miss Mallory had just left his shop."

Still...

I knew how the police worked from that first inquiry case with Brodie. Admittedly it was possible that their methods had improved since. They were under a new interim chief inspector after Mr. Abberline was persuaded to take an '*extended departure.*' Yet, it was also possible, as I knew only too well, that they had simply not asked the right questions.

"Might it be possible to see the body before the family makes their arrangements?" I then asked.

Mr. Dooley's gaze narrowed. "I might be able to make arrangements at the Yard where the young woman's body was taken."

"Are you making inquiries then on behalf of the family, or perhaps the young woman's fiancé?" he asked. "I'd not want to read about it in one of your books, Miss Forsythe. No offense, mind you. But it could bring about undue attention and questions."

"Not at all, Mr. Dooley," I assured him. However, I didn't reveal who our new '*client*' was.

"Have the police spoken with the family?" Brodie asked.

"Not as yet, but in due time, out of respect for their loss," Mr. Dooley replied.

"Perhaps we could assist in that," I suggested and received a dark look from Brodie.

"Unofficially?" he asked. "The MET is short-staffed, as several lads left after the difficulty with Abberline. It seems some of them may have willingly 'overlooked' some matters in favor of the man. The new fellow is said to be 'cleaning things up,' as they say."

"Perhaps as consultants," I then suggested. "The old saying, '*many hands make light work.*' And it might be helpful as well to speak with Mr. Eddington. Perhaps he can provide some insight into the matter."

Mr. Dooley looked over at Brodie.

"There would be only a small compensation in it, if any at all. But I suppose I could call it that if there should be questions. We have more than our share of crimes to follow, and you do have experience with such things. You would have to agree to share anything you learn with me."

"Of course," I replied. I chose to ignore Brodie for the moment. I could imagine what he was thinking.

Mr. Dooley nodded. "Well and good, then. I'll make arrangements for you as 'consultants,' and send word when it's been arranged. When would you like to begin?"

"The sooner the better," I replied, keeping my thoughts to myself as we had already started.

"Consultants, is it?" Brodie asked after Mr. Dooley left.

"It was all I could think of in the moment, so that we might not encounter obstacles. Particularly where the family is concerned."

"Yer determined to humor the girl in this, then."

"Humor her?" I replied with some pique. "Hardly. You know her as well as I. Do you think she will be content to simply sit idly by while the police go about their business?

"She was quite fond of Charlotte Mallory. If we were to simply coddle her or placate her with excuses, I would not put it past her to simply take herself off and make her own inquiries. She hardly has the experience for that, particularly here in London. She doesn't know her way about here, and there is the other part of it," I added.

"Such as?"

"She is part of our family now. The least that we can do is make a few inquiries of our own on her behalf. There is the fact that she has hired us." I threw that in for good measure. "And, since you are acquainted with Sir Mallory, it would make it easier for us to call on them."

That dark gaze bore into mine.

"Three against one," he shook his head. "And all of ye are women. I know well enough that ye will go on yer way whether I say yea or no."

I smiled to myself. He did know me quite well.

"*Consultants* it is," I declared of our new titles. "Once Mr. Dooley has made arrangements, we need to visit the yard," I plunged on ahead before he could object.

"It might be helpful to call on the printer as well," I said now, from in front of the chalkboard where I had made a few notes.

"Perhaps there was something Charlotte might have said, perhaps she had seen someone on her way to the shop... I wonder if Mr. Brimley might be available to assist," I added of the chemist who had been invaluable in past inquiries.

To some people he might have been a bit off-putting, with his experiments and body parts in jars and choosing to serve the people of the East End rather than taking up a medical practice in a better part of London. But I had found him to be quite brilliant and an excellent source of valuable information.

"He does have a great deal more experience with bodies and wounds. He might be able to tell us something more than the police surgeon. And we will need the name of the constables who were the first to arrive."

Mr. Dooley called the office later that day and informed us that he'd made arrangements for us to visit the police holding-facility at Scotland Yard.

Brodie reminded him that we would also like to speak with the constables who were called to the print shop when Charlotte Mallory's body was found. Mr. Dooley said that he would have the man stop by the office the following morning before he went onto his shift.

I had contacted Mr. Brimley, the chemist, as we waited to hear from Mr. Dooley.

"*Another body is it, Miss Forsythe,*" he commented. "*I suspected that it had been too long since our last adventure into the crime of murder. Of course I will meet you. The murder of the young woman, you say? Most exciting.*"

Even though it was later in the day, we agreed to meet at the old Scotland Yard that afternoon, arrangements having been made by the family to have Charlotte's body removed to a private location the following day.

"I know you have been acquainted with Mr. Brimley for some time," I commented after we found a cab and gave the driver the location of the old Scotland Yard. "But it has occurred to me that he does seem to acquire great satisfaction in viewing dead bodies."

"Just as ye seem to have a penchant for adventures, no matter where it takes ye?" Brodie suggested. "Museums, hiding out in coffins, trapped in the old city beneath Edinburgh, or perhaps the Greek Isles?"

I did see his point, although I wouldn't give him the satisfaction of knowing that I had a distinct dislike for rummaging around in musty museums or coffins, and I had to admit that I was concerned that I might not make it out of the caverns below Edinburgh alive. As for the Greek Isles?

That was an adventure all by itself. I was eighteen years old at the time, off on my first adventure. My guide had suggested that I might like to visit Crete rather than trudging along with my travel group to more ruins. And...

It was the '*and*' part—a dark-eyed stranger with that thick mane of hair, older than the guide, who was quite enthusiastic about leading me astray.

I could have pointed all of that out, including the part that he was obviously to blame for. However, that was another adventure to come, or several of them as it had turned out. And now...

We arrived at the old Scotland Yard with what was referred to as the 'holding rooms' on the ground floor at the back of the building where there was access for the police vans to drop off the latest collection of bodies. It was just across from the 'yard,' where horses were still kept in spite of the new motorized inventions that had begun to appear on the streets of London.

Brodie stepped down from the cab, then assisted me and paid the driver. We went to the back entrance, where Brodie informed the constable on duty that Mr. Dooley had arranged for us to visit the morgue.

The man checked a clipboard with papers then nodded.

"There will be another man joining us," Brodie told him. "By the name of Brimley."

"Right you are, guv'ner. And may I say it's good to see you again, Mr. Brodie."

He nodded in acknowledgement. "And yerself as well, Mr. Macky."

With that we stepped into that imposing building where Brodie had once been charged with murder and imprisoned.

I sensed rather than heard the deep breath he took and could only imagine his thoughts at that memory. I reached out and wrapped my hand around his.

"Let us see what we can learn to find Charlotte Mallory's murderer."

That dark gaze met mine, lines of anger easing from his face. His hand tightened on mine.

"Aye."

Four

MR. BRIMLEY promptly arrived and joined us, along with the police surgeon who had been made aware of our arrival, as we entered that room where bodies were taken, usually an assortment of those found in the river for one reason or another—murder or suicide. It was not uncommon.

There were only two additional tables with sheets drawn over this late afternoon. However, the night awaited.

The surgeon who usually inspected the bodies brought there determined the cause of death, if that was possible, and then released them, identities unknown most usually, for burial in the pauper's graveyard. On other more rare occasions, as in the case of Charlotte Mallory's body, they were held for families to make the necessary arrangements.

Arrangements. Now there was a polite word that I thought was most odd. It usually referred to floral arrangements, enormous bouquets of hydrangeas that the staff at Sussex Square spread about the manor, or other bouquets that James Warren, my sister's fiancé, had sent her.

It had a different meaning here. How bodies were to be dispensed, tagged like a sack of potatoes, thrown into the back of a wagon or funeral van as the case may be, then carted off.

From a family of some position, Charlotte Mallory's body would no doubt be given all due respect. Most probably in the front parlor of the family residence at Knightsbridge for viewing. A tasteless 'arrangement' with friends and family passing by.

Be over and done with it, to my way of thinking as I recalled my own preference for a Viking send-off.

"Ye are not a Viking," Brodie had pointed out when we had that particular previous discussion.

"Nevertheless," I told him. "I'll hold you to that."

He had looked at me with more than a little amusement. "I suppose with that red hair, ye might have a bit of Viking blood. I'll have to remember that, given the knife ye carry. However, ye will undoubtedly outlive me as well as everyone around ye. After all yer great-aunt is eighty-five years old."

She had left specific instructions in that regard as well, my sister declaring at the time that we were both heathens.

So here we were, and I couldn't help but wish a Viking send-off for Charlotte Mallory—off in a blaze of glory, so to speak, no weeping, whispering melodrama with mirrors draped in black.

The surgeon cordially greeted us, however he frowned when he greeted Mr. Brimley—professional disdain, no doubt.

Mr. Brimley had attended King's College medical school, yet chose to administer to the poor in the East End as well as his scientific endeavors. I would have trusted him with my life. In fact, I had previously. The narrow-eyed surgeon sniffed his greeting as if Mr. Brimley was beneath him, as he began his own inspection of the body.

He drew back the sheet over Charlotte Mallory's body. She was still clothed. He pointed out the stain on the front of her gown.

"As you can well see, the manner of death was a single wound here, with a blade. The location and the amount of blood lost indicates that the knife severed a major vessel or organ, with death very soon after."

"Was there any indication of any other disturbance to the

body?" I asked, even though Mr. Burke's newspaper article had provided that information. By that, I thought it important to know if she had been intimately assaulted.

The surgeon frowned. "There were no indications of any other assault, Miss Forsythe," he bit off rather sharply.

"We'll not keep ye longer, sir," Brodie informed him. "We'll make our observations, then be on our way."

Clearly dismissed, the surgeon sniffed again. Perhaps a cold or some other misery with the wintry weather that had set in?

After he had gone, Mr. Brimley set about making his observations as well, while I set about taking down notes.

Brodie frowned as he made his own inspection of the body, gently easing Charlotte Mallory's head back and turning back the collar of her gown.

"No bruises," he commented. "What have ye found, Mr. Brimley?"

"A single wound with great force and most definitely the cause of death. The person was substantially taller by the angle of the wound as you can see here, and the slight bruising just above where the blade penetrated," Mr. Brimley indicated. "That would indicate that he was forced to lever the blade up when he struck, rather than straightaway. And the force of it that severed internal organs was most likely made by a man."

He proceeded to make other observations as I made notes.

"Hmmm, yes perhaps," he commented more to himself as he inspected one of the young woman's hands. He then took a vial of liquid from inside his coat.

"Something I came across that might tell us more," he explained.

He proceeded to scrape under the fingernails of both hands with a small knife then wiped the blade on a towel he retrieved from a cart beside the examination table. He then doused the towel with the grayish liquid.

"It would seem that she either didn't fight her attacker, or had no opportunity." Mr. Brimley looked up. "The chemical causes a reaction when it comes into contact with blood. It turns blue. There is no indication of it here as I would have expected."

"What else can ye tell us, Mr. Brimley?"

"The nails are not broken, which could mean as the surgeon indicated, that it was all over very quickly with no time for her to struggle against the murderer. However, there is what appears to be a thread just here." He indicated the nail of a finger on her other hand.

"I will need to look at it under a microscope." He retrieved the thread and tucked it into an envelope that he always carried.

Fascinating, I thought as I made additional notes.

"And there are scuff marks on her boots," Brodie added.

As I knew, that might or might not mean anything. However, Charlotte had been from a well-placed family and it seemed unlikely that her boots would be so badly scuffed, as opposed to someone who lived on the streets.

It did seem that Mr. Burke might *not* have been quite so thorough in his observations for that newspaper article. There had been no mention of scuff marks.

It appeared that our observations were at an end as a young constable appeared at the entrance to the holding room.

"A representative for the family has arrived for the body."

"Of course," Brodie replied. "We are quite through."

"What are ye thinkin'?" he asked as I stood in front of the chalkboard after we returned to the office on the Strand.

Only Brodie would ask what I thought.

"It is possible that piece of thread might tell us something," I replied. "Or perhaps it's nothing more than a thread from her gown." I continued to stare at the board.

"There is not much to go on. I suppose it could be useful to visit the print shop where she was found. It does appear from what we saw at the holding facility that Mr. Burke is not as well informed as he believes he is."

And not the first time, I thought to myself. A case of dubious journalistic skill for sensationalism.

"She was to be married. I wonder if her fiancé might know of anything in the matter," I added.

"It might be useful to speak with him," he agreed. "As they were not yet married, he will not be directly involved in the final arrangements." He frowned.

"What is it?"

That dark gaze studied me. "I know yer feelings in such things, to be sent off in a burning boat."

I sensed an objection that he hadn't spoken of before.

"However, perhaps there is something comforting to have a place to go, to be with them for a time."

I was fairly certain I knew where this came from. His mother had been placed in one of dozens unmarked graves at the edge of Greyfriars Kirkyard in Edinburgh. There was no way to know precisely where she had been buried, no headstone to mark the spot.

He had gone there and then left, unable to mourn her as he would have liked, to have finally been able to tell her—if one believed in such a thing—that he had found the man who killed her.

I laid the chalk on the rail at the bottom of the chalkboard, then went to where he sat across from the desk.

I was nine years when my mother died. My memories of her were filled with love, even though there was sadness as well. I could not say the same of my father. There were too many difficult memories of him.

They were both buried in the Forsythe family crypt. I refused to go there, although I knew that my sister had.

She was considerably younger than I, and her memories of that time were vague, if at all. She was not the one who found our father in the stables where he had taken his own life, and had almost no memory of him except a shadowy figure who was rarely present and then suddenly gone.

I did understand that going to the place where they were buried provided some measure of comfort for her. For myself, my memories of our mother were my comfort unlike those last memories of our father. But I knew it was different for Brodie.

He had never known his father. As for his mother? It was, I supposed, bittersweet. She had died quite young and tragically murdered. He had finally been able to find the one responsible, but I knew that made the loss no less painful, and then not even to have a marker at her grave...

"I think it's not where a person is buried," I told him, "but the memory you have of them, that is more comforting. Something they always use to tell you..."

"*You are my brave, beautiful girl. You must be brave for your sister.*" My own mother had told me more than once.

"There when it was dark," I pulled another memory up. "And it seemed there were creatures in the shadows. Or the touch of her hand when she smoothed your hair back." I could imagine it with that thick mane of dark hair as I brushed it back.

"There inside you where no one can ever take it away."

He took my hand then and kissed it, that dark gaze fastened on me.

"As ye are inside me now."

We didn't return to Mayfair that night. Instead, we ate supper at the public house as we had so many times. I then took a box with supper back to the office for Mr. Cavendish and Rupert the hound.

Afterward, I placed a call to Sussex Square and spoke with Lily. I informed her that we had begun our inquiries as promised, with a reminder that clues often led to other clues and we would be proceeding in the morning. An inquiry case was not something that resolved overnight.

"How is she?" Brodie asked.

"Impatient. She wants answers, and we don't have any yet."

I caught the look he gave me. "That sounds familiar."

"I want to speak with Burke, and then pay a visit to the print shop."

"Ye dinna trust the newspaper man?"

"It's not a matter of trust. It's a matter of profit, selling as many newspapers as possible. He may know more that he's planning, for future issues. I want to know what he knows."

"I pity the poor man."

I ignored that comment. "What of Mr. Eddington, Charlotte's fiancé?"

He nodded. "I'll call on Sir Mallory's office and see if he will speak with me. It is a difficult time to be certain. It would be helpful to know if he intended to meet Miss Mallory that evening. However, he may refuse to speak with me."

"Not that it has ever stopped you," I pointed out.

It was late into the evening by the time I had made the last of my notes.

Brodie stoked up the fire in the firebox as I straightened his desk, which was buried in paperwork—a copy of the Times, a bill from the coalman, and other odd bits and pieces—which he claimed to know exactly what was there in a disheveled heap.

"What are ye about, lass?" he asked as I went into the adjacent room and turned back the blankets, then slowly removed the pins from my hair.

I was not good at early mornings, most particularly with only a faint sliver of light at the edge of the window shade, the cold as the fire in the coal stove had died down during the night. I burrowed closer to Brodie.

There was something to be said for the relative peace and quiet of the town house at Mayfair, with Mrs. Ryan's efforts in the kitchen in another part of the house, perhaps the smell of coffee brewing...

As opposed to the baying of the hound, and the noticeable creak of the door in the outer office.

"What the bloody hell?" Brodie exclaimed as he retrieved his revolver and left the bed while I curled into the warm place he had left that smelled faintly of cinnamon.

I heard another muttered curse, then "What the devil?" as there were sounds of the outside door suddenly jerked open.

It did appear that I wasn't going to get more sleep.

"Oh! Good mornin' to ye, Mr. Brodie."

I recognized that voice and the unmistakable Scots accent in spite of the months of lessons with her English tutors.

I swung my legs over the edge of the bed, taking the covers with me.

It was probably best that I rescued Brodie, though I was hardly dressed for callers. My camisole and bloomers were undoubtedly far more than he was wearing.

I went into the outer office, in my knickers and discovered him in his long woolen drawers and nothing else.

Quite a stirring sight. If not for our guest, I might have persuaded him to return to bed. As it was...

"Good morning, Lily," I greeted her.

She had set upon a tray of biscuits left from supper the night before, a sign that she had not eaten before departing Sussex Square.

"Do we need to pay the coachman?" I inquired.

She shook her head. "Mr. Hastings brought me."

I would have to have a conversation with him about allowing her to ride all over London in the wee hours of the day. It simply wasn't safe.

"I had my knife as ye told me," she announced as she took another biscuit from the plate.

Oh, dear. It did seem as if she was developing some familiar habits.

Lily sat at the small table in the main office, doing quite well with the biscuits. Brodie had disappeared back into the adjacent bedroom undoubtedly to make himself more presentable, dressed as he was in only his underdrawers.

However, it wasn't as if Lily hadn't seen a man in a state of undress in her former life in a brothel. "Is there coffee?" she asked.

Brodie had emerged from the bedroom somewhat more appropriately clothed, although his shirt was still unbuttoned as he hastily tucked the tails into his trousers. A most stirring sight.

"At this bloody hour? Only if ye know how to make it," he informed her.

Not a challenge for someone of her vast experience. She crossed the office, seized the pot from atop the coal stove, then filled it with water from the pitcher.

I watched with growing amusement as she rummaged about, found the tin of coffee, then added several spoonfuls and set it on the stove.

Brodie made a sound, crossed the office barefoot, made another sound, and then proceeded to add coal to the stove and stoked up the fire.

Lily returned to the table and seized another biscuit, looking at me thoughtfully as if there was nothing unusual about bursting in unannounced when it was barely light outside.

"I've been thinking..." Lily announced.

Brodie groaned. "Ye can find me at the public house." He returned to the bedroom, put on his boots and made a half-hearted attempt to tame that mane of dark hair.

The outer door to the office snapped shut behind him.

"Someone twist his tail?" Lily inquired, then with a look at me, "Did I interrupt somethin'?"

"Sit," I told her as I went to the stove where the pot now simmered. I badly needed coffee.

My relationship with Lily was... somewhat undefined. I was not old enough to be her mother—well, not unless I started quite young. I suspected our friendship needed some refining, as she was now my ward. Which brought me back to the present situation.

I had brought Lily from Edinburgh with an arrangement to provide her with an education and the ability to provide for herself. And admittedly, I was quite fond of her.

Brodie and I had agreed to make inquiries regarding Charlotte Mallory's death, which seemed warranted under the circumstances. When we had information that could be helpful we would provide that to Lily, as we would with anyone, client or no. However...

"Yer peeved at me," she said, most observant as I sat at the desk with cup in hand and thought how best to handle the situation.

She wasn't a child, therefore scolding her as one was not appropriate. Nor was she a woman full-grown, even with her background. She had learned to survive with spirit, determination, and grit, as my friend Templeton called it. A term she picked up on her tour through the United States.

Lily most certainly had that.

Brodie had marked our unmistakable resemblance and perhaps that was part of the reason we usually got on so well. I say *usually*. It did seem as if I now needed to step into another role with her.

'Stepping in it' conjured all sorts of images that had to do with horses and other animals.

Very well. I had made this commitment, best to determine the appropriate way to handle the present situation. I started with a question, as I was most curious.

"I'm surprised you made it past the hound, and the office door was locked."

"The hound weren't no problem. He's right friendly if ye bring a bit of food with ye."

The apple and the tree came to mind.

"*Wasn't,*" I corrected her.

"That's wot I said."

With memories of my own distaste for lessons, I didn't belabor the point.

"The lock at the door?" I reminded her.

"That weren't no problem. I picked it, just like ye showed me."

Oh dear. She was most observant. This was not going at all well.

"Only to be done in the case of a necessary situation," I reminded her.

"It was necessary. I wanted to speak with the two of ye about my idea."

"It is not yet seven o'clock of the morning. Couldn't it have waited?"

"I wanted to make certain I spoke with ye before ye were out and about for the day. But with Mr. Brodie takin' himself off like that... Do ye think he was put out?"

That was undoubtedly an understatement.

"I will speak with him. I'm certain he will understand. Now, the reason you're here?"

"I want to help."

There it was. A flash of emotion in that blue gaze, the firm set of her mouth, the care for a friend tragically lost.

I fully understood. It was not unlike my determination when my sister had disappeared and her maid brutally murdered.

"Where do you propose to start?" I asked her, fully aware that any attempt on my part to explain the specifics of murder would only be met with stubborn resistance. A trait I had also been accused of possessing.

She looked around. "I suppose here at the office..."

"And?"

"Ye've said there are clues in an inquiry case," she pointed out, obviously thinking to win a point with my own words.

"Of course. How do you propose to find those clues?"

"I would go to the print shop. She might have said something to the owner that could provide a clue."

"And if there was nothing he could provide, what then?"

If the brain was a set of wheels, I could almost hear them turning, as her mouth set in a frown.

"I would speak with the police."

"They are not known to cooperate in private inquiries." If not for Brodie's connections after several years with the MET, we would not have been able to obtain some of the information in our past inquiry cases.

"I suppose I would have to rely on ye and Mr. Brodie and what yer able to learn."

"Precisely."

The frown deepened. "I see yer meaning. I suppose it's because I dinna have the experience and no one would be willing to meet with me because I'm a girl."

"You are a young woman, not a girl any longer," I pointed out. "However, it often does not matter what your age is. It is a fact that I must often find a way to out-smart or out-maneuver someone from time to time. It is something you will undoubtedly confront at some point."

"Mr. Brodie?" she asked.

That was an entirely different matter. I had discovered that it was not usually possible to do either where Brodie was concerned. It was difficult to keep one step ahead or even astride with the man because of his experience. Unless, of course, he allowed it.

"He has a great deal of experience in these things. Along with things that he has learned, often the hard way."

"Ye think it is too dangerous for me, and yet ye make inquiries with him."

"It is dangerous. However, I have learned a great deal along the way."

"I could learn."

I realized that the argument could go on and on. She was most obstinate.

"That is the most important part. There is a great deal you must learn before undertaking such a thing."

"I know how to read and write now, and I'm good with numbers."

"What do you know about people, beyond what you learned at The Church in Edinburgh?" A most unusual name for a brothel, but there it was.

"Wot do ye mean?"

I explained what I had learned about human nature in my travels and the inquiries I made with Brodie. The lies people told, what motivated them, who they might be protecting, where I went to find information—the newspapers, libraries, museums, and galleries. And those moments that became dangerous.

"I know wot yer sayin'. I need to learn more. It's only that, I want to help find the man who did this."

I heard the tears in her voice, and knew those same feelings so very well. I rounded the desk and put my arm around her shoulders.

"You will be able to in time, if that is what you choose."

Although I would not have wished wading through the dregs of humanity and depravity for her. That was a conversation for another day.

"Or perhaps you could join the theater like my friend, Templeton."

"How long will it take before I can join in yer inquiry cases?"

I answered with a question of my own.

"How long will you take to finish your lessons?"

"Aye, lessons first then."

"And no picking locks at six o'clock of the morning," I took the opportunity to make that point. It could be dangerous."

"I get yer meanin'."

She had obviously seen the revolver Brodie held when he came from the bedroom, that protective 'street instinct,' as he called it.

"Can ye at least tell me what's to be done next?"

At last I was able to persuade Lily to return to Sussex Square, if somewhat reluctantly. I then joined Brodie at the Public House for breakfast, as I was starving.

"Ye sent her on her way?"

"Eventually," I replied over potatoes and sausage. "You might have stayed to assist in persuading her."

"How did she know where to find the key to the office?" he asked by way of avoiding a response to that.

I thought how best to answer that question.

"It's possible that it was unlocked from the night before." I tried that excuse and received a glare.

"I checked it myself," Brodie replied.

Best to get it over with, I thought.

"She picked the lock."

"Now, I wonder where might she have come by that skill?"

"Perhaps at The Church," I suggested. "It is something that might be useful..." I was definitely on thin ice here.

It was undoubtedly good that we were in a public place. Brodie made that sound I was quite familiar with and simply shook his head.

Five

AFTER BREAKFAST Brodie put out a call to the office of Sir Mallory. He hoped to speak with Charlotte Mallory's fiancé in spite of the fact that it was a difficult time. While I set off for the print shop where she was found murdered.

The shop just off Oxford Street was well known around London as a place where one might find fine stationary and also have invitations and announcements printed. A royal warrant was in the bow window that fronted the street, a clerk looking up as I entered the shop.

I knew it well from having ordered invitations for my great-aunt's eighty-fifth birthday celebration. The main shop was on the ground floor with the presses, cartographers, and artists that the owner retained on the second floor above.

The owner of the shop was Hiram Adams. I was greeted by his son Geoffrey, whom I remembered from the year before.

"Lady Forsythe. It is a pleasure to see you again. You're here regarding Lady Lenore's invitations... They are not quite ready."

Ah, the wedding, full steam ahead.

"Not this morning. Either she or Lady Montgomery will make arrangements to have them delivered."

"Of course. How may we serve you today?"

I explained the reason I was there, mindful of the fact that some people can be put off by inquiries made by a woman about things such as murder, something I had encountered from time to time. I had simply learned to ignore questions from those I spoke with, and only found it necessary to mention Brodie on a handful of occasions. The title I had the unfortunate luck to be born with, courtesy of my father, very often opened doors that not even Brodie could have opened short of picking a lock.

As it was, I simply explained that Mr. Brodie and I were making private inquiries on behalf of a client in the matter. That was usually enough.

"I understand," Geoffrey Adams replied. "Dreadful business and in front of the shop. Such a tragedy."

He was about to close for the day when he heard a woman scream and discovered that Miss Mallory had been attacked in front of the shop. He ran out and saw the man and woman who had found her body.

"Did you recognize them?" I asked in the chance that, if so, I might be able to question them about what they had seen.

"Not at all. It seems they were passing by and found the young woman."

What could he tell me about what he saw then? On the street? Perhaps someone rapidly leaving the area afoot, or by carriage?

"The man from the newspaper asked the same questions," he replied, no doubt referring to Theodolphus Burke. "I didn't see anything before it all happened. I had returned to the back to retrieve an order for another customer. There was just that poor young woman who had just picked up her order here—Miss Mallory. Wedding invitations, so very tragic."

"Did she mention any difficulty? An encounter on the street before arriving that might have bothered her?" I then inquired.

"It was the usual conversation when a customer picks up an order," Geoffrey Adams replied. "She seemed very pleased with the invitations when I showed them to her. She paid for them. Then she was on her way to post a letter across the way. She asked

if the office was still open. There was something in her manner..."
He shook his head.

"Was there anything else?" I asked.

He shook his head. "The constables were here then, taking care of the body and asking questions for their report. There wasn't much that I could tell them, as I was in the back of the shop when the alarm went out and hadn't seen anything."

"You said there was something in her manner when she inquired about the post office hours. Did she say anything about that?"

"No, I'm sorry."

I then asked if there was anything else that he remembered from that night, anything that might seem insignificant.

He started to shake his head once more, then stopped.

"There was this. It seemed odd afterward," he replied as he went to a side table and returned with a slender porcelain vase with a single red rose in it.

"The woman with her husband who found Miss Mallory, said that this was lying across the body when they found her. It was in the gutter after the constables left. They didn't seem to think it was important."

"Did she have it with her when she came into the shop?"

He was thoughtful for a moment. "I don't remember seeing it. I suppose it is possible that she encountered a flower seller nearby after she left. They're usually about even late into the day."

The way he described it, it was almost as if...

It was a morbid thought, still the fact that he didn't recall Charlotte having the rose when she entered the shop made me question how she had come by it. Then the description from the man and woman who found her, that it was lying across her... As if the murderer might have placed it there?

I contemplated that possibility as I sat at the desk in the office on the Strand.

I had explained to Geoffrey Adams that Brodie and I were

making private inquiries on behalf of a client regarding Charlotte Mallory's murder, and asked if I might have the rose.

I had no idea what it meant, if anything, yet the circumstances seemed most curious. It now sat on the desk across from my usual place opposite Brodie when he was there.

It was badly wilted and much the worse for having been tossed aside, drooping over the top of a glass jar that had once held a healing salve that Mr. Brimley had provided for Brodie during one of our inquiries.

I stared at the chalkboard where I had made notes of my visit with Mr. Adams. There were more questions than answers along with the particularly nagging question, who would want to harm a young woman from a prominent family?

And not for the usual reasons that we encountered in other inquiry cases. Most particularly in a part of the city that was heavily patrolled by the MET. It made no sense, but then as I had learned, murder rarely did.

As I had discovered in the past it was usually not random. There was always a reason behind such a horrible act. It was merely a matter of finding what that reason was, and the person who had committed it.

Greed? Passion?

It seemed that neither of those were the reason in Charlotte Mallory's case. According to the police surgeon's examination, there was no intimate violation. And she still had her handbag with a good number of coins in it. The motive obviously was not robbery.

What then had been the reason for such a heinous crime?

Motive, means, opportunity.

Two were obvious. The opportunity had been outside the print shop, where Charlotte Mallory had gone unescorted. The means had been that single knife wound. That brought me back to the question of motive.

I had learned from Brodie that it was a matter of digging

deeper, following even the most obscure or seemingly unimportant piece of information.

He had not returned since our parting, there was no note left about as had become his habit when he went off to follow up on some other bit of information.

Therefore, I decided to call on Mr. Brimley and see if he was able to learn anything from that cloth fiber he had found under Charlotte's fingernail.

In turn, I left a note for Brodie—something that was quite foreign to me, yet something I discovered that I liked very much.

He had explained it, *"When ye go off on yer own, a simple note would do. If ye get into a stramash, then I can help ye, lass."*

I had never before felt the need to leave a note with anyone, except for my great-aunt. I respected her, it was as simple as that.

However, I did have to admit that when making our inquiries on behalf of a client, even if that client was Lily, things often took an unexpected turn. In the past I had found myself in a difficulty and only by good fortune, and perseverance on Brodie's part, had I escaped relatively unscathed.

Well, there was that one incident in our first inquiry when I had been shot. I did have to admit that was not a pleasant experience. And now?

As we were both learning what this new relationship between us meant, I realized that he was right about certain things. Not that I would have admitted to all of them. However, leaving a note seemed a small concession to my previous way of doing things. And he had seemed most accommodating when I pointed out that he might do the same.

I locked the door behind me as I set off. On the street below the office, Mr. Cavendish summoned a driver for me.

"When you have time, miss, there is a matter I would like to discuss with you," he said as a driver circled round his hansom cab from across the street, then angled his rig through the usual midday traffic to pull alongside the curb.

The request seemed somewhat unusual and he seemed

almost...shy about it. And that was not a word I would usually think of regarding Mr. Cavendish.

"Of course. Is there some difficulty?" I asked.

"No, not at all," he assured. "It is simply a matter I need some assistance with... regarding a lady, you see."

A lady? I didn't actually see what it was, but I liked Mr. Cavendish, né the Mudger, very much. He had obviously led an adventurous life, now relegated to that platform, but with a keen sense of loyalty to Brodie and me. Not to mention Rupert the hound. I was happy to assist with something that seemed important.

"It can wait," he said then. "You're obviously off and about on some matter of importance."

"When I return?" I suggested.

He nodded and rolled back from the edge of the curb as I climbed into the cab.

Mr. Brimley's shop was just up from the docks in one of the poorest parts of the East End. There he dispensed medications for ailments, set broken bones, and assisted women 'in need.'

It was where he also made his own scientific inquiries with specimens in jars or under a microscope, and on occasion had removed a bullet from a wound. I could personally attest to his skills as a surgeon.

His assistant, Sara, greeted me as I arrived. She was quite young, but wasn't at all put off by the sight of wounds, broken bones, or other ailments among those who sought Mr. Brimley's care. She would make a good surgeon, he had declared, with a natural curiosity about the human body.

Mr. Brimley was in the back of his shop, his *laboratory* as he called it, with that shelf the length of one wall for his microscopes, pill-press machine, and camera that he had previously acquired.

"Ah, Lady Forsythe," he greeted me, looking up from a steel tray before him on the counter opposite, wearing magnifying goggles and looking much like an enormous bug seated on the stool before the counter.

"I was hoping to speak with you or Mr. Brodie today."

"You have something regarding the thread you discovered?" I had been hopeful although fully prepared that the thread might have been too small to reveal anything that might be useful.

"Indeed."

He removed his goggles, very similar to the ones my aunt wore when she was driving about London, terrorizing people on the streets in her automobile.

These goggles were quite different as Mr. Brimley had explained. The lenses were actually magnification glass, to provide him a means of studying something other than through the much smaller lens of a microscope. It worked quite well when studying body parts, he had informed Brodie and me.

"Something important?"

"That would be for you to determine," he replied. "I have it here for you to take a look." He pulled out a stool before the countertop, checked the viewer of the microscope, then stood back.

I sat atop the stool, removed my hat, then peered through the microscope onto the glass slide below. With the magnification of the lens, it looked as if I was staring at a large log, which in fact was the fiber Mr. Brimley had retrieved.

"You might want to focus it," he suggested pointing out the knob at the side of the microscope.

I adjusted it for a clearer look at the fiber.

"It's dark blue," I commented.

He nodded. "What else do you see?"

"It's quite smooth." I looked up from the microscope.

"You have a keen eye, Miss Forsythe. What might those two things tell you?"

"The garment was dark blue, possibly wool, perhaps high quality by the smoothness of the fiber, possibly from a cut or tear in the fabric. From our examination of the body at the mortuary, Charlotte Mallory was wearing a burgundy-colored gown with jacket over, not dark blue."

"My guess would be that it is a very fine worsted wool, and with the color, the sort found in a gentleman's very fine coat," he concluded.

Fine gentleman's clothing.

"Mind you, she could have come by it before her encounter with the murderer."

It might mean something, or nothing. I thought of her fiancé, Daniel Eddington, or possibly another student she had called on before going to the print shop, or any other possibility where she might have come in contact. Except for that one glaring detail.

"Under one of her fingernails, Mr. Brimley?"

"There is that, and quite firmly lodged there as well. Almost as if..."

I finished the thought. "As if she had reached out when she was struck down, in an attempt to defend herself, or clutching at her attacker's coat after he struck.

"And one more small detail," he replied. "Take another look. Most particularly at one end."

As I did, he reached out and turned the knob at the side of the microscope. It gradually emerged, something I had not noticed. A small sliver of something embedded in the end of the fiber.

"The remnants of silk thread," Mr. Brimley said then. "Whoever the man was who wore that coat, is most definitely a gentleman of some means."

I made my notes before leaving his shop. I had no idea yet what any of it might mean, if anything, about Charlotte Mallory's murder. It was possible that the fiber and thread were from a coat she had thought of wearing then decided against it. Or possibly from that of her fiancé, Daniel Eddington. I needed to know more.

I returned to the office on the Strand to discover that Brodie had returned as well.

He had met earlier with the two constables who first arrived outside the print shop when Charlotte Mallory's body was discovered.

Someone, perhaps Mr. Cavendish, had brought luncheon from the Public House across the Strand. Brodie, dear man, had placed the platter atop the coal stove to keep it warm.

It was their version of workingman's stew, chunks of meat and potatoes with a portion of carrots and celery pieces. The sort of meal that was fairly inexpensive and would stick to a man's or woman's bones through the rest of the day, not to mention that it warmed one on a rainy, cold day.

I retrieved the rose, much the worse for wear, and placed it in a pitcher of water. Brodie looked up from the desk and frowned.

"A token of affection?"

"It was found at the curb where Charlotte Mallory was murdered. According to the man and woman who found her, it was lying across her body. Why would someone do that?"

"Perhaps she had it with her."

"Mr. Adams didn't recall it being with her when she arrived at the shop."

I set the pitcher on the desk then went to the coal stove.

"Oh, bless Mr. Cavendish. I'm starving."

"Not the Mudger. I brought it back from the Public House. The damned hound almost took my leg off for it."

"That will teach you to next time bring a cake or biscuit for him."

I smiled as I brought the plate to the desk and sat across from him. "It serves you right for speaking badly of him. He does have a particular liking for the stew from the Public House."

"He has a particular liking for anything that is not moving," Brodie replied.

It was a frequent comment.

"What else were you able to learn from the printer?"

"It appears there was nothing unusual about her visit. She wasn't upset nor did she indicate that she was fearful of anything. She paid for her print order—invitations for the wedding, then left. It was just after that the man and woman made him aware that something had happened."

"She gave no indication of any difficulty?"

"None, so it would seem that the attack might have been the first encounter," I replied. "I then paid a visit to Mr. Brimley, most interesting."

Brodie looked up from a piece of paper he had been studying. "Aye?"

"The fiber that he found under Charlotte Mallory's fingernail was most distinctive."

He frowned. "Distinctive?"

"A very fine, dark blue worsted wool, along with silk thread at one end. As if Charlotte might have clutched at the man's sleeve."

And not at all what I had first thought, that this crime might have been the sort committed by the Whitechapel murderer.

"That could be useful," Brodie admitted.

I angled a glance down at the paper in front of him. "What have you there?"

"The police report from the night of the murder."

At my look of surprise, he explained. "Mr. Dooley made a copy of the report. His handwriting is... Let us just say that it's a wonder he made inspector."

"Let me have a go at it. I've had some experience... Mr. Munro's writing leaves a great deal to the imagination."

"Well, when ye learn things on the fly, often times with the local police after ye and no proper schoolin', ye make do with wot ye can."

"Your own handwriting as well?" I replied as his was no better, a surprise that he had made inspector.

"In code perhaps?"

"Ye are a cheeky lass." He pushed the paper across the desk. "See wot ye can make of it."

I had to agree that the writing was quite... unique. However, with past experience with Brodie's handwriting—it did seem that he had a habit of mixing up letters, I was able to make out most of the words in the report.

"There wasn't anything unusual noticed about the body,

there were no witnesses other than the man and woman who found the body, nor from the shopkeeper. It does seem as if the murder was recent, as the body was still warm." I looked up.

"Nothing unusual? That cannot be all... something is missing, and there is no mention of the rose."

"Constable Dwyer is young, only in service of the MET for less than six months," Brodie replied. "Details come with experience. I wasna able to speak with his partner as it was his day away."

"And in the meantime, the murderer is still out there, and we have nothing to go on."

"Not precisely."

"How *not precisely*?"

"There is always something to be learned, even when it appears there are no clues."

We'd had many conversations during our partnership since that first case. I was always fascinated by the way his mind worked. Of course, much of it came from his experience with the MET, previous inquiry cases, and the fact that he'd lived on the streets for a time.

"What have we learned?"

"First, the body was not disturbed other than that one wound. Second, it would seem that she didn't fall to the sidewalk after the attack but was lowered most carefully according to what the young constable told me." he added.

I listened fascinated.

"Then there is the flower, which was found, laid across the body, ye say. Not the manner of something simply discarded or dropped by the victim. And ye said the shopkeeper didna notice that she had it when she called at the shop for her purchase."

And not a crime of passion, at least not in the sense of what had been proposed about the Whitechapel murders. I was fascinated, not the first time, by his observations and possible conclusions.

"It would seem that Miss Mallory was not frightened or alarmed," he continued. "She did not cry out, and other than that fiber Mr. Brimley found, it does not appear there was a violent struggle. Then for her to be lowered to the sidewalk with the flower, almost as if..."

"As if?"

"It's just a thought, however it's as if she was being laid out most proper possibly for someone to take notice. Not in the usual manner I have found in the past."

Not in the usual manner. What did that mean, I wondered? Very strange.

"It seems that the burial is to take place on Saturday." He handed me the afternoon edition of the Times, folded to the society page with the announcement and the location of the burial, along with a poem about a parent's remembrance of a child:

'Too soon, sweet child, whose music touched the soul. I will listen to the morning and hold you once more.'

That did seem a bit overdone, however, I supposed each to his own. And it had mentioned Charlotte's talent in music. I did wonder who might have written it.

Sir Mallory perhaps? From his reputation prosecuting criminals I wouldn't have expected such flowery words. Possibly written by Charlotte's mother?

Saturday. Four days after she was killed, the usual day of the week for those of certain status in society to be buried, and most expeditiously out of concern for disease.

Those not of a certain status were usually buried on Sunday, with unclaimed bodies either placed in a pauper's grave or simply dropped into the Thames. An unpleasant memory that, from our first inquiry case.

"A Viking ceremony would be far more efficient," I commented.

"Ye are such a heathen," Brodie replied. "The funeral is necessary for people to mourn," he pointed out.

"I think it would be much better to appreciate someone when they are alive," I replied.

"Has anyone ever told ye that ye have a peculiar way about such things?"

"My sister believes it's quite barbaric," I admitted. "However, my great-aunt is of much the same opinion."

"Of course," Brodie replied. "I'm surprised she hasna decided to go out with yer ancestor's sword and shield in that boat she has in the salon at Sussex Square."

"She has mentioned it, however I believe now that she intends for Lily to have the sword. Once she's *traveled on*, as they say."

"Traveled on?"

I heard the skepticism at his voice. "Ye believe there are those who dinnae?"

"According to Templeton, many simply transition into another life," I replied, something I had given a great deal of thought. It did answer some questions for those who claimed to see spectral objects and heard things go bump in the night.

"Transition?"

"Entering another life," I explained, at which Brodie's eyes rolled back. "To take care of things left undone, or to make amends for some transgression. For others I suppose it could simply be their refusal to leave this world."

"Templeton," he commented, with that sound I was most familiar with as he left his chair and rounded the desk.

"Witches, goblins, and spirits in the night as well, I suppose?"

"What do you believe?" I asked, since we had not previously had that conversation.

"I've seen too much of death and not experienced a spirit after, even though I might have wished it." He brushed my cheek with his fingers.

"I believe in what I can see and touch."

"I shall have to haunt you when I return," I replied.

I wondered if I would be able to feel such things as the touch of a hand. I would have to remember to ask my friend.

FRIDAY

THERE WAS someone I wanted very much to meet with, as regarded our case and most certainly not for any other reason—Theodolphus Burke with the Times newspaper.

He had managed to arrive at the print shop quite expeditiously for his story in the newspaper when the call went out after Charlotte Mallory was found murdered. He did seem to have a talent for arriving first on the scene of a crime, thereby putting out the story before the other newspapers.

I did have my suspicions about that, perhaps payment changing hands to the watch captain as Brodie had once suggested. However, I wanted to see if there was anything I might be able to learn from him that he hadn't written about.

"Do ye want me to accompany ye?" Brodie had asked as we both dressed for the day.

"I can handle Mr. Burke. You can be somewhat intimidating."

A dark brow, the one with the scar, angled sharply.

"Intimidating? Ye have never been the least intimidated by meself."

"That is because I know what that look actually means when you look at *me* that way."

"Usually when ye've done somethin' ye shouldna, that put ye in danger."

"And other things..." I reminded him.

"Ye are shameless, Mikaela Forsythe Brodie."

Yes, well... I did write that off to that encounter on the Isle of Crete a handful of years earlier. As my great-aunt would say, most stirring!

Brodie hoped to speak with the other constable who had arrived at the print shop the night that Charlotte Mallory was murdered. The man lived in the Commons, one of a dozen buildings for working-class tenants.

Constable Erskine was older, with a great deal more experience working the streets. A handful of years before, he had been called out to the Whitechapel murders.

"Do ye have the revolver with ye?" Brodie asked as I set off from the office.

"Surely you don't think I will need it."

"I'm not worrit about *ye*, lass. I'm more concerned for Burke. I would hate to have to explain to her ladyship that ye have gone off and killed the bugger for his insults."

I promised not to leave a trail of blood. Theodolphus Burke might be condescending even outright insulting, however, he simply was not worth what it would take to put him out of everyone's misery. And there was the fact that he might know something important to our inquiry case.

I arrived at the Times offices early in the morning and before he had taken himself off on his usual rounds searching out his next story. Then, usually back to the newspaper office, I had recently discovered, to write up whatever nasty bit of rumor or salacious gossip he was able to obtain for a column that he also wrote under a pseudonym when there was a shortage of robberies or murder.

No one was spared his vitriol, certainly not myself. He had been quite amused to learn that I was the author of the Emma

Fortescue novels. He had called my Emma Fortescue adventures much like Alice's Adventures in Wonderland:

"Lady Mikaela Forsythe's literary efforts, disguised as Emma Fortescue, are amusing, though obviously a product of her privileged imagination. What woman of her breeding and family name would risk her life dueling with swords?"

Indeed.

When I arrived at the Times building, the clerk at the ground-floor desk contacted the second floor, where Burke had a desk.

"If you would wait, please, Lady Forsythe." He indicated a sitting area in the foyer. He was congenial enough and I thought I recognized him, then dismissed it.

I was not good at being put off. However, I was there hoping to find out what Burke might have learned in his poking about, determined to write the full story about Charlotte Mallory's murder. I decided, as my great-aunt once said in a similar situation, to 'play nice.'

I eventually heard the persistent jangle of the phone, very near an hour later, and the young clerk informed me that Mr. Burke would see me now.

"Lady Forsythe!" I heard him call out as I reached the second floor from the direction of the private office he had been given.

"Or, should I say Mrs. Brodie? There has been that rumor about the city. To what do I owe this dubious pleasure? Isn't there a ladies' tea to be attended somewhere?"

"Oh, it almost slipped my mind, perhaps a new inquiry case, someone's lost Pomeranian?" I inquired.

Odious man. I pushed back the urge to reach for the revolver, and greeted Burke with a smile instead, determined to *play nice*.

We exchanged the usual pleasantries. He even congratulated me on my latest novel.

"Always entertaining. And you and Mr. Brodie tracking down dangerous criminals."

"While your gossip column seems to be a great success," I complimented him.

The truth was that he had managed to humiliate several members of society, particularly Lady Braithwaite by exposing the affair she was having with a much younger man.

While I hardly thought it was of any great interest, my great-aunt had thought it highly amusing.

"Lady Braithwaite is at least sixty years old and the young man is rumored to be no more than twenty-five. I do hope that she is enjoying herself."

There had been no mention of Lord Braithwaite who was very near eighty.

"I have no idea if he's still alive," my great-aunt added at the time. *"The last time he attended one of my soirees he did have the smell of camphor about him or some other preservative, and some difficulty moving about."*

The follow-up to that bit of gossip had been the revelation that Lady Braithwaite had departed for their country estate at the time, with her much-younger 'companion,' who was reported by said newspaper writer to be her riding instructor.

Riding instructor. Most amusing.

Never mind that winter approached when weather prevented riding about the countryside. That did raise the question of who was instructing whom? And in what?

"To what do I owe the pleasure of your company, Lady Forsythe?" Burke replied now as he returned to his desk and sat down after our greetings.

"And what is this I hear about your recent marriage?"

I decided to simply ignore him on that last one. I had learned in the past that the less said the better when it came to Theodolphus Burke. Yet, I was not beyond dangling a bit of information to gain more information that he might have.

"I read your article regarding the murder of that young woman, Charlotte Mallory," I began. "It is getting so that it is not safe for a woman to be about London at any time of the day. It reminds one of those dreadful Whitechapel murders that have never been solved."

That sharp gaze narrowed.

"Yes, most dreadful. But what is your interest, Lady Forsythe?"

"Mr. Brodie and I have been asked to make inquiries in the matter." I replied. There was no reason to keep secret something that he would learn for himself from his own sources on the street.

"Hmmm. And you wish to know what I know, on behalf of your client."

"It does seem as though we might be able to assist one another," I replied.

"You have information?"

I heard the doubt in his voice.

"It might be beneficial to both of us, and you would, of course, be able to write the article once the murderer is caught."

"What sort of information?"

"It would require your sharing information you might have as well," I reminded him. With no guarantee of course that he would. Except for a bit of bribery.

"And it would be a shame for one of the other dailies to post their article first."

"Are you suggesting a partnership, Lady Forsythe?"

Not bloody likely, I thought. Yet, something that would entice him to share and I would do the same.

"Not precisely," I replied. "But perhaps something to help each of us. I want to find answers for our client, and you want information for your articles for the Times. We might both benefit," I pointed out.

At the same time, I was hoping that printing the information that Brodie and I had been able to learn might entice someone to come forward with something they saw or heard.

"What is it that you believe you have discovered, Lady Forsythe?" The derision in his voice was obvious.

"A question first. Have you been able to learn anything from the man and woman who found the body?"

He shook his head. "They have refused to speak with me. Some sort of bad experience with someone from the newspapers in the past."

Considering what was usually printed, often for purposes of sensationalism with a bare smidgen of fact and subsequent sales, I wasn't surprised. However, that might provide Brodie and I with an opportunity.

"What about anyone else who was on the street at the time?" I then asked.

"That is two questions, Lady Forsythe."

That smile, much like the Cheshire Cat. He was enjoying this part in this exchange.

"But I suppose there is no harm in sharing," he continued. "There was a man going about lighting the street lamps who might have seen something. I haven't been able to locate him as yet."

While many street lights were now electrified along the major thoroughfares in London, gas street lamps were still found in other parts of the city. Was it possible the man might have seen something?

"I have been forthcoming with information," Burke pointed out. "Now it is your turn, Lady Forsythe."

The derision was still there in his voice with a hint of curiosity.

I had given a great deal of thought to what I might tell him, from what little we knew about the murder.

The entire purpose of my visit was an attempt to learn anything that might help us, as I had explained to him. I didn't give a fig about his ambitions. However, I was not willing to share the information Mr. Brimley had discovered.

He was a friend, and I was not willing to reveal him as a source for information in our inquiries. It was impossible to know as yet what that blue woolen fiber meant, if anything. That left one thing that I was willing to share.

"It seems that there was something possibly left behind by the murderer," I caught the sudden interest even as Burke sat back casually in his desk chair.

"What would that be?"

"A flower was found at the scene of the murder." I watched for any indication that he already knew about it. I saw only vague amusement.

"A flower?"

"A red rose," I replied.

He stared at me from across the desk. "That is the information you have?"

"From what I was able to learn she didn't have it with her when she entered the print shop. It was found on her afterward."

"And you believe it could be important."

He obviously didn't think that it was important. I was beginning to question how Theodolphus Burke had reached the place in his career that he had.

"It was placed across her body in a particular manner," I explained. "Almost as if..."

"As if what, Lady Forsythe?" He rose from behind his desk with notepad in hand. "You cannot be certain that she didn't purchase the flower after she left the print shop. Now if that is all, I have a deadline to meet, which you might understand."

The man really was full of himself. I rose from the chair across from him. It was obvious that our meeting was at an end. I paused at the door, then left him with a parting thought.

"It was after dark and there was no flower seller in the area," I informed him what I already knew from my conversation with Mr. Adams at the print shop.

I left him with a parting thought, though certain he would dismiss it.

"It's almost as if the murderer was leaving a message."

With that I closed the door behind me rather forcefully.

Condescending, arrogant man! I thought as I took the stairs instead of the lift back to the ground floor.

"Good day, miss," the clerk called out.

I thanked him, then left the building.

As irritating as Theodolphus Burke was, I had given him information that could be useful. It was not my responsibility if he chose to ignore what I had told him. As for myself, I had learned two things that could be important.

The man and woman who found Charlotte Mallory's body had refused to speak with him—something I could most definitely understand.

Yet, they might be willing to speak with Brodie and me, in order to find the person who had committed the murder. Their names had been on the copy of the police report that Brodie made.

The second piece of information was regarding the man who had perhaps been on the street at the time—the lamplighter, whose route that night included the street in front of the print shop.

I found a driver and returned to the office on the Strand. Brodie had returned as well, and he was not alone.

"The housekeeper gave me your message, Mr. Brodie," the man dressed in casual work clothes seated across from him was saying. "Came as soon as I could find a driver, and thanks to ye for the coin to cover it."

Brodie nodded, looking up as I crossed the office and removed my coat.

"Thank ye for coming as quickly as ye did. This is my associate, Miss Forsythe."

We had previously discussed how I was to be introduced to potential clients or others we worked with.

Lady Forsythe seemed pretentious unless it was a situation where it might be advantageous, at which time it could be used with no hesitation on my part.

Brodie had pointed out that my given name, Mikaela Forsythe, might seem too informal, particularly with those he objected to treating me so familiarly.

As for my married name, Mikaela Forsythe Brodie, that might create issues as well. He had pointed out that while he very much liked the sound of it, there were those he had encountered in the past, of a criminal sort, who would like nothing better than to get back at him through his wife.

While I wasn't concerned about it, he was, that was the reason that he usually introduced me as his associate, Miss Forsythe.

"This is Constable Erskine," Brodie provided. "He was on the call the night of the murder."

Constable Erskine nodded a greeting. "That I was." He turned back to Brodie, effectively dismissing me. I was used to that sort of thing, but that didn't mean that I liked it.

"It is good of you to assist us," I told him.

There was that nod again, with a faint smile this time.

"I don't know what more I can tell you, Mr. Brodie. I see you have a copy of the report." He gestured across the desk to the copy Brodie had made.

"I had my partner give the information to the night officer when we got back from the Yard."

"I thought there might be something that wasn't in the report," Brodie suggested. "Something that might have been said or noticed but didn't make it on paper. Would ye take a look?" He turned the copy of the report about and slid it across to Constable Erskine.

He pulled a pair of spectacles from his jacket pocket and put them on, then began reading the copy of the report, occasionally reading aloud, then continuing on.

"Pretty thing, she was," he said with a frown as he stared down at the copy of the report. "And holding that flower."

I exchanged a look with Brodie but said nothing.

Constable Erskine was thoughtful. "When I first saw her lyin' there with that flower across her, it reminded me..."

"What did it remind you of?" I asked.

He shook his head. "Somethin' a long time ago perhaps, and

it was just for a moment. An impression, you understand, that flower just under her hand. Almost as if..."

"Wot do ye remember, Mr. Erskine?" Brodie prompted him.

He shook his head. "After seein' this sort of thing over twenty-five years... You know how it is Mr. Brodie; you don't want to see any more of it. Just doing my job, responding to the calls when they come in, waiting for the day when I can retire.

"What you did, leaving after only a few years," he continued. "I should have done the same, but we had three young ones at home then. They're all gone now, and I've only eighteen months left. Then, I'm out on my pension."

"Is there anything else you remember from that night," Brodie replied.

"Were the street lamps lit nearby?" I asked.

He nodded. "They'd been lit some time before. It was the reason we had no trouble seeing that she was already dead, and that wound as well." He hesitated.

"There were a handful who gathered about in that way that a crime draws attention, and then the man from the newspaper."

"Mr. Burke from the Times," Brodie provided the name.

He nodded. "That's the one, got there before we arrived. Thought it was odd at the time. But you know how it is, guv'ner."

And something that Burke hadn't bothered to mention. I wasn't surprised.

From working with Brodie, I was aware that a handful of the more successful writers for the newspapers had their 'sources' on the street. Those who often knew of a crime before the police or anyone else, and then sold the information to the newspapers.

It was rumored that the one who had committed the crime might report it to a well-known newspaper reporter, and make a fee from it.

Did that also include murder?

I had no doubt that Burke had his own sources scrabbling about the streets of London, those of a low sort. Perhaps those same criminals who took him information.

It did explain how he was able to be the first one to write about the latest crimes for the Times.

Might that include the murder of Charlotte Mallory?

Seven

LILY WANTED to attend the funeral for Charlotte Mallory.

"I never been to a proper funeral before. Leastwise not for one like her," she said when we spoke of it.

"She was my friend. I hear it helps sometimes, being able to say good-by and all."

"Then by all means, you should attend," my great-aunt told her when we had the conversation. "I liked her very much as well. We shall both go. I will have Mr. Hastings bring round the coach."

The funeral service was at St. Paul's church in Knightsbridge, with burial service at Brompton in Kensington.

I had been to funeral services before, for one reason or another, in spite of my long-held preferences for a Viking send-off. However, this was Lily's first experience with the rituals of the upper classes.

Her previous experience with such things had been in Edinburgh, when one of the 'ladies' who worked at the 'Church' had succumbed to a malady and was taken off to burial in a common grave.

There didn't seem to be any memory before that, perhaps of some relation, before she was taken in by the madam at the

'Church,' first to run errands, as so many orphaned children found themselves, then as a 'ladies' maid' as when I had encountered her there.

Brodie and I arrived separately at St. Paul's church where we joined Lily and my great-aunt. I clasped Lily's hand as we entered the church.

"I never seen nothin' like this," she whispered, as we took our places inside the church. "It's like a castle."

It was quite imposing and beautiful, I suppose, if one was into that sort of thing, with that tall edifice now draped in clouds. Inside, tiled panels around the walls of the nave depicted different religious scenes, lit by dozens of candles in tall sconces. Pews lined both sides of the chapel.

"Sir Edward and Lady Mallory," my aunt whispered with a look at the front pew as the service began with the casket front and center. And beside Lady Mallory, was a young gentleman whom I presumed to be Charlotte's fiancé, Daniel Eddington.

Lady Mallory was dressed all in black as was the custom, with a veil over her face, frequently reaching under with a handkerchief. Sir Mallory was stoic, if a bit distracted, with a frown amid thick jowls that I imagined those in the Queen's court confronted in his profession as barrister.

He seemed impatient, even perhaps annoyed, as if the service was an intrusion, leaning forward to pass some comment along to Daniel Eddington who merely nodded.

Charlotte's fiancé was a pleasant-enough looking young man in spite of his somber expression and the frown under a neatly clipped mustache. I could only imagine how difficult this must be for all of them, when it was a wedding they had been planning with those invitations Charlotte had picked up from the print shop.

I had expected some long, drawn-out sermon about the cruelties of life and was surprised not only at the brevity of the service, but the tone as well.

The Anglican priest spoke of qualities of those who brought

light into the lives of others, then spoke specifically of Charlotte's gift of music that she shared with her family and students.

It was very uplifting in spite of the circumstances as the priest described a young life ended too soon. Afterward, the casket was removed with the Mallorys following behind for the burial service in Kensington.

Coaches lined the thoroughfare as we arrived at Brompton Cemetery. The rain that had held off through the morning seemed to wait as we accompanied Lily and my great-aunt to the graveside.

There the priest from Brompton Chapel gave a brief service for all those who had gathered. There must have been thirty or forty in attendance to pay their last respects at the graveside. No doubt due to the Mallorys' standing not only in society, but Sir Edward's legal work.

Mourners filed past... couples, older gentlemen with whom he had no doubt served as a barrister, Mr. Eddington briefly responding as he stood as before with Sir Edward. Both men were stoic and somber, greeting those who passed by with a brief nod. Mrs. Mallory, small, with sagging shoulders, occasionally nodded at someone she apparently knew, a gloved hand reaching out.

"So many flowers," Lily commented. "It looks like all the flowers in London are here."

"Hmmm," Aunt Antonia replied. "Sir Mallory is quite well known."

Lily frowned as we joined the other mourners.

"I'd like to say something to her mother and father, but I don't know what's proper."

I offered what I thought might be meaningful for her as well as for Sir Edward and Mrs. Mallory.

"Perhaps a word or two about what Charlotte meant to you. That she was a friend as well as your instructor."

She seemed to think about that.

"Come along dear. I shall go with you," Aunt Antonia told

her. "At my age, I've had a good deal of experience with this sort of thing." She glanced over at me.

"Not that I intend to have a funeral for others to wail and carry on over," she added.

With a look from Lily, I decided to accompany them.

"I'll wait for ye at the coach," Brodie told me. "Take my umbrella." He handed it to me. "Ye seem to have left yers behind, as usual."

It was just a light rain, one he and Munro would have called a fine soft rain, but I knew quite well what London weather could turn to.

I caught up with Lily and my great-aunt as they reached Sir Edward and Mrs. Mallory where they stood beside the white casket as others moved ahead, some placing flowers atop the casket.

Lily glanced at me and I nodded my encouragement as my great-aunt expressed her sympathies first, then waited for Lily to say what she wanted to say.

"Miss Charlotte was my friend," she began hesitantly, then seemed to find the rest of the words.

"I wanted ye to know that she made the most beautiful music I ever heard."

Not an eloquent speech but simple words from the heart. I was very proud of her.

Mrs. Mallory acknowledged her with a nod from behind her veil. Beside her, Daniel Eddington nodded, while Sir Mallory remained silent.

"Come along, dear," Aunt Antonia told Lily. "Or we will be thoroughly soaked with the rain."

It had definitely decided to make an appearance as Lily took my great-aunt's arm and they made their way from the burial site along the footpath back to the coaches, with others who paused to place bouquets of flowers on the casket.

There were more lilies and orchids with other winter flowers, in arrangements of all manner, size, and shape. It certainly seemed that Charlotte Mallory had touched many lives. Or perhaps it was in deference to Sir Mallory, as many of the mourners were older and perhaps professional associates.

He obviously knew a great many people and it seemed that they had come to pay their respects—ladies in appropriate mourning attire, with men in fine frock coats and top hats crowded under umbrellas as they paused, spoke briefly to Sir Mallory then moved on.

Eager to join Lily and my aunt, I might have missed it among the sea of lilies and orchids, except for the bold color amid white, pale pink, and lavender. Stark contrast to the usual funeral arrangements that surrounded it, a single red rose lay across the casket.

A red rose! A coincidence?

I left the line of mourners and immediately looked about for anyone who might have placed it there. Who would have left a single red rose?

Possibly Daniel Eddington? Mourning the loss of the young woman he hoped to marry?

Yet I had seen him place a bouquet of lilies on the casket just before my great-aunt had given her condolences.

"Mikaela?"

Brodie had doubled back, no doubt after Lily and my great-aunt had arrived at the coach.

"The rain has set in and her ladyship and Lily are waiting." He took one look at my face.

"What is it?"

I kept my voice low as other mourners passed by. "There, atop the casket."

That dark gaze narrowed as he saw the rose.

"Aye," he replied, then scanned the mourners who slowly moved past the casket, and others who lingered for the opportunity to say a word of sympathy to the Mallorys.

That dark gaze met mine.

"It could be a coincidence."

"You don't believe in them any more than I do. Why would someone leave a single red rose?"

"Did ye perhaps see who might have left it?"

I shook my head. "No, it could have been anyone. Is it possible that the murderer is here?"

If so, it was bold, arrogant, almost as if... the murderer was sending a message?

What message? And could it possibly have to do with Charlotte Mallory?

The rain had increased, and mourners that hadn't already departed quickly gave their condolences then left, making their way along the muddied path to their coaches.

Sir Edward and Mrs. Mallory also departed, with Daniel Eddington, leaving only the attendants who slowly lowered the casket into the grave, taking that sea of flowers and that red rose with it.

"There's nothing to be done here," Brodie said, holding his umbrella over both of us.

We were the last to leave the graveyard, Sir Edward and Mrs. Mallory, walking slowly ahead, Daniel Eddington behind them.

I glanced back as we reached the coach, but the only thing I saw were the graveyard workers who worked quickly to close the grave as the rain thickened. Everyone else was gone.

We didn't speak of what we saw on the ride to Sussex Square, with no idea what it might mean, if anything.

We accepted my great-aunt's invitation for a late luncheon. Lily was unusually quiet, barely touching her food.

"What is bein' done to find who kilt her?" she suddenly blurted out.

Not exactly dining table conversation, I thought, with a look at my great-aunt.

"It's quite all right," she assured everyone, then with a look at me.

And to put an end to any objection on my part... "As I recall you were given to speaking out when anything was important, or not. This is quite important."

When I would have given her a simple answer, for the most part because we didn't actually know anything yet, Brodie's hand closed around mine, stopping me.

"We have both been making inquiries on behalf of Miss Mallory," he explained. "To the police constables who reported to the crime that night, and Mikaela has spoken with the reporter at the Times who wrote the article for the newspaper. He was there afterward.

"We dinna have any answers as yet," he added. "But there are other persons to question who may have seen something that night.

"I know yer feelin's in this," he continued then, much like a father, I thought. And God knows he did understand, perhaps better than most.

"It's difficult to wait, when ye've lost someone ye care about. But I will say that one small piece of information usually leads to another, then another. And ye must know that this one," he looked over at me for emphasis, "is verra stubborn and determined."

Lily's sad gaze met mine.

"We both are," Brodie assured her. "And we will find the one responsible. I promise ye. As far as ye are concerned, it's important that ye continue with yer lessons just as if Miss Mallory was here. She would want ye to do that."

She seemed to think about that. "May I be excused?" she politely asked.

"Of course, dear," Aunt Antonia told her. "Perhaps Mikaela might join you in the sword room if you feel the need."

Lily nodded, rose from her chair and laid her napkin on the table, just as any properly raised young lady might.

"I have found that a bit of exercise with a sword is a great reliever of frustration," my great-aunt announced. "And as I recall, for you as well, my dear," she told me.

"Something that you should be aware of, Mr. Brodie," she added.

"I've already witnessed her skill in that regard," he replied, as we heard the first sounds of music from the music room.

"I do believe that is Chopin," Aunt Antonia announced.

Concerto No. 2, to be precise, and Lily performed it exquisitely. I knew that from countless agonizing hours I spent with my own music teacher very near the same age as Lily.

It was another of the talents I somewhat lacked, along with any artistic ability with oils or water colors. And the reason I was often given to question whether Linnie and I had the same set of parents.

My sister had acquired all the artistic ability, while I much preferred...

"The sword room and hiking about the forest in the north of Scotland?" Brodie commented when I mentioned the vast difference between Linnie and myself, as my aunt's coachman took us back to the office on the Strand.

"How could two sisters possibly be so very different?" I had asked.

"It would seem that ye favor her ladyship," he replied. "Considerin' the stories ye've told me when she was a young girl. And no doubt, bein' raised by someone of her nature might have rubbed off on ye a wee bit."

That dark gaze found mine through the shadows in the coach from the lanterns that Mr. Hastings had lit against the gloom of the day.

"We must find the person who did this," I replied, my throat suddenly tight. "For the Mallorys and Charlotte's fiancé, and of course for Lily. This is very hard for her."

He reached across the space between the two seats and took my hand.

"Aye, ye understand, lass. We both understand."

. . .

"A red rose," I said aloud, as I sat at the edge of the desk across from Brodie and stared at the chalkboard after returning from Sussex Square and the funeral service earlier for Charlotte Mallory.

In addition to the few pieces of information that we'd gathered, I had made a separate list of possible motives.

It was late and the weather was beastly. We chose to spend the night at the office rather than return to Mayfair.

It was very near midnight when I went to bed, while Brodie chose to continue to work in the adjacent office.

That was very much like him with a case, even when there were few clues as in the murder of Charlotte Mallory.

He went back over everything, a habit from his days with the MET—the time that the body was found, others who might have been on the street that early in the evening. And that rose.

He was inclined to be skeptical about the rose we had seen on Charlotte Mallory's casket at Brompton. However, while skeptical since there were dozens upon dozens of floral arrangements there, I knew from experience he didn't dismiss it.

For myself, it was more useful to lay everything out, make my lists, and then put information on the chalkboard.

I suppose it was the reason we worked so well together, suggesting possibilities—his experience from the streets, mine from growing up in what was referred to as *polite society*. If one could call murder polite!

It was sometime later, after I had retired for the night, when sounds from the office wakened me, and I realized that Brodie was not alone.

I pulled on my skirt and shirtwaist, then stepped into the outer office, the wood floor of the office cold beneath my bare feet.

Brodie was at the desk, a deep frown on his face. Inspector Dooley stood across from him, his own expression grave. He glanced up at the sight of me.

"Beg pardon, Miss Forsythe. I thought Mr. Brodie should know."

In spite of the fact that he was now a police inspector, Mr. Dooley continued to greet Brodie formally from their time together with the MET.

"The call came in barely a half hour ago, and by the sound of it..."

"Aye," Brodie replied, then with a look over to me, "A young woman has been found dead in St. James's Park with a wound similar to Charlotte Mallory."

"She wasn't found right away, due to being short-staffed of constables at the park," Mr. Dooley explained, "as there's never any crime to speak of in that part of London, and what with the weather last night and all.

"And strange it was. The constables who eventually found her found a flower laid over her, almost as if the killer had placed it there."

"Was it a red rose?" I inquired, even as my thoughts refused to consider that it might be. It was too much of a coincidence.

Mr. Dooley's gaze narrowed. "It was. Just that one red rose, and enough to make someone like me, who has seen a great deal on the streets, uneasy.

"Laid out like she was and with that one red rose, like it was some sort of ceremony."

"Or sacrifice?" I suggested.

That dark gaze met mine. I could see by his grim expression that he had the same thought.

"Have ye identified the woman?" he asked.

Mr. Dooley nodded. "By way of a previous report we had from two days ago that she had gone missing. It was a bit difficult with..." He hesitated with a look in my direction. "Beg pardon again, miss. The body was somewhat deteriorated."

"It's quite all right Inspector Dooley." Evidently the young woman was in an advanced state of decay.

"Who filed the missing person report?" Brodie asked.

"The father, Judge Harold Cameron, made the report."

"There's a bit more," Dooley continued. "Even with the time o' night the body was found, the interim chief inspector, Mr. Graham, insisted on returning to the office."

"Graham?" Brodie seemed surprised.

"You may recall the man from your work with the MET. It's to be a temporary position until Mr. Abberline returns..."

Brodie was as surprised as I was. Chief Inspector Abberline, whom Brodie had what might be politely considered difficulty with in the past, had been put on suspension after a previous inquiry case of ours.

"I heard something of it," he acknowledged.

According to Brodie, Mr. Graham was well liked among the inspectors of the Metropolitan Police, as well as most police constables.

He had apparently worked his way up through police ranks, and was considered to be a fair man who obviously wasn't put off by making himself available, apparently even at this time of the night.

And it seemed that due to his experience as a constable, and then an inspector working the streets, he wasn't above participating in an investigation instead of delegating it to others, as Abberline had.

"I assume there is more to this," Brodie commented.

Mr. Dooley nodded. "He knows that you have been making inquiries regarding the Mallory murder. And now, a second murder with similar circumstances." He hesitated.

"Go on, Mr. Dooley," Brodie told him.

"He's a good man, and most of the men would like to see him permanent in the position."

"Get on with it, Dooley."

"He asked me to bring the copy of that report and inquire if you would be willing to meet with him later this mornin' regarding the two cases."

Brodie's eyes narrowed. "I know ye well, Dooley. There's nothin' that goes on at the Yard that ye dinna know about, and I've been grateful for yer assistance in the past. Now, tell me wot ye know of this."

"The word is that he wants you to join the police investigation in the matter of both murders."

Eight

"WILL you agree to join the investigation with the Metropolitan Police?" I asked after we arrived at the townhouse in Mayfair that same morning, to dress more appropriately after the meeting with Mr. Dooley at the office on the Strand only a few hours earlier.

Brodie had agreed to meet with Chief Inspector Graham at ten o'clock out of courtesy, given his respect for the man who had been given an almost impossible job. He was now the temporary replacement for Chief Inspector Abberline during his suspension.

"He's a good man, in an impossible situation. And now with two murders, one victim bein' the daughter of a prominent barrister, the other the daughter of an equally prominent Judge of the Court."

Mrs. Ryan provided breakfast, then we both dressed for the appointment. Brodie insisted that I attend the meeting as well, since the original inquiry case for Lily, if one could call it a case, was in the matter of Charlotte Mallory's murder.

"And?" I prompted him. I could tell there was more to the thought behind the frown and that hooded dark gaze, as I pushed his hands aside and proceeded to tie his tie for him.

"I dinna know how ye figure the damned thing out," he grumbled. "It makes me think how ye might have learned it."

He does have a habit of grumbling when he's deep in thought, particularly in the matter of an inquiry case.

"A bit jealous, are you?" I teased.

"That has nothin' to do with it."

Oh, really, I thought, as I wove the end of the silk tie—he did loathe them—under, over, and through, then smoothed the silk.

"It's not proper for an unmarried lady to know such things. And ye were unmarried when ye first tied me own tie."

"Then you are complaining that I knew how to tie one, and you didn't," I concluded.

"I have no use for the damned things!"

"I am well aware of that. Still, it does make you look..."

There was that frown again.

"Quite handsome, especially with the glare. As if you were some brigand who might carry me off and have his way with me."

That stopped him. "Brigand?"

"A man of dubious reputation," I translated.

The glare slowly melted. His hands closed around mine.

"I'd much rather carry ye off than meet with the 'Interim' Chief Inspector of the Metropolitan Police."

"It won't hurt to listen to what he has to say."

"That he wants me to join their investigation—ye know my feelin's in that regard."

"Of course, dear," I replied. That dark brow with the scar through it arched at my reply.

"Wot is yer meanin'?"

"Chief Inspector Graham sent Mr. Dooley with a request for you to meet with him. He knows you from past experience. He also obviously knows that you may very well have information regarding Charlotte Mallory's murder."

"Wot else?"

"I would imagine that he's being watched very closely, with Mr. Abberline set aside for the time being."

"Go on."

"It seems to me that you are in a position to name your own

rules and requirements, and still proceed as before. After all, you are no longer under the authority of the MET."

"Has anyone ever told ye that ye have a curious mind for such things?"

"I believe that I may have heard that once or twice before."

We arrived promptly for our meeting with Chief Inspector Graham. I say *we*, as Brodie insisted that I was to be included.

We walked into the old building of Great Scotland Yard police quarters, and I immediately experienced a sense of déjà vu. I had read about it previously, proposed by a French philosopher, that sense of having done something exactly the same or being in a place where one had been before.

I very definitely felt that now, upon entering the Great Scotland Yard, which would eventually be moved to new headquarters very near the Tower of London. But for now, as in the recent past, the sounds, the smell, and the cloying feeling was there as it had been when I had first come there during the investigation into my sister's disappearance.

And then there was what Brodie had suffered at the hand of Chief Inspector Abberline, a most despicable man. I was hopeful that he might not return to the position.

"What is it?" Brodie asked.

"It's just that…being here again, after what happened."

That dark gaze met mine. "Aye."

I tried to push back the memory of the last time I had been to this place, yet it was impossible—the sight of him imprisoned in a cell at the back of the building, beaten and bloodied.

"If ye'd rather go some other place and wait until I've met with the man, I understand."

I shook my head. "We do this together."

I could only imagine what it took for him to return here.

He frowned. "Aye. We'll hear wot the man has to say. Then decide what's to be done."

I had not previously met Mr. Graham. Yet, Brodie seemed to at least have an admirable opinion of the man. Fair and reasonable, he had described him on the coach ride to the series of buildings at Whitehall Place that comprised Old Scotland Yard.

Still, I thought it couldn't be demolished soon enough. Not that I was one to hold a grudge over Brodie's experience there. Not bloody likely!

Mr. Graham was a pleasant-looking man, in his late forties by Brodie's estimation, with greying hair that had receded somewhat, side whiskers, and quite neat in his appearance. The smile that greeted us was cordial.

"Mr. Brodie, thank you for agreeing to meet. And Lady Forsythe. Your successes in your inquiry cases precede you. But of course, I am not surprised, Brodie. You have shown yourself most admirable in the past in service to the MET in spite of... certain circumstances."

Did I detect an apology in the greeting? Not in so many words, as evidenced by the chief inspector's careful glance at the young constable who had accompanied us to his office.

"You may go now, Mr. Hughson," he dismissed the constable.

The careful smile broadened after the man had gone.

"It is damned good to see you Brodie. After certain things, mistakes that were made..."

"Best left in the past, sir," Brodie replied somewhat formally.

"We have both walked the streets and apprehended some fairly dangerous sorts. I believe that we can dispense with formalities."

Brodie merely nodded an acknowledgement in a way I had seen before, and now here as well. He was after all a Scot.

"Please sit, both of you." He offered to have coffee brought. Brodie declined.

"Perhaps best to get on with the point of yer request to meet."

"Yes, I do understand," Graham replied, and I did sense that he understood very well Brodie's guardedness.

"You have taken an inquiry case in the matter of a young woman who was found dead several days ago, Miss Charlotte Mallory. May I ask who your client is?"

"You may ask," Brodie replied.

I looked over at him with some surprise. We had not discussed the need to keep Lily out of this. I need not have been concerned.

"That is a confidential matter," Brodie then added.

"I understand. However, in the interest of finding the person or persons responsible..." Mr. Graham suggested.

Brodie's silence was his answer.

"Very well," the chief inspector continued. "She was the daughter of..."

"Sir Edward Mallory, barrister," Brodie finally replied. "The dailies published the information."

He said nothing of the copy of the police report, and I did wonder if Mr. Graham was aware that it had been made available to us.

He nodded. "Yes, of course, the dailies. That brings us to the matter regarding my request for this meeting. As you are aware from Mr. Dooley's call on you in the middle of the night, there has been another murder of a young woman under somewhat similar circumstances."

Brodie merely nodded. He was deliberately letting the chief inspector continue, to reveal as much as possible about the latest murder in an attempt to learn what we could from the meeting.

"As I'm certain Dooley shared with you, the new murder victim, Margaret Cameron, is the daughter of Judge Harold Cameron. The circumstances are frightening and quite similar.

"It does seem that the two murders may have been committed by the same person, which brings us to my request for this meeting.

"With your experience, I don't need to explain the high importance of these two cases and the urgency to find the one responsible. In that regard, I'm proposing a joint investigation.

"You have resources from your time with the MET as well as in your private work, which is commendable," he continued, "while I have the resources of the Metropolitan Police and the vast experience of many years of service. Not to mention that you are one man, and the MET is well over thirteen thousand constables and inspectors who are on the streets of London daily. A collaboration of efforts could be highly successful."

Collaboration? Joint investigation?

I could only imagine what that might look like.

How would new clues be handled?

The MET might have several thousand constables, however the rampant crime that still plagued the streets of London spoke to their efficiency. Or lack thereof. And then there was the question of authority in the joint investigations.

There were dozens of questions, none of which solved the murder of either young woman. I could only imagine the paperwork that would be required, perhaps daily filing of reports. And precisely how were we to obtain information from those working the cases at the MET?

I looked over at Brodie. His expression was unreadable in that way that gave nothing away of his thoughts. Yet, I could imagine what some of them might be.

The chief inspector, temporary that he was, was suggesting an alliance that would put Brodie back in partnership with the very organization, under the authority of Chief Inspector Abberline, that had caused Brodie to leave the MET some years before. And recently, he had been imprisoned by Abberline under false charges and brutally beaten during a private investigation.

I knew precisely what my answer would have been, under the same circumstances, something polite but very direct.

Still, I was fully aware that certain connections Brodie had within the MET had been valuable in the past. Maintaining those relationships was a delicate balance as it was.

Most certainly Mr. Dooley, who had recently made inspector. And Mr. Conner as well. Although now retired, he had no great affection for the MET after over twenty-five years of service.

All three had seen a great deal on their time on the streets. However, Brodie's experience had exposed a darker side of the

MET that included unscrupulous tactics, even revenge against fellow inspectors.

"Yer proposal has merit," Brodie tactfully replied. "However, there are several questions to be answered. Who would be in authority? What sort of structure between the both of us do ye propose?

"As ye well know time is often crucial when investigating a crime and gaining the trust of those on the street most critical as that is where information comes from. I do understand the urgency in particular in this matter, with the deaths of the daughters of two prominent members of the legal system who want answers."

"I understand that you might need some time to consider this, and to discuss it between you," the chief inspector commented.

"As to the authority in the matter, you would, of course, have authority over your own part of the investigation, including any sources you rely upon, with the provision that there would need to be a sharing of that information."

"And from the MET as well," Brodie replied.

"That would be the purpose of such an arrangement," Mr. Graham acknowledged. "I do realize that you have reservations about such an arrangement considering past issues. However, in the interest of finding the person who has committed these horrible crimes, perhaps..."

"I appreciate the consideration, sir," Brodie told him. "And I do understand the important nature of the situation. However, joining the two investigations might hinder as well as help in the matter."

Mr. Graham turned to me.

"Surely you see the advantage, Lady Forsythe. Particularly in consideration of the past inquiry into the disappearance of your sister."

"You may not have fully known the situation, sir," I told him. "I was forced to turn to Mr. Brodie for assistance when it became obvious that I could not rely on the Metropolitan Police. The only reason she was found safe was through his efforts."

"I wasn't aware, Lady Forsythe. Nevertheless," he turned back to Brodie. "We need your assistance in this... *I* need your assistance."

The chief inspector came out of his chair and rounded the desk.

"You are no doubt aware of recent *events* here at the MET, regrettable events, and I do not blame you for your reluctance. The truth is my position in the office is temporary. I have no ambitions for higher position as others do. I know of your recent experience here."

I looked over at Brodie to see his reaction, but there was none, only that dark, steady gaze, while I felt anger all over again just at the memory of it.

"The truth of the matter, just between those present, is that if it is left in the hands of others... I have no confidence that the murderer will be found.

"It is sad to say that the MET is in disarray. Men perform their shifts with many looking the other way from things they see on the street while others—good men—are put in harm's way. I want the person who has committed these horrible murders caught, and I will do whatever is necessary to see the matter done."

I did not know the man, even though Brodie had spoken highly of him. He was in an unenviable position no doubt. However, I believed him.

He seemed, much like Brodie, one of those 'good' men, forced to beg in order to find the person who had murdered Charlotte Mallory and now Margaret Cameron, for it did appear that it might very well be the same person.

"There would be conditions for sharing the investigation," Brodie said after much consideration.

"Very well. What are your conditions?"

"If we are to participate, we are to have access to all reports submitted to you, along with any in the past regarding the murders. We will provide a report as necessary."

Mr. Graham nodded.

"Lady Forsythe is to be included in this."

Once again there was a nod, which surprised me, considering the usual objections about a woman taking part in such things, even outright contempt.

"Most particularly, Inspector Dooley is to be part of this, and he will answer only to me."

Mr. Graham slowly nodded once more.

"Is that all?" he asked.

It was not.

"Most important," Brodie replied. "Lady Forsythe and I will make every effort to find the one responsible for the murders. But we answer to no one in this. Not even yerself. That is not negotiable."

I fully expected the chief inspector to object, or in the very least to make his own conditions. I was surprised when he did not.

It may have spoken to the seriousness of the matter and expectations that the murders be resolved as quickly as possible. Or possibly something else between the two men.

If Brodie was surprised that there was no objection, he gave no indication.

"You drive a hard bargain," Mr. Graham eventually replied.

"That is the only bargain I will accept," Brodie replied.

"What you're asking for violates several rules and regulations of conduct and procedures of the MET."

Brodie's response was in his expression. There would be no compromise.

"Very well," the chief inspector finally said. "Agreed." Then, in a slightly sarcastic tone. "I suppose that you want this in writing."

I stood as Brodie rose from his own chair, the meeting very

obviously at an end. He paused at the door to the chief inspector's office.

"Ye are a Scot, Mr. Graham."

"My father and mother as well." He watched Brodie with open curiosity.

"Yer word on our arrangement will do," Brodie told him as we turned to leave. "And I will hope to see Mr. Dooley with the police report. Then we will begin."

The chief inspector took out a pen and wrote something on the back of what appeared to be a calling card.

"You may need this." He handed it to Brodie.

"Will he keep his word?" I asked as we reached the street and Brodie signaled for a cab.

"He will."

Or? I thought.

The answer to that was obviously in that comment: '*Ye are a Scot.*'

I knew what it meant between Brodie and Munro, a loyalty that was bone deep between the two of them. A promise once made would never be broken.

It was part of who they both were, that Scottish background, relying upon each other to survive on the streets as young boys. Even now.

If one was to need the other, that one would be there, no questions asked. And the secrets they shared?

I was somewhat new to the arrangement. Yet I was learning what that loyalty meant and grateful for it.

Bone deep. That brought all sorts of situations to mind that I might not want to question too thoroughly about the past.

As far as the here and now, it did seem that initially Mr. Graham intended to keep his word about those 'conditions' Brodie had told him.

And that calling card that Mr. Graham had given him. It declared that Brodie was to be given every consideration and full cooperation, along with Mr. Graham's signature.

. . .

Within an hour of our arrival back at the office on the Strand, Mr. Dooley arrived with a large envelope in hand.

"I don't know what you told the man." He handed the envelope to Brodie. "He said ye were to have the report in the matter of the Cameron murder, anything else that you ask for, and that I am to consider myself part of your investigation for the time being."

Mr. Dooley shook his head as he sat across the desk while Brodie opened the envelope and read through the police report on the Cameron murder.

"Forget I said anything about it," Mr. Dooley added. "It's probably best that I don't know the reason."

Nine

THE POLICE REPORT that had arrived with Mr. Dooley was quite thorough.

It stated the approximate time two constables were dispatched from their area to investigate a body found in St. James's Park by an individual named Edgar Peabody.

Mr. Peabody, a London wine merchant, was returning from a late delivery to one of the residences at the edge of St. James's Park, and might have run over the body of the young woman if one of his horses hadn't shied away.

No one else was seen in the area at the time, which indicated that Margaret Cameron might have been abducted and killed at another location.

Other information in the report included the single knife wound that had obviously killed the victim almost immediately, and a note regarding a flower, later said to be a red rose, laid across her body.

"What do ye know of the two constables who were called out when the body was found?" Brodie asked Mr. Dooley.

"Good men, both. I've walked the street with John Hix. The other one is young but has good reviews from his superiors.

"Where is the young woman's body at this time?" he then asked.

"The family requested that it be taken to their private physician in Westminster."

"We will want to see the body, even though the report appears most thorough."

"I thought you might, Mr. Brodie. I've already sent word to the physician's office that you would be calling on him in the matter."

Brodie nodded. "How was the young woman originally identified?"

"There was a post with her name on it in the lady's bag she carried. With that information, the family was notified."

"Was there anything else found in the young woman's handbag?" I asked.

"There were several coins along with a comb. She was wearing a watch pin on her jacket as well, but no other jewelry."

Several coins and a watch pin, none of it taken by whoever had attacked and killed Margaret Cameron. It appeared that robbery was not the motive.

"Any indication of an assault of an intimate nature?" Brodie asked.

Color appeared on Mr. Dooley's face. "There was no mention of it by the police surgeon on his examination of the body."

Brodie looked over at me. "We will want to see the body as well."

"What can I do to assist?" Mr. Dooley inquired.

"Best see what you can learn about the wine merchant, Mr. Peabody. His reputation, any other encounters with the police, the reason he was making that late delivery, and if he saw anyone else about before the constables arrived."

"There might be something to learn about the location he made that delivery," Mr. Dooley added. "I'll see to that as well."

"I ask that ye not discuss anything with anyone at this time. Not even the chief inspector."

"He's a good man," Mr. Dooley replied.

Brodie nodded. "However, two young women have been murdered. One is the daughter of a Judge of the Court, the other is the daughter of a prominent barrister. For now, we keep everything we learn private until we know more."

"You have my word, sir. I'll be off then. I will let you know as soon as I have information."

Brodie stopped him at the door. "We dinna know wot this is about. However, with two murders involving two prominent families, best watch yer back."

Mr. Dooley nodded and then left.

"Wot are ye thinkin'?" Brodie asked after he had gone.

"It would seem that robbery was not the motive. Then there is the rose that was found on the body. And now a second murder once again with a rose left behind. I assume it is not a coincidence?"

"Aye, verry likely not a coincidence. We should call on the Mallory family's physician this afternoon, before the young woman is buried."

"Might Mr. Brimley be able to assist?" I asked.

"I'll put through a call for him to meet us there."

In spite of the late time of the afternoon and the usual London traffic on the street that often made navigating the city that time of day quite difficult, we made the trip to Westminster in good time. Mr. Brimley had arrived just prior, and met us on the street.

"Another murder?" He looked at the brass nameplate beside the door in the main entrance. Discreet, tasteful, with the name Alan Cameron, Physician. Otherwise, the brownstone building, with tall street-side windows and that dark green door with a brass bell beside, might have been any fashionable residence found in Westminster, or Mayfair for that matter.

Brodie and I looked at each other. Cameron—not an uncommon name. Still, was it possible the physician was a member of the young woman's family?

That would explain the reason her body had been released from the Yard so quickly and brought here rather than a mortuary.

"I know the man," Mr. Brimley explained. "I studied with him at King's College. Seems to have done well for himself."

A woman in a starched black dress met us at the door. Brodie gave her our names. She showed us into what was a waiting room that could have been someone's formal parlor.

"I will let the doctor know that you are here."

Dr. Cameron eventually appeared. He was of average height, approximately fifty years of age, I would guess. He was clean-shaven except for side whiskers, with light brown hair that was beginning to gray.

"I was told to expect you," he said with a brief glance at Brodie. "I'm certain you understand this is a very difficult time. You are with the Metropolitan Police?"

Brodie didn't bother to explain that it was a private inquiry which might have been a bit confusing.

"We appreciate your assistance in the matter," he replied. "You may be acquainted with Mr. Brimley," he made the introductions.

"From King's College," Brimley provided.

"I'm sorry, I do not remember. You are a physician?" Dr. Cameron inquired.

"My work took me in another direction, sir—research. However, from time to time I assist as I can."

I thought his answer quite clever—considering the small laboratory at the back of his apothecary shop. And truth be known, I would have trusted his medical skills over any other, and had. The bullet wound in my shoulder had healed most excellently.

"I asked Mr. Brimley to accompany us for his expertise in certain matters that could be helpful," Brodie explained and left it at that.

Dr. Cameron nodded somewhat distracted, I thought.

"We will need to see the body," Brodie told him and presented the card that the chief inspector had given him.

"Of course," Dr. Cameron replied, still quite distracted it seemed. Or was it something else?

"If you will come this way."

We followed him down a hallway past what appeared to be his private office, past another room with door closed, then toward the back of the brownstone.

"This is a most dreadful situation."

We had finally reached a set of double doors at the rear of the building.

"You must understand. The victim is my brother's daughter. He asked that her body be brought here rather than the police morgue."

Brodie and I exchanged a look. This was a development we had not anticipated. But what did it mean?

"I assure you we will make our observations as quickly as possible and not cause any undue difficulty," Brodie assured him.

I was not at all certain what that was supposed to mean. But it seemed to address Dr. Cameron's concerns, as he led us into the large room that appeared to serve as a surgery, with overhead lights, a variety of instruments on a metal side table, and of course, an examination table with a sheet drawn over.

"We appreciate your concerns and your assistance in this," Brodie told him, by way of excusing him so that he and Mr. Brimley could conduct their own examination of the body without the accompaniment of Dr. Cameron.

"I see. Yes, well I do have an appointment to prepare for. I will be in my office. You will let me know when you have completed your observations?"

Brodie assured him that he would.

Viewing dead bodies was never pleasant, but over time I managed to steel myself accordingly. It was the unexpected discovery that very definitely had a way of unnerving me. That first shock that eventually gave way to sympathy and the curiosity when we were investigating a case.

My first encounter had been that body in the Nile River on one of my travels, covered in flies.

I reminded myself this was not the Nile, and the body under that sheet was not some poor nameless soul who, it was later discovered, had been a river pirate gone afoul of others.

This was a young woman at the beginning of her life, cruelly murdered and then left at the edge of St. James's Park like so much refuse tossed away.

I prepared myself in the usual way, with the thought that the most important thing now was to find the murderer, as Mr. Brimley reached for the edge of the sheet that covered her body and drew it back.

Margaret Cameron wore a badly stained blue walking skirt with a short jacket over. Her dark blonde hair was tangled with leaves and twigs.

Her shirtwaist was stained with blood as was to be expected given the circumstances of her death.

"How long would you estimate that she's been dead?" Brodie asked.

"Perhaps three to four days. You say she was found at St. James's?" He proceeded to carefully open the front of her jacket.

"The wound is here." He gently probed the cut fabric of the jacket and the shirtwaist underneath.

"A knife wound, just there under the ribs. Here is something interesting."

He retrieved an instrument from the side table and gently probed the wound.

"The blade was approximately five to six inches and there was just the one wound. It would have severed a major artery, and very likely internal organs. Death would have been very quick with the loss of so much blood. It's difficult to determine anything more, as there has been loss of some tissue, creatures in the park perhaps," he explained. "Animals and other things, worms and such."

Yes, of course, I thought as I listened. Worms.

"Three to four days," Brodie commented. "Then, she would have been murdered very soon after Charlotte Mallory."

"There is this as well," Mr. Brimley drew our attention once more as he examined Margaret Cameron's fingers.

"There appear to be some sort of small puncture wounds."

I looked at Brodie.

"Could it be the sort of puncture wounds that might come from the stem of a rose?" I asked.

"Perhaps or possibly from something as she reached out and then fell."

According to Mr. Dooley, a rose was found on Margaret Cameron's body, the same as Charlotte Mallory. However, in looking about the doctor's examination room, there was no sign of it. Nor had Dr. Cameron made any mention of it.

I found her handbag that had been set aside. According to the police report, it contained substantial coins, the same as Charlotte Mallory.

Once more, a young woman murdered, and robbery apparently was not the motive.

"Is there anything else?" Brodie asked. "Anything found under her nails that might indicate a struggle with her attacker?"

Mr. Brimley shook his head. "Such a pity. So young and those out there that would do such a thing."

Doctor Cameron had returned. "Will that be all then?" he asked.

"Was there anything else found about the body when it was brought here?" Brodie inquired.

"No, nothing," the doctor replied. "If you are quite finished, I am expecting an appointment that I must prepare for."

An appointment? This late in the day?

"Of course," Brodie replied as we prepared to leave. He turned back at the door.

"Ye are Judge Cameron's brother, are ye not?" he asked.

"Yes," he replied. "My brother was drawn to the law, while I preferred the practice of medicine."

"And you have been most successful it would seem," Brodie commented, with a slow look about the examination room and then a look into the outer office, with its expensive furnishings usually found in the front parlor of someone of some means.

"I have been most fortunate. As Mr. Brimley can attest, I received the finest education at King's College, as well as four years of study at the medical school in Edinburgh."

"That would include research as well?" Mr. Brimley inquired.

"Yes, the finest in research and new treatments."

It was then the woman in the black gown appeared at the entrance to the examination room.

"If there is nothing else, I will be leaving now, Dr. Cameron."

"Yes, of course, Miss Phipps," he replied.

"May we see you home, Miss Phipps?" I inquired with a sudden thought. "It is quite late of the afternoon, and one can never be too careful." The body on the examination table, case in point, I thought.

I caught the look Brodie gave me at the offer to accompany her. She was obviously surprised.

"Thank you, no," she cordially replied. My flat is only a short way from here. No need to trouble yourselves. Good evening."

I made a mental note of that.

I caught a glimpse of her through the open doorway to the front office, slipping on a long coat and then tucking an umbrella under her arm.

"We will be leaving as well," Brodie told the doctor. "I thank ye for yer time."

Out on the street Brodie waved down a cab for Mr. Brimley, then held back.

"And good evening to ye, Mr. Brimley."

He nodded. "And you as well, Mr. Brodie. Miss Forsythe."

When he had gone, Brodie took me by the arm and pulled me

away from the light of the streetlamp and into the shadows just beyond, as the lights in the doctor's office were extinguished. We waited. In very short order, a coach arrived.

"That is convenient," I whispered. "Particularly when one is expecting the arrival of someone for an appointment?"

The doctor came out of his office, set the lock on the door, then climbed into the coach.

"And private coach at that," I commented. "And perhaps time enough to put through a call to someone beforehand?"

"My thoughts as well," Brodie replied. "It would seem that the good doctor was in somewhat of a hurry," he added.

"Come along, before the good doctor returns." He left our hiding place there in the shadows and retraced our steps back to the entrance of the doctor's office.

He handed me the hand-held light he always carried.

The lock took some effort, but eventually we heard the faint click of the tumblers and he pushed the door open. I stepped past him into Dr. Cameron's darkened office.

We relied on the hand-held light rather than turn on the electric, so as not to draw suspicion by anyone who passed by.

As I moved about the office in the beam of that light, I asked myself, where might someone dispose of something?

Brodie went to the examination room and closed the door. There was a sudden sliver of light at the bottom of the door as he turned on the electric. I continued the search with the hand-held in the outer office.

There was a table and four chairs, a set of wood cabinets against one wall, and the desk Miss Phipps obviously occupied. Atop the desk was a desk calendar, an ink pen in a holder, and a leather-bound book that turned out to be an appointment book.

Most interesting, there was no appointment shown for that time of the afternoon, in spite of what Doctor Cameron had told us.

I searched the drawers of the desk and found nothing unusual other than the doctor's stationary, appointment cards, a card file with what appeared to be patient names, many whom I recognized, and other items that might be found in a business office.

After searching all the drawers, I searched under the desk and found the rubbish container. I pulled it out.

"There was nothing in the examination room or in a private room beyond where the doctor might stay over late at night with a patient who needs care."

"I seem to have found something." I held out a thick wadded piece of paper.

I unfolded it and the contents spilled out onto the desk—a badly crushed red rose.

"Aye," Brodie replied. "So ye have. Bring it along... we're finished here."

I carefully folded it in that piece of paper then slipped it between the pages of my notebook.

The question was, what did it mean that a single rose had been found on the bodies of both Charlotte Mallory and Margaret Cameron. Furthermore, what did it mean that Doctor Cameron chose not to disclose the rose I had just found, even though it was noted in the police report?

"He wouldn't have known that," Brodie pointed out. "But the question remains, why was it thrown out?"

"And," I added, "where was the good doctor going after he said that he was expecting a late appointment?"

Ten

I HAVE DISCOVERED in our inquiry cases that when it comes to crime, nothing is trivial or unimportant. Everything discovered, each clue, often leads to something else, and then something important.

It was, as I pointed out to Brodie, very much like a jigsaw puzzle, one piece led to another until the whole picture emerged. So far, we had only a few random pieces to this puzzle and none of them connected. Yet.

Which led me now to pace before the chalkboard in the office on the Strand where I had made new notes after returning from our visit with Dr. Cameron.

We had learned two very important things:

One: the good doctor had specifically said that nothing else was found on the body other than a few coins in Margaret Cameron's handbag.

Two: We had, after much searching, found the rose in the rubbish container in the front office by Miss Phipps's desk, very near the same as the flower found on Charlotte Mallory's body.

Either Miss Phipps had thought it unimportant and simply tossed it away, or there had been a deliberate attempt to get rid of it either by her or Doctor Cameron. Then there was the doctor's immediate departure after we left.

I contemplated all of this as Brodie sat at the desk, going over the police report Mr. Dooley had provided. Then the service bell at the landing rang.

Supper had arrived. I was starving.

Brodie went out onto the landing, and returned with the supper Mr. Cavendish had brought from the Public House across the way. It was neatly wrapped in brown paper and then in a paper bag to make it easier for Mr. Cavendish to navigate the Strand without losing it.

He did have a penchant for crossing the Strand at a dangerous speed that terrified coach and cart drivers as well, with Rupert the hound usually close beside amidst shaken fists and colorful curses.

"Meat pies!" I exclaimed of that hearty fare found in most working areas of London. And those from the public house, prepared by Miss Effie, who had become a good friend, were most excellent.

"And for Mr. Cavendish as well?" I inquired, as she usually sent along supper for him.

"Aye," Brodie replied. "He and that disgusting hound were well into their pies in the alcove when I retrieved our supper."

"Has he said anything yet?" I asked.

"About wot?"

"Miss Effie," I replied. "There is most definitely something going on there."

That dark gaze met mine as he set a paper carton before me on the desk.

"Miss Effie and Cavendish?"

"Hmmm," I replied as I savored the meat pie. "They have been spending a considerable amount of time together."

It was so like a man not to notice these things.

"Miss Effie and Cavendish?" he repeated.

"It is quite obvious. He even inquired what sort of candy she might like."

He had set his fork down and stared at me.

"She leaves the door to the storeroom at the Public House open for him when the weather turns," I pointed out. "And he has most definitely improved in his attire."

"When might this have happened?"

"It's been going on for several months. They are both unattached, after all." Although I supposed the hound might be considered an attachment.

I was well into my meat pie, and enjoying it immensely.

"It is possible, you know," I added. "Even with his infirmity. He is quite robust."

"Robust?" he repeated.

I smiled to myself. I was enjoying the conversation. I angled him a teasing look.

"The old saying, where there's a will, there's a way?" I suggested.

He shook his head. "Ye are shameless."

I rose from my side of the desk and returned to the chalk-board. I studied the lists of clues we had discovered, along with the evidence from the two murders.

"Two women, both from well-placed families, found murdered. Both women killed in the same manner, no apparent struggle, nothing of value taken, and no other physical violation." I turned back to where Brodie sat at the desk.

"Is it possible the murderer was known to them?"

He took out his pipe and filled the bowl with tobacco, then lit it. I did love the smell of pipe tobacco.

"Perhaps. Or it might be that the man was so well-dressed—considering that fiber Mr. Brimley discovered—that they felt no cause for alarm."

I looked at what was left of the second rose we had discovered in Dr. Cameron's office.

"A rose was found with both victims," I continued. "A red rose." I was thoughtful.

"A red rose is a symbol of passion, usually given by a man to his lover, but that does not seem to be so in this case."

"Ye seem to know quite a bit about that," Brodie commented as he poured two tumblers of whisky, then rose and approached where I stood before the chalkboard. He handed one to me.

"Two apparently random murders within a few days of each other, a red rose found on each body." I took a sip and continued.

"Either Miss Phipps or Doctor Cameron attempted to dispose of the one found on Margaret Cameron. And let us not forget that he stated that he was awaiting an appointment that late in the day—obviously an excuse to get rid of us, and then his sudden departure in a private coach."

"Wot?" Brodie asked, that dark gaze watching me. He did know me so well.

"Something in Dr. Cameron's manner," I replied

"Yer woman's instinct again, perhaps?"

There wasn't the usual teasing tone this time when he said it. It did seem that it might be possible for Angus Brodie to learn something. And from a woman! Oh, my.

"It was something in his manner." I attempted to explain what it was that I had sensed. "He seemed..."

"Preoccupied? Perhaps uneasy?" Brodie suggested.

"Yes! Very much so. Almost as if..."

"As if he knew more than he was telling us, perhaps even hiding something."

I turned to him. "You sensed it as well."

"It comes with experience. Ye see enough crimes, the people who commit them and others, and ye pick up on things. Congratulations, Mrs. Brodie. Ye've learned a great deal."

It was so like a man to give himself a pat on the back and take full credit.

"It could simply be natural instinct," I pointed out. "It is said that women most particularly seem to have that."

"Women's instinct?" he replied.

"It was through instinct that I decided you might be qualified to assist in pursuing my sister's case," I pointed out.

Never mind that the initial recommendation had come from my great-aunt. That was beside the point.

"Instinct?" he repeated.

"On the surface you hardly seemed the reputable sort," I explained. "However, you proved yourself most adequate." I had sensed other things about Angus Brodie at the time, but this was enough to share for now.

"Adequate?" he replied.

One look at that dark gaze and I knew quite well the reason that I tolerated that insufferable Scot manner. That and the other reason of course. No other man I had ever known valued my thoughts and ideas, and... that woman's instinct.

We had determined that in spite of the two recent deaths and what would normally be the appropriate period of mourning, we needed to speak with the families of Charlotte Mallory and Margaret Cameron for any possibility that there was something they might be able to share something that would shed light on their deaths. Difficult as it was, it needed to be done.

I have found in the past that my official title as Lady Forsythe did have a tendency to open certain doors, and I was not opposed to using it.

Nor was I opposed to using my great-aunt's name of Montgomery when it came to doors that might be firmly closed for one reason or another, most particularly when it came to an official investigation. It could be off-putting.

"What was the response when ye made the request to meet with Sir Mallory?" Brodie asked as our driver navigated traffic across London to the Mallory residence in Knightsbridge.

The telephone call that I put through had been answered by a servant who politely but firmly informed that due to a recent family loss, Sir Mallory was not receiving any visitors.

I had then asked to speak with Sir Mallory and gave my formal name, Lady Mikaela Forsythe. There had been a sudden silence from the person at the other end. It was then that Sir Mallory responded and proceeded to explain the same, and surely I understood.

I politely informed him that we were making inquiries as part of the official investigation by the Metropolitan Police, and added that I was certain he supported that, given his professional position and in the interest of finding the persons responsible.

I then added that if it was not convenient to meet with myself and Mr. Brodie, that the current chief inspector would need to meet with him in the matter at his office.

A polite but curt response followed that he would be able to meet with us at ten o'clock of the morning.

"Ye are quite ruthless," Brodie commented now.

"The pot calling the kettle black?" I replied as we sped across London toward our meeting with Sir Mallory.

When we arrived, we were met at the main entrance of the Mallory residence by the head butler, who announced our arrival in a voice I recognized from that telephone call.

"Lady Forsythe," he acknowledged now, with an expectant look at Brodie.

"Mr. Brodie," he provided the introduction. "Consultant with the Metropolitan Police."

That did seem the best way to describe his association with the MET. We were immediately shown unto the formal library to await Sir Mallory.

The residence was draped in black, as was to be expected of a household during a period of mourning.

Black crepe had been hung across the front entrance, mirrors were draped in black or turned to the wall. There were dozens of bouquets of flowers about the front parlor as we passed by. However, not a red rose in sight.

While we waited, I glanced at Sir Mallory's preference for reading. Not that I thought I might find one of my books on the shelves behind his desk, however I have always found it interesting to glimpse a person's preferences. It can tell a great deal about them.

There were two shelves filled with books regarding the law, which was to be expected. There were also books on the history of English rule from the time of the Conquest through the sixteenth century—Aunt Antonia would have been amused at that, since her ancestors filled the pages of English history.

There were also books on military campaigns, including the war with the American colonies, and a half-dozen volumes by Mr. Dickens. A most interesting variety, and in itself gave me some insight into the man who had acquired the reputation of being one of the most well-known and successful barristers in England.

That brief conversation over the telephone and the glimpse into his preferred reading did not prepare me for the man who eventually joined us in the library.

I had expected someone lean, perhaps even gaunt, the events of the past days heavy in the lines on his face.

Sir Edward Mallory was somewhat portly, immaculately dressed, with what I thought to be deceptively cordial features, thick brows drawn together and a frown on his mouth.

From things my great-aunt had told me, he had to be very near sixty years old. His suit was black, as was to be expected, however except for that, there was an energy about the man that belied age and circumstances, a man very much in control. Perhaps that came with his profession.

"I was told that you would be calling. You must forgive my man, Mr. Hobbs. He was doing his official duty at this very difficult time for our family." He turned to me.

"You were at the service for my daughter earlier this week."

We exchanged brief pleasantries, if it could be called that under the circumstances. He invited us to sit in the thick upholstered chairs before his desk.

"And we have met before," he acknowledged Brodie. "In your work with the MET, I believe."

Brodie nodded. "I gave evidence it two cases regarding clients that you represented at the time."

"Yes, I remember, and I want you to know that I will assist now however I can. The person who is responsible must be found and held to account."

We discussed the events of the evening that Charlotte Mallory was killed, her appointments that day, and that she was to meet her fiancé for supper at Rule's after leaving the print shop.

"There was no difficulty that you were aware of, between her and Mr. Eddington?" Brodie inquired.

"No, of course not. The wedding was to be in January. He is a fine young man, with my office, as I'm certain you're aware. He is devastated, absolutely devastated over this, as you can no doubt imagine."

"There was an item found at the location where Miss Mallory was attacked." Brodie then approached the subject of the rose and what it might mean.

"A flower," he clarified.

Sir Mallory shook his head. "I had heard that. I can only assume that my daughter received it from her fiancé or perhaps purchased it."

"Has there been any difficulty with anyone you might have represented professionally in the past?" Brodie asked.

I caught the faintest change of expression at Sir Mallory's face. Perhaps it was nothing at all. Still...

"None that I am aware of," Sir Mallory replied.

Knowing Brodie, there would be more questions.

"I know that this is a very difficult time," I commented. "However, I wonder if I might I speak with Mrs. Mallory? To again express my condolences."

I stood and waited expectantly.

"Of course, Lady Forsythe. Mr. Hobbs will show you to the parlor. I believe that she is still there."

I found Mrs. Mallory sitting before a fire, the pallor on her face much the same as our previous encounter at the funeral for her daughter.

Mr. Hobbs introduced me.

"Yes, I remember," she acknowledged. "It is good of you to call, Lady Forsythe. There have been so many the past two days, all very kind."

I didn't bother to point out that this wasn't a social call.

She seemed... fragile, with a small writing table beside her that included notes she was no doubt writing in answer to condolences they had received.

I expressed my own once again at the loss of her daughter as tea was served, then waited until the butler left.

I did hate intruding when one was grieving, however I thought there might be something Charlotte mentioned in recent days that could be important.

"My family, most particularly my ward, was very fond of Charlotte," I began. "She was so very talented and caring."

There was a faint sad smile. "My sister was quite talented as well."

I nodded. "I know that so very well. My sister is quite artistic, while I do well to draw simple stick figures."

That common experience seemed to ease the formality between us, and I decided to try something that Brodie had once explained, that might provide a way to ask Mrs. Mallory questions.

"My sister and I are very close and I remember how devastating it was when she disappeared," I commented. "And then her companion at the time was found dead."

I chose not to use the word 'murdered.' It was such a harsh word and while it applied to both situations, I wasn't of a mind to be cruel.

"It was such a difficult time," I continued. "However, I was determined to find those responsible, as well as find my sister."

She nodded, and I took that as my cue.

"There was so little information at the time," I began. "Yet, slowly, and with the help of Mr. Brodie, we discovered one clue, and then another."

"I do remember reading something of that in the dailies," Mrs. Mallory commented. "So very difficult. And you eventually found her?"

"Yes, and equally important, we were able to stop the persons responsible from hurting anyone else and see that they were held accountable. There were clues that were invaluable in finding them."

Granted, I might have exaggerated a few of the aspects of that first case, yet it was very near the truth. And I did see a subtle change in her manner at the mention of holding the murderers accountable, the way the tension seemed as she leaned toward me.

"And your sister? She is well."

"Quite well. Our great-aunt is currently assisting her in planning her wedding."

"Lady Antonia Montgomery," she commented. "I know of her from the society pages."

"Through that ordeal," I continued, "I learned how very important even the smallest detail can be in ending a very dreadful situation."

"What sort of insignificant information?"

Rather than go into details about that case, I stayed with generalities that might bring a memory of something Charlotte had shared with her.

"A place my sister planned to visit, an encounter she mentioned, something that seemed unimportant when we last spoke, yet provided insight into something important."

She nodded. "I was helping her plan her wedding. So many decisions to make... far more than I remember from my wedding to Sir Mallory—the church, invitations to be sent out..." She hesitated and the tears came.

"She had gone to the printer's shop. I told her that we could have them delivered, but she wanted to check them one last time...

there was a mistake the first time." She pulled her handkerchief from the sleeve of her gown and blotted at the fresh tears.

"And of course there were the flowers to be decided upon," I commented in an attempt to draw the conversation forward.

"Oh, yes," she replied, composing herself once more.

"Red roses?" I suggested.

"Red?" She looked at me with a different expression, confusion at first, and then something else.

"It seemed that she might have purchased one from a flower vendor that day. Or someone gave it to her? Mr. Eddington, perhaps?" I gently suggested.

"I don't know anything about that," she replied, pressing her fingers against her temple.

"It was something the newspapers printed..."

She stood abruptly, and I caught her uneasy glance toward the parlor doors that had been left open.

Had someone been listening to our conversation?

"Thank you for your condolences, Lady Forsythe," she said, quite formally. "If you will excuse me."

She didn't wait for a response but immediately left the room. Not in that slow manner I might have expected of someone in mourning, but more like someone fleeing a fire.

As I returned to the library it seemed that Brodie's conversation with Sir Mallory was also at an end.

"I have told you everything, Mr. Brodie. Now I must insist that you leave us in peace."

Brodie bowed his head in acknowledgement, his expression cordial. However, that dark gaze that briefly met mine was sharp.

I expressed my condolences as well. And as if on cue, the head butler appeared.

"A coach is waiting," Mr. Hobbs informed us.

How convenient, I thought. He had thought to call ahead, so that there would be no delay when it was time for us to leave.

Eleven

"YE VISITED with Mrs. Mallory for quite some time," Brodie commented as our driver pulled away from the residence, Mr. Hobbs standing sentry at the entrance to make certain that we left.

"Hmmm." I wasn't certain what I had learned, if anything.

"The poor woman is grieving," I explained. "She and Charlotte were apparently extremely close, and planning Charlotte's wedding to Daniel Eddington."

"Aye, to be expected. However, ye managed to speak with her at length and obviously learned something."

"It is more an impression than something specific that she said."

"Is that anything similar to yer *woman's instinct*?"

"Or, perhaps a police investigator's sense of something when interviewing someone?" I suggested.

I caught the twitch of a smile at one corner of his mouth. It did seem that at least he knew when not to argue the matter.

"Ye were saying."

"I explained the situation of our first inquiry case, how difficult it was, that even the smallest clue was important."

"Sharing yer experience, no doubt."

"You were the one who explained that it is important to build rapport, that it might bring about something remembered."

"I will have yer promise that ye won't be explaining other details about things we have shared."

"Whatever do you mean?" I asked with wide-eyed innocence.

It was endearing to hear that he didn't want me sharing the more intimate aspects of our relationship. Not that I would. As for a man? I had heard rumors of conversations men had among themselves.

"What else did ye speak of?"

"The planning of the wedding. I asked her if Charlotte intended on having roses for her wedding flowers... red roses."

That dark gaze angled toward me. "That is direct. What was her response?"

"There wasn't one. Yet, her manner immediately changed. She became quite agitated when I mentioned red roses, and ended our conversation."

"It might simply have been that the poor woman was over-wrought over the death of her daughter."

"It was not that," I insisted. "I know what I saw. She became quite upset, and then seemed to think that someone might have been listening to our conversation.

"She left, and there wasn't an opportunity to question her further. What were you able to learn from Sir Mallory?"

"The man has not changed since my encounter with him some years before in a case that was brought before the court. He has a reputation for being thorough and aggressive, and has won several well-known cases before the court."

"What did you sense about him in your conversation?" I caught that narrowed gaze he directed at me, and couldn't prevent a smile.

"I *sensed* that he perhaps knew something that he chose not to share." He shook his head. "There was no prying it out of the man, and ye saw his manner when ye returned after yer conversation with his wife."

"You believe that he knows something about his daughter's murder?"

"Perhaps. And perhaps Daniel Eddington might be able to tell us something about that."

"This has undoubtedly been devastating for him as well," I replied. "To be planning a wedding and then it all ends with a funeral. When will you speak with him?"

"This afternoon if it can be arranged, and before Sir Mallory has a conversation with him. Unless he already has."

"Do you believe that he would encourage him to withhold information? For what reason?"

"That is what I would like to find out."

I was thoughtful as we returned to the office on the Strand.

"We will need to speak with Judge Cameron as well. Aunt Antonia might have some connection there through Sir Laughton. He is quite well acquainted with those in law. And I do need to visit Lily."

"What will you tell her?" Brodie asked.

"The truth. That we have little information so far. But we did promise to keep her apprised of what we learned, and I will not leave her dangling. She is not the dangling sort."

"No, she most certainly is not. Much like someone else I know."

Traffic was particularly congested even past the noon hour. The weather that had threatened to set in since early morning gathered ominously over the city. Ladies with shopping baskets over their arms hurried about the marketplaces. Draymen who usually made deliveries after hours clogged the thoroughfares with their carts and wagons as they rushed to get in one more delivery for the day.

All the while workers and shopkeepers took precautions against the high tides from the river that were expected with the heavy rain.

In the past, the lower floors of buildings along the river front had flooded, furnishings were destroyed, and people displaced.

The best to be done was to seek a higher floor then clean and repair the damage.

For those of the professional sort with offices on the high streets, sandbags were brought in by the score and placed in strategic positions to divert the heaviest runoff.

We arrived back at the office on the Strand. Brodie paid the driver as Mr. Cavendish wheeled up from down the sidewalk, Rupert the hound beside him.

"Wot do ye say about the storm that is coming?" Brodie asked.

Mr. Cavendish cast what might be described as a weather eye toward the sky. He was quite an authority and usually quite accurate. Although I supposed that predicting rain over London was much like predicting that the sun would rise of a morning. It was a constant.

"Felt it earlier in my bones, Mr. Brodie," he shrugged. "We're in for a good solid rain."

He hooked a thumb over one shoulder in the direction of the sand bags that were being delivered across the way.

"It's early in the season yet. But there will be a big one comin' later. There always is most usually after the holidays, and those sandbags won't be enough. You remember the one five years past?"

Brodie nodded. "Aye. Good to hear this storm won't be that bad."

"Do you believe him?" I asked as we climbed the stairs to the second-floor landing.

"He's been right most every time."

So much for Dr. Merryweather with his leeches in bottles that supposedly predicted a change in the barometer before a storm, even though the predictions had been printed in the dailies according to my great-aunt.

And then there was the weather bureau founded by Vice-Admiral Fitzroy after his retirement from the Royal Navy. He gathered information from across Britain and compiled it along with maps. Somewhat more accurate than leeches in a jar.

Brodie put out a call to Judge Cameron's office and was informed that Daniel Eddington had left earlier but would be returning for appointments that afternoon. It seemed that even death was not a reason for time away from work. Brodie made an appointment.

"I want to be there when he returns," he commented.

"And I need to make notes from our visit with the Mallorys, and then I should go to Sussex Square. I promised Lily that I would let her know what we've learned. If I don't, I fully expect her to return here and demand an update. She can be most insistent."

He gave me an amused look. "Verra much like someone else I know."

"I have no idea what you are talking about," I replied.

He rose from behind the desk and leaned over where I sat.

"Ye are a cheeky lass."

Oh, that wicked smile.

"When is your meeting with Daniel Eddington?" I asked as a diversion.

"He's to return by two o'clock this afternoon," Brodie replied, not the least *diverted* as he brushed my cheek with his fingers.

"It is the middle of the day," I reminded him.

"Aye, it is." Which was immediately followed by a curse as the bell on the landing sounded insistently.

"Food!" I enthusiastically announced, as Mr. Cavendish had departed for the Public House just after we returned.

"I need to have a word with the man," Brodie grumbled.

"You may have a word with him after we've eaten," I replied. "For all the good it will do you."

"He does seem to have a fondness for ye," he added as he went to the door of the office.

Lunch indeed! Potatoes with tender cooked meat—I was not

a fan of fish. And there was cobbler, almost as good as Mrs. Ryan's.

"Oh!" I exclaimed as I opened the brown paper sack. "Bread that is still warm from the oven."

"I dinna know the reason ye are not the size of one of yer aunt's coach horses," Brodie remarked as I divided the luncheon then handed him a bannock.

"I believe it might be hereditary," I commented as I enthusiastically ate. "My mother was quite slender. And our great-aunt is most slender as well, for a woman her age, and she still has a hearty appetite."

He sat across from me at the desk.

"I may need to increase our rates to clients in order to feed ye."

"*Dinna fash*, Mr. Brodie. I am quite capable of providing food for both of us."

"Aye."

I heard that faint grumble, a complaint, if I wasn't mistaken.

He had been most vocal in the past about providing for both of us, with no need for my money unless it was something I particularly wanted.

It was, of course, something most men took quite seriously—their ability to be the provider of the family. And a Scot, even more so. I handed him another bannock.

"I can afford food for the both of us," he insisted. "Along with Mr. Cavendish. I draw the line at the hound."

"You may draw the line wherever you wish," I replied with a smile.

Brodie left afterward to keep his appointment with Daniel Eddington.

I remained to add notes to the chalkboard, then departed for Sussex Square.

Lily had taken Charlotte Mallory's death very hard. Charlotte had been the first friend she had since arriving in London. True friends were few and far between, as I knew all too well.

For me, even with our recent difficulties, I knew that Brodie was a true friend, as I was to him.

As for Lily, she kept her true feelings with most people carefully hidden. She was slow to trust, something else I could identify with as well.

Mr. Symons, my great-aunt's head butler for over forty years, greeted me as I arrived.

"Good day, Miss Mikaela. It is always good to see you." He glanced past me as the coachman gathered the team to return to central London.

"Mr. Brodie is not with you?" he said with a slight frown.

Since my sister and I first arrived at Sussex Square, he had appointed himself not only guardian of the door, but guardian over two young orphan girls as well.

"He had business to attend to."

"Very well, miss."

"Is that Mikaela?" Aunt Antonia called out. "Do join me in the ballroom, dear." Her voice echoed down the long hallway.

As I handed off my coat and umbrella, I looked at Mr. Symons, usually an accurate source for whatever was happening at Sussex Square.

"She has been with the wood carver most of the morning," he explained in that stoic manner that I was familiar with.

"Wood carver?" Repairs of some sort or perhaps a new piece of furniture?

"I believe it is about the dragon's head," he replied with a faint roll of the eyes.

"I see. Thank you, Mr. Symons." Of course, I didn't see at all and could only imagine what I might find as I headed in the direction of the ballroom.

"Here you are," my great-aunt exclaimed as she sailed across the enormous hall that had seen entertainments, feasts, and perhaps a sword fight or two over the generations since it was built several hundred years earlier.

It was one of a handful of original estates in London that had survived and dated back to that original ancestor, William the Conqueror.

"We are quite through here. Thank you, Mr. Sturgess, for your thoughts and suggestions. I should like to see a drawing by next week along with a schedule for the work. We are planning a wedding before Christmas. I don't imagine that I will have need of it until after that."

"Of course, madame." Mr. Sturgess nodded as we passed. He did seem a bit pale.

"New furnishings?" I inquired, thinking of the reception after Linnie's wedding that our aunt insisted be held at Sussex Square. Perhaps a new banquet table or two?

She smiled as she took me by the arm and we sat at one of the long tables that had been in her family for centuries, complete with a few battle scars.

"I believe we have enough to accommodate a few hundred guests," she replied. "I requested Mr. Sturgess's thoughts regarding a dragon's head for the boat."

She made a sweeping gesture to the Egyptian boat that had graced the ballroom since another reception she had given the year before.

"I do want everything to be as authentic as possible when I sail off."

As in that Viking funeral she had spoken of since I was a child, complete with sails aflame as she sailed off to... wherever she intended to sail.

I was convinced that she would have her way in this, and thought it a perfect way to end one's *stay* in this life, as my friend Templeton had explained it.

She communicated with the somewhat disagreeable spirit of Sir William Shakespeare. Particularly when one of his plays was not being represented as he thought it should.

Of course, that is if one believed in spirits in the afterworld. I left that particular door open and thought a Viking send-off was quite exciting. It did seem as if my great-aunt had taken that notion to a new level.

"A dragon's head?" I asked with growing interest.

Aunt Antonia smiled. "It is all quite daunting for Mr. Sturgess. His work came highly recommended by Captain Turner, and he should know, with his experience on different vessels."

Captain Tom Turner was a long-time acquaintance. He had a lengthy career, sailing between England and the Orient on all manner of ships. He had lost a leg during an encounter with pirates in the South China Sea, and retired to the canal boats he owned in Richmond.

It was there we had met. He brought cargos of fresh food from the countryside in the spring and summer, then returned with passengers traveling to small villages along his route to escape the heat and smell of London.

Linnie and I had made his acquaintance years before on one of those excursions. More recently, he had provided important information in that first inquiry case when Linnie disappeared.

He was gruff and could be quite churlish. However, much like the hound, he had a particular liking for sweet biscuits, which I had been known to take to him. We got along quite well.

"Yer not like the other ladies that take a trip to the country, with their frilly parasols, fancy gowns, and a bothersome piece of fluff for a dog," he had once told me.

I took it as a compliment. However, he had not met Rupert, who also had an appetite for sweet biscuits.

"Mr. Sturgess's work?" I inquired, as I studied the sailboat that was obviously the subject of her latest project.

"He and his assistants have worked in the shipyards and created some of the most intriguing figureheads for sailing vessels," my great-aunt explained. "And for the royal family over the years."

Oh my.

"I was most interested if he could create a dragon figurehead for the sailboat, to be utilized for my send-off."

Startled, I look at her with some concern.

"Not to worry, my dear," she assured me. "I am in perfect health, much to the consternation of my personal physician. However, one must see to these things while one can or have it left to others. Although," she continued, reaching over to pat my hand. "I know that I may count on you to see my wishes carried out."

"What did Mr. Sturgess have to say about it?" I asked, relieved that her interest was not due to her impending demise.

"It seems that it could be quite complicated, although not beyond his abilities. Still, he did suggest that I might simply have a Viking longboat built at the shipyard. Although I shouldn't need one of any great length. It would burn far too long. Do you think a smaller version would suffice?"

I could imagine the issue with a longboat, Viking invasions of the past in mind, and that sort of thing.

"A smaller one might be best," I suggested.

If this was anyone other than my great-aunt, I might have thought the conversation most bizarre. However, I was quite used to what some might have called her eccentricities.

My view of it all was, at her age and with rumored enormous wealth, she should be able to do whatever she wished. As long as it caused no harm, or caused her to be arrested.

Not wanting to wander further into the depths of that conversation, I inquired where Lily was.

"I believe she's in the sword room with Mr. Munro. After presenting her with that knife for protection, he insisted on showing her how to use it. They've been at it for some time. It does remind one of when he showed you how to handle a blade."

The sounds from the sword room reached me long before I arrived at the entrance. It did seem that a robust lesson was under-way, including a few colorful curses from Lily.

I slipped inside the room and quietly closed the door behind so as not to disturb. I did want to see how she was progressing without drawing attention, Lily being somewhat younger than I was with my first lesson.

They maneuvered around each other in mock attack with Munro in the role of the villain as he came up behind her and attempted to overwhelm her. Lily drew the knife from the pocket in her gown, efficiently sidestepped, turned, and thrust at him.

"Take that, ye bloody varmint!" she told him.

Lesson number two, I thought—never assume that the initial strike would subdue the attacker, as Munro seized her wrist, pinched it, and the blade dropped to the floor. She retaliated with a punch to the nose.

Munro grunted and suddenly stepped out of arm's length, with a somewhat surprised expression.

"That will do for the day," he announced, massaging his nose. It was then that Lily saw me.

She scooped up the knife, folded it, dropped it into her pocket, then ran excitedly toward me.

"Did ye see, miss?"

I assured her that I had with a glance at Munro, none the worse for it, but still rubbing his nose.

"I best see to the accounts," he said as he moved toward the door. "Ye still have a lot to learn, miss."

"A blow to the face is not the best option," I commented when he had gone. "The objective should be to remove yourself from being that close to the attacker."

It was something I remembered well and had improved upon afterward.

"Mr. Munro said ye learned something called self-defense on one of yer travels," she commented. "Would ye teach me?"

There were moments when I felt that I had been somewhat remiss in my responsibilities after bringing Lily to London. Even though Lily had assured me that the arrangement for her to live at Sussex Square suited her quite well.

Here she had a somewhat normal household. I emphasize the word *somewhat*, whereas for me to continue working with Brodie might find me at the office on the Strand at all hours. Or, at the town house at the end of the day, or anywhere in between following up information for a client.

And I suppose that for Lily, as it had been for my sister and me, Sussex Square was far more interesting with the things my great-aunt was always into.

"Very well," I told her. "I can show you the basics, and then a move that will almost guarantee that you will be able to subdue an attacker and then flee if necessary."

Two hours later we were both exhausted, my hair had come down, and my forehead was damp from the exertion. Lily was much the same, but with a very determined look on her face.

"Wot about that move ye were goin' to show me?"

She was a very quick study, focused on everything I had showed her. Not to mention that she, like Brodie and Munro, had learned a great deal on the streets of Edinburgh. She was also quite slender and a bit smaller, as I gauged her height and weight.

"Very well. We'll stage a mock attack," I told her. "You're to come at me, face-to-face as if you intend to strike me."

She looked at me with a hesitant expression. "Are ye certain ye want to do this?"

"Quite certain. I will play the part of a lady out shopping and you are to approach me as if you intend to take my handbag."

She grinned, and for just a brief moment it seemed that I glimpsed myself at her age.

I took my position, pretending to be shopping among the displays of swords and shields along the wall.

As we had discussed, she approached in a most innocent manner, and then suddenly lunged for that imaginary handbag.

I caught her by the wrist with my left hand then launched a mock blow toward her face with the heel of my other hand. My final move was to sweep her completely off her feet with my right foot, dumping her on the floor with a stunned sound as the air left her lungs.

She made a muffled sound as the color slowly returned to her face. I held out a hand to help her back to her feet. She glared at me.

"Ye might have given a warning," she exclaimed as she finally took my hand.

"Would you give a warning to someone who came at you on the street?"

"No," she replied, then said, "I want to know how ye did that."

"With a great deal of practice," I replied. "And I left out the last part."

"Wot is that?"

"The part where I am no longer there but safely away."

I agreed to show her how it was done, along with the series of moves that led to it.

"The heel of your hand to the nose is far more effective than a punch with the fist. It will momentarily distract your attacker, and then you can sweep his feet out from under him."

"Where did ye learn to do that?"

"A fellow traveler introduced me to it. She was a very independent woman and often traveled alone. She had learned it in the Far East."

"Does Mr. Brodie know about it?"

That was a conversation for another time, as we left the sword room and returned downstairs, where my great-aunt sat at a table in the solar with rain washing the glass walls in late afternoon gloom.

"How is Mr. Munro?" I inquired.

"He will survive," my great-aunt replied with an amused expression. "Was it Lily or you who landed the blow?"

Lily confessed. "That was before Miss Mikaela showed me how to sweep someone off their feet," she added with what could only be described as keen excitement.

What might have passed for a decanter of tea sat on the table, along with a pitcher of lemonade. I discovered that her 'tea' was actually some of my aunt's whisky with water.

My aunt poured a glass of lemonade for Lily as I explained to her what we had learned with our inquiries so far.

"That man with the Times—Burke, I believe is the name—has certainly been writing about the murders a great deal," Aunt Antonia commented. "It does have the entire city of London astir, very much the same as the Whitechapel murders that have never been solved," she commented.

"It does remind one of another murder some years ago, it must be very near five years now. You wouldn't know of it," she continued. "You were off on one of your travels at the time."

"There was quite a to-do about it at the time," she added. "The man was eventually caught through someone who saw something or some other such thing."

"Was there a trial?" Lily asked.

"Oh, yes. Such a tragedy the way it all turned out," my great-aunt went on to explain.

"What happened?"

"It seems that the man who was accused of the murder—Ormsby was the name from the Ormsby family as I remember it—had been spurned by the young woman."

"Spurned?" Lily asked, scrunching up her nose as she had a habit of doing.

I smiled to myself, obviously a new word for her.

"She rejected him, and according to the Gazette at the time, he killed her in a fit of passion," my aunt explained. "Such a tawdry affair. He was eventually caught, charged with the murder, and taken to trial.

"Was he hanged?" Lily asked as I took a biscuit from the refreshment plate and continued to listen to the story. Aunt Antonia thoroughly enjoyed the moment.

"That was the scandal of it," she replied with great drama. "The man's family acquired the services of the best lawyer money could buy for his defense, and apparently the witness in the case disappeared."

Lily frowned. "How could he disappear?"

"That, my dear, is a very good question. The judge had no choice but to dismiss the case."

"What happened to the man who murdered the young woman? That was the end of it? He got away with murder?" Lily exclaimed.

"Not precisely," Aunt Antonia replied. "The young man was found dead with a broken neck sometime later, an apparent accident while out riding in Rotten Row."

"Rotten Row?"

I had to laugh at Lily's response to that, not to mention her expression at the odd name.

"It's in Hyde Park," I explained. "Gentlemen and ladies ride their horses there when the weather allows."

"Seems like justice was served, filthy bugger."

We did need to work on improving Lily's choice of words, however I caught my great-aunt's amusement.

"Yes, quite," she replied with a chuckle. "But that was not the end of the tragedy. Just after the trial, the young woman's mother died, from grief according to the newspaper, and the father perished in a fire at the family business that had been in London for decades—a coffee import company, as I recall.

"Of course, there were those who said that the family must be cursed, though I never put any stock in that," she continued. "Such a tragedy to have suffered so much loss. And the mysterious part of it all," my great-aunt added with great suspense, "according to the newspapers at the time, a bouquet of flowers was delivered to the young woman's grave each year for several years on the anniversary of her death."

"Who would send them?" Lily replied. "Everyone was dead."

"That was the mystery. No one seemed to know. However, I am most grateful that there are people such as Mikaela and Mr.

Brodie with their private inquiries, who find those who commit these dreadful crimes."

I appreciated the vote of confidence; however, I wasn't quite as confident as my great-aunt, in consideration of the few clues we had.

Was the murderer perhaps a spurned suitor as Charlotte Mallory planned her wedding to another? Or was it something else?

And what of Margaret Cameron's death? With that rose that had been left on each body, it seemed obvious the two were connected. But how?

I was hopeful that Brodie might learn something from Daniel Eddington that could provide a clue, perhaps something Sir Mallory wasn't aware of that might prove important.

Twelve

BRODIE

HE ARRIVED at the offices of Sir Edward Mallory Esq. for the appointment he had requested with Daniel Eddington, who was a partner in the law office and had been the fiancé of Charlotte Mallory.

He gave no specific reason for the appointment, but had simply stated there were legal matters he needed to discuss, not far off the truth. He did not want to alarm Eddington by stating the actual reason, that he was a consultant for the Metropolitan Police. The clerk might have refused altogether to schedule the appointment. He had encountered that before and it just made things more difficult.

He checked the time on his pocket watch as he stepped down from the cab. He was somewhat early, but it gave him the opportunity to visually take in the Mallory office very near Hyde Park.

It was a brownstone in the Georgian design, as Mikaela called this particular building style, with tall windows that faced onto the street and a half-dozen steps that led to the main entrance behind a wrought-iron fence. A brass nameplate beside the entrance announced that he had arrived at the offices of E. Mallory and Associates, Legal Consultants.

It was the sort of building with that discreet façade that spoke of success in the court, prestige, and money. Not the sort of representation that he could have afforded if those charges against him had not been dropped, courtesy of Sir Avery Stanton of the Special Services.

As he had learned long ago, wealth meant power, power meant success, and it seemed by that address and appearances that Sir Mallory had been very successful in his chosen profession as one of the most powerful lawyers in London.

The clerk at the front desk greeted him with a critical glance at his coat and an appropriately subdued expression, the sort he had seen countless times among those of the upper classes.

"You have an appointment, sir?"

Brodie nodded and gave his name. "Mister Eddington will be expecting me."

"I will let him know that you have arrived," the clerk curtly replied, then disappeared down the hall that led from the front entrance to a series of doors and a set of double doors at the end.

The interior of the offices gave off that same air of success and wealth, with thick carpet on the floor, gleaming dark wood furnishings that included the clerk's large desk, and several over-stuffed chairs of the sort at Lady Antonia Montgomery's residence.

Two gentlemen sat in muted conversation beside a fireplace surrounded by wood-paneled walls lined with requisite framed portraits. One a likeness of Sir Mallory.

The others were older individuals, including one he recognized as the former prime minister from pictures in the dailies, and a more recent one of the current prime minister. The nameplate below the portrait gave his name, Sir Robert Gascoyne, as a former legal associate.

Wealth meant power.

It was a lesson he'd learned on the streets as a boy and never forgot in his time with the MET, and then in his private inquiries. People used their wealth for power.

And then there was Mikaela Forsythe, who contradicted everything he had learned about those of her station.

"Mr. Brodie?" The clerk had returned. "Mr. Eddington will see you now."

He followed the clerk down that hallway with that thick carpet under his feet to one of those doors.

The clerk knocked and then showed him into the office of Daniel Eddington, who had recently been made a full partner in the prestigious law firm, according to Mikaela. No doubt in anticipation of his marriage to Charlotte Mallory, and then as a new member of the family. And now, that had all ended with the young woman's death.

Mikaela didn't know anything about Mr. Eddington, however, her great-aunt had 'heard' things around London regarding the man who was being introduced about the city as the heir to the Mallory legal firm.

"I've read his name mentioned connected to several cases," Lady Antonia had mentioned. "Quite an ambitious young man, and heir apparent to the Mallory dynasty, as there was only the daughter and no son to inherit. Everything I have heard is that he is being molded in the manner of Sir Mallory."

And according to her own solicitor, Sir Laughton, the young lawyer had acquired that same ruthless manner when presenting a case at court.

The office Brodie now entered was not large, but it spoke of that influence. And power? What did that tell him about the man who rose from behind that desk?

"Mr. Brodie, previously with the Metropolitan Police, now in the private inquiry business. I would usually say that it is a pleasure to meet you, however under the circumstances..." Eddington added. "I am not surprised by this visit. I am aware that you have spoken with Sir Mallory about this dreadful situation. Are you here in some official capacity?"

Situation, Brodie thought, not unfamiliar with the way some people put things in little boxes. The man's fiancée had been murdered, and it was a *situation*.

He had encountered that sort of response before, that way of putting a label on something, then tucking it away. Again, he found himself thinking of Mikaela, not at all of the same cut of cloth, as one on the street would say. How had she escaped it? But he knew.

Those early things that had a way of shaping a person. The good along with the bad that became like a shadow that followed one everywhere, and made them who they were.

In that they were verra much similar as they were different, and he could well imagine how she would approach Mr. Eddington—direct, her questions sharp, insistent upon answers, not above using her station.

He was of a different mind in the matter and the reason he chose to make his appointment.

"Aye, a most difficult situation." He was deliberate in his choice of words. Eddington had anticipated that they would meet and, as they say, his guard was up.

"Ye have my condolences, sir. I know this must be a verra difficult time. And of course, ye would want to assist in whatever way ye can to find the one who has done this dreadful thing to ye."

He caught the immediate change in Eddington's demeanor, the way his mask as Mikaela called it, slipped and a different expression from that of the aloof legal counsel appeared.

"I can imagine how difficult this is," Brodie said with great sympathy, quite simply because he could imagine it.

"Can you?" Eddington's voice caught. "To have been planning our wedding and now... Are you married, Mr. Brodie?"

"Aye."

"And if this happened to your wife? Can you imagine how it must be, Mr. Brodie?" Eddington demanded, his hold on self-control seeming to crumble.

He could, of course, particularly with the work they shared.

Of all the things he'd experienced and come through, and the things he'd done, that was the one thing Angus Brodie knew he could not bear.

He would be like a madman and he would hunt down the person who had hurt her, no matter the cost. It was that simple.

Aye, he could imagine it.

"It is the reason I am here. To find the one who has done this. If there is some way that ye might be able to help us, something that Miss Mallory might have spoken of, some encounter that perhaps frightened her."

Daniel Eddington seemed to gather himself once more. "You must forgive me, Mr. Brodie. Of course, I will help in whatever way that I can."

Over the next hour, he asked those questions and watched Daniel Eddington with the experience of having spoken with countless people over the course of his time with the Met. He noted the way Eddington held himself, each gesture, the emotion that came and was then forced back, and listened to the perfect control in the answers he gave.

What he was seeing was either genuine grief with an effort to maintain control. Or something else?

"How long have ye been with Sir Mallory's firm?" he then asked. He caught that faint hesitation again.

"Very near twelve years," Eddington replied. "I represented my first client shortly after being asked to join the office."

A knock at the office door ended their meeting as the clerk returned and announced that Mr. Eddington's next appointment had arrived.

"If that will be all?"

It was not a question, but polite dismissal.

~

MIKAELA

I had told Lily as much as I could about our inquiry into Charlotte Mallory's murder before leaving Sussex Square. She was quite stoic as she listened. There was no need for me to explain to her that our information, so far, was quite thin. We had very little to go on.

"Ye will be able to find the one who did this, won't ye?" she had asked afterward. "Ye always find them."

I appreciated her confidence in us, but knew that there were some cases that went unsolved. I didn't want to mislead her. Still, it was early in our inquiries, and I was hopeful that Brodie might learn something from Daniel Eddington that could be helpful.

"It is early in the case," I explained. "We have additional people to speak with. There is always the possibility that one will be able to provide important information."

She had accepted that, yet I saw something behind that striking blue gaze that I had glimpsed once before, when we first met. Determination.

It was late afternoon now, as I arrived back at the Strand, the office above darkened.

"Aye, Mr. Brodie has not returned yet," Mr. Cavendish informed as he wheeled out from the alcove. Rupert the hound followed at a trot to show me his latest conquest—an old boot that had been thoroughly mauled and chewed.

I gave him a pat on the head, and did hope there hadn't been a foot inside that boot.

"I was just on me way over to the Public House," Mr. Cavendish announced. "Might I bring supper for you, miss?"

"Perhaps for Mr. Brodie," I replied. I had eaten an early supper with Lily and my great-aunt before leaving Sussex Square.

"Right you are," he nodded, then waited.

"Is there something else, Mr. Cavendish?"

"I'll just wait until you reach the office, miss."

I gave him a surprised look.

"Mr. Brodie's instructions, now that I'm workin' for him. Not that I wouldn't otherwise."

"Instructions?" This was something I wasn't aware of.

"He said that me and the hound were to make certain that you were safe up at the office with the lock set. What with them poor women murdered, and other crime about the city. Can't be too careful."

He patted the front of his short coat, somewhat shorter in his case due to his infirmity.

"He said that I was to use this if it came to it." He produced a knife, of the sort that might have come from Munro and similar to the one I carried.

"The hound, he naturally has his own weapons," he added.

I could have sworn the hound grinned on the sidewalk beside him, flashing those 'weapons.'

It seemed that I now had two bodyguards. It was quite amusing in the extreme. However, I had seen the swiftness with which Mr. Cavendish maneuvered that wheeled platform. Legs and ankles would certainly be in danger. As for the hound, there was that grin.

It did seem that Brodie had taken precautions once again. It was that over-protective nature of his that I had decided I simply had to accept. One could take the man out of Scotland, but not the Scot out of the man. And I had to admit that I did like those other aspects of Angus Brodie.

"Very well, Mr. Cavendish," I replied as I climbed the stairs to the second-floor landing. "Please convey my greetings to Miss Effie."

He grinned, almost as wide as the hound, and then he was off, the hound remaining on guard duty, with his boot at the bottom of the stairs.

Along with other changes at the office under the new owner-ship, locks had been changed including a bolt, with keys provided by the locksmith, who had been less than forthcoming regarding who had ordered the new locks when Brodie had questioned him.

I now carried one of the two matching keys as I wondered again about the new owners and how long we might remain. It did seem with that rather elegant sign that it might be arranged. Although one could only speculate what the new rents might be.

I turned on the electric just inside the entrance that was also one of the recent improvements, then closed the door and smiled to myself as I set the lock according to Mr. Cavendish's instructions.

The office was cold with the weather that was expected. I quickly removed my coat and scarf, then crossed to the stove and filled the hopper with coal.

I soon had the fire going, then crossed over to the desk and turned on the electric desk lamp eager to read that letter found in Charlotte Mallory's handbag that the police had found. Mr. Dooley had sent it over.

I noted the name on the outside of the envelope—C. Walmsley, Guildford, Surrey—and took out the letter. It was dated the same day Charlotte Mallory was murdered:

Mrs. Walmsley,

I am in receipt of your letter of November 18 in addition to your previous letter of 4 June.
I cannot understand the reason you are doing this.
I must ask that you have no further contact with me in the matter.

Charlotte Mallory

Who was C. Walmsley? There was no way of knowing with that address on the outside. Only that Charlotte Mallory had written—*Mrs. Walmsley,* on the letter itself.

Yet, I had learned several things in those few words.

One: Mrs. Walmsley had contacted Charlotte some months earlier and then again on 18 November.

Two: There was something in that original letter that had

alarmed Charlotte, even though she chose to ignore it. Then she had received a second letter.

I obviously had questions.

Who was C. Walmsley of Guildford?

What had she written in those letters that had upset Charlotte Mallory?

What did any of it mean to our current inquiry case?

I remained at the office rather than returning to Mayfair, so that I might discuss those contents with Brodie when he returned.

It was quite late when he finally arrived. After meeting with Daniel Eddington, he had then met with Mr. Dooley regarding the information he asked him to obtain.

"Ye should have bolted the door," he commented as he hesitated in the open doorway, watching the street below, an icy gust of wind swirling into the office as the weather arrived.

"Mr. Cavendish was standing guard in the alcove below after returning from the Public House. And the hound was quite content to guard the stairs," I informed him with some humor.

It was apparently wasted as he continued to watch the street below, his eyes narrowed.

"What is it?"

"A man across the way, watching the office."

The Strand was never empty, no matter the time of day or night. It was at the edge of the theater district just a short distance away, along with a handful of taverns, the Public House, and other establishments.

I approached the entrance and glanced down at the street. While the weather and the time of the night had sent most people home, there were still several afoot and others in cabs who hurried against the cold and the rain that had started.

I saw no one across the way who lingered in spite of the weather. Whoever it might have been was now gone. Brodie closed and bolted the door.

"Mr. Cavendish brought supper from the Public House," I told him. "There on the desk."

He made only the barest acknowledgement, obviously deep in thought as he set his umbrella aside and removed his neck scarf.

"I ate earlier with Lily and Aunt Antonia," I mentioned. "I told Lily as much as I could about our inquiries." I tried again.

"What were you able to learn from Mr. Dooley?"

He still hadn't touched the covered plate on the desk, but stood before the chalkboard where I had made additional notes after reading that letter.

"He was finally able to locate the wine merchant. He's driven that route for the past five years. He gave the same description of the man he saw but thought nothing of it at the time, as it was only late afternoon that day."

And then in that way when he was thinking of two things at once.

"Ye read the letter..."

In addition to the contents of that letter, I also told Brodie about my conversation with my great-aunt. And once again, I had the impression that he was barely listening, if at all.

Then, in that way he has, he looked up and asked what I thought the information my great-aunt had shared might mean. Infuriating man.

"I have no idea what it means," I replied. "It hardly seems likely that the same person committed that murder five years ago, and now again. After all, he's dead."

"The letters that Charlotte Mallory received might tell us something," Brodie commented then. "If she kept them."

"I will contact her mother in the morning, if she will even agree to meet with me. She seemed most fragile when we met before."

He had finally eaten supper, or at least some of it. The rest was left for the hound in the morning.

He was most definitely preoccupied with something.

"What of your meeting with Daniel Eddington?"

"As to be expected, the young man is in mourning. He seemed

most cooperative, however there was little he could tell me about that day."

Someone else might have missed it, but I picked up on it.

"Seemed?"

"Aye, something didn't seem quite right."

It really was too tempting to ignore.

"Your instincts, of course."

That dark gaze narrowed as he reached out and grabbed me by the wrist.

"*Fear treun*," he replied in Gaelic with that thick Scots accent.

"And what might that mean, Mr. Brodie?" I asked as he pulled me close.

"Ye are a brave one," he replied with a low growl as he buried his hands in my hair.

Thirteen

WE STAYED the night at the office. I returned to Mayfair in the morning in my attempt to meet with Mrs. Mallory, while Brodie hoped to meet with Judge Cameron.

There were still questions as well over the urgency with which Doctor Cameron had left his office that previous evening, along with no mention of the rose that we had found after we returned to his office.

The patient appointment was obviously an excuse to end our meeting with him. What did that mean? And where had he gone after he left? Did it have something to do with our meeting with him?

As of yet, more questions than answers. Still, I was hopeful there might be something to be learned from a meeting with Mrs. Mallory.

However...

"*Mrs. Mallory is not receiving telephone calls or visitors at this time,*" I was informed in a typically upper-class response from the butler.

I gave him my name, using my formal title, and ended the call.

Mrs. Ryan appeared at the entrance to the front parlor.

"I am on my way to put in the weekly order with the grocer," she announced. "Will Mr. Brodie be joining us for supper?"

The obvious answer would have been that I couldn't be certain.

"I will be preparing my Irish stew," she added.

It was a favorite of Brodie's, never mind that she was thoroughly Irish and frequently reminded him of it.

"Of course," I replied. The truth was that if he didn't take supper at the town house, Rupert the hound would eat quite well afterward.

"Is there anything else in particular, miss?"

"Some of your sponge cake would be greatly appreciated." Brodie was fond of it, as was Rupert.

"I'll not see it wasted on that beast of a hound," she declared.

"And perhaps some of your biscuits?"

I was in the midst of going over the notes in my notebook when the telephone jangled sharply from the stand in the hallway.

On her way out, Mrs. Ryan answered the telephone and informed me that the caller was Mrs. Mallory.

"*I can only speak briefly,*" she hurriedly explained as I picked up the earpiece.

Out of concern that she might be overheard by the servants? I did recall her watchfulness the day we met at the Mallory residence.

I quickly gave her the address for the office on the Strand, then added, "Charlotte received two letters, one several months ago, and one quite recent. It might help if you were to bring them..."

There was a polite response that could mean anything to someone listening at the other end of the call, then the call abruptly ended.

I had no way of knowing when, or even if, Mrs. Mallory might in fact be able to meet me, yet I went upstairs, quickly dressed, then called for a cabman.

. . .

"Mr. Brodie left earlier," Mr. Cavendish informed me when I arrived at the office on the Strand.

"Did he say where he was going?"

Mr. Cavendish shook his head. "I did hear him tell the driver to take him to the Old Bailey."

It seemed that, failing Judge Cameron's cooperation in setting an appointment, Brodie had decided to go directly to the courts. He was determined to speak with him in spite of the difficult situation over the death of his daughter.

Mr. Cavendish handed me the newest issue of the daily. The latest article by Theodolphus Burke filled most of the front page. The deaths of two London women were now being called the Rose Murders. Mr. Burke was determined to elevate his career no matter what it took—sensationalism, mostly repeating what had already been printed about the two murders.

I then climbed the stairs to the office and read the daily. The details of the first murder were repeated, then the second murder as well. There was speculation with the writer of the article 'following leads to discover who had committed the dreadful crime, possibly at risk to himself.'

It was quite dramatic, yet when reading the article, it became very obvious Mr. Burke had nothing new to write about.

I put the daily aside and then spent the next hour reorganizing my notes on the chalkboard, then adding a note about meeting with Mrs. Mallory. Then I created a second list of inquiries yet to be made that might provide additional information.

It was very near midday, and I had arrived at the conclusion that Mrs. Mallory was not going to appear when the bell on the landing rang out.

Most unusual, Mrs. Mallory had arrived in a rented hack rather than a private coach. She now stood hesitantly on the sidewalk speaking with Mr. Cavendish, the hound at his side. I did hope that Rupert didn't greet Mrs. Mallory in the usual way. I had visions of her screaming then collapsing on the sidewalk in horror.

He did have a way of greeting people, myself included when I first made his acquaintance, that was somewhat off-putting. As a child, I was constantly around dogs and quite used to their ways.

The hound was different, and I had long suspected that his usual greeting was a deliberate move to establish dominance. As for myself, I had firmly established that I would not put up with such ill-mannered habits.

An old boot, some poor creature brought back from the streets, were one thing. Rudeness was quite another.

I quickly descended the stairs to rescue Mrs. Mallory, and discovered there was no need. She had the situation firmly in hand, or rather her umbrella that Mr. Cavendish held for her as she knelt on the sidewalk murmuring several endearments, her gloved hands stroking the hound behind the ears. She looked up as I hastily arrived, prepared to reprimand the hound.

"He is quite a marvelous fellow, isn't he," she said in a soft voice. "Once one looks past the soot and mud."

"Beg pardon, you must forgive him," Mr. Cavendish started to apologize as the hound made himself prostrate on the sidewalk in front of Mrs. Mallory.

"He's spent his life on the streets with no manners or care for others until Miss Mikaela came. He does seem to have a preference for the ladies."

Mrs. Mallory slowly stood and brushed her hands down the front of the black coat she wore over a black gown.

"I have discovered that animals are better than most people," she said in a soft, thoughtful voice. "And always honest. My daughter loved animals." That sad gaze met mine.

Together we climbed the stairs to the office.

Althea Mallory, as she insisted I call her, explained that she had left her private coach and hired a driver who brought her to the office on the Strand, so to avoid any questions about her visit with me.

How very sad, I thought, that she was forced to take such steps so not to be discovered, or questioned by anyone. Her husband perhaps?

I thanked her for agreeing to meet with me as I poured tea and placed several of Mrs. Ryan's biscuits on a plate. I set them on the small table I had recently added to give the office a less... *sparse* appearance. After all, Brodie and I did spend a great deal of time here.

"My husband has spoken regarding Mr. Brodie's efforts in two of his cases in the past," she began the conversation. "I was not aware that he had taken on an associate until our meeting the other day."

"It was in the matter of the disappearance of my sister," I then explained. "I have never been one to stand aside when there is something that I might be able to do. I am often reminded," I thought of Brodie, "that it might very well be a flaw."

"Perhaps," Mrs. Mallory replied. "However, it seems a flaw that very likely saved your sister's life."

I had not revealed all the details of that sordid affair. I deliberately left out the part where I had shot the woman at the center of the conspiracy. I was aware that sort of thing could be somewhat off-putting.

"I did appreciate your sharing that with me," she told me. "This morning when I received your telephone call, it helped me to understand what I had to do. I was hesitant at first. Everything the last few days has been so very... difficult."

I wanted to ask what finally changed her mind about meeting with me, but I realized that she needed to tell me, to say it in a way I did understand all too well.

"You said something when you came to our residence. That if the situations were reversed, your sister would do the same for you."

As different as we were, as difficult as that might be for some to believe, I was convinced that Linnie would do the same for me as I had done.

"The thought that brought me here was that if my situation was reversed with my daughter, I would want her to do everything to find who did this to me." She reached inside her handbag then.

"I have no way of knowing if these will be helpful." She took out the two envelopes that were mentioned in that letter found with her daughter's body.

"Charlotte was put off by the first one. You will note the date when you open the envelope. We both thought it nothing more than someone attempting to make money off the information. It was written right after..." her voice broke softly. "It was right after the engagement was announced."

"And no doubt written about in the newspapers," I suggested.

Mrs. Mallory nodded. "She chose to ignore it. I thought she had thrown it away until the second letter arrived all these months later. She came to me about it. That is when I discovered that she kept the first letter.

"This second letter made her angry with the things that were written, and she decided to respond to it, even though I attempted to persuade her to ignore it as she had the first one."

At a glance at the two envelopes, it did seem that the person who had sent them—C. Walmsley in Guildford, was the same person whose name was on the envelope Charlotte Mallory intended to post late in the afternoon the day she was murdered.

"Will these be helpful?" Mrs. Mallory asked, her voice stronger with hope.

"Everything we can learn is helpful," I replied, knowing that she needed something to hold onto amidst such terrible loss.

"Does this name mean anything to you? Might your daughter have known this person?"

She shook her head. "She had no idea who the person is or the reason they would write to her with the things that are in those letters. You will see how disturbing they are when you read them."

She was thoughtful again. "When this is over, I would like the letter returned that was found... with her. It is the last thing that she wrote."

I promised that I would see that it was returned to her.

She drank the tea I had provided as she stared at the chalkboard.

"The name of the person who sent those letters is on the board," she commented.

"I find that notes about every aspect of a case helps me organize my thoughts," I replied.

"You wrote them?"

I nodded. "Mr. Brodie's writing leaves a great deal to be improved."

There was a faint smile. "He is fortunate to have such an accomplished assistant."

"He might question that from time to time... however, we manage to work through our differences."

She looked at me with obvious confusion.

"Mr. Brodie is my husband," I explained. "We work together in the cases that we are asked to take."

"How very extraordinary," she commented.

Extraordinary was an interesting word, and for the first time I glimpsed past the sadness and pain of the past days.

"There are moments I am not certain that he would agree with you on that."

The smile deepened on another thought. "My father was a barrister. My brother as well. I have always been fascinated by the law. However, Sir Mallory pointed out a long time ago that it was not a profession for women."

There was something wistful in her voice and I thought how *extraordinary* it would be for a woman to be a lawyer defending clients in English court.

"I should be returning home now," she said, as if reminding herself. "I didn't intend to be away so long. I must return before..."

I instinctively sensed she was about to say, before Sir Mallory returned at the end of the day.

"Of course," I replied, easing her past the moment. I could

not imagine being caught in such a relationship, and thought of my own marriage, quite unusual, different than anyone might have called appropriate for one of my title and station.

I realized that I would not have had it any other way.

I had Mr. Cavendish signal a cab for her. He rang the bell when it arrived. Mrs. Mallory put on her coat and gathered her umbrella.

She stopped at the door and turned before leaving.

"I envy you, Lady Forsythe." She looked around at the office, the simple but comfortable furnishings, then added, "No matter what it takes, find the person who murdered my daughter."

To say that my meeting with Althea Mallory was not at all what I expected was very much an understatement.

As sad and horrible as the circumstances of the case, I sensed beneath the black mourning clothes that she wore and the sad expression from a pain that would never—could never—go away, was a strong woman.

I liked her very much and ached for her loss. I hoped that Brodie and I could at least bring her peace by finding the person responsible.

I stayed at the office to await Brodie's return and some word as to whether he had been successful in obtaining a meeting with Judge Cameron. I spent that time reading the two letters sent by someone by the name C. Walmsley in Guildford, Surrey.

The first letter was more of a brief note and was dated 4 June 1891. It included a clipping from the Times of London with the announcement of Charlotte Mallory's engagement to Daniel Eddington. It was brief and quite cryptic:

"People are not what they pretend to be."

I opened the second envelope. The message with it was even more cryptic, almost a warning, as those few words seemed to leap off the page:

"Secrets and lies are the devil's work."

I then read the newspaper article that had been sent with it. It had been written by a writer with the Police Gazette at the time by the name of Alvin Morris and reminded his readers about the trial of a young man from a prominent family who had been accused of the murder of a young woman.

The subsequent trial had been dismissed along with all charges against the man for lack of evidence. The young man's name was Ormsby!

I sat back at the desk chair, trying to make sense of it all.

What did someone, apparently a woman by the name of Walmsley who lived in Guildford, Surrey, know about that ten-year-old trial and a young man by the name of Ormsby? Further, for what reason had she contacted Charlotte Mallory with that cryptic note? Because of the wedding announcement? A warning? But for what reason?

What did the woman know? Or was it a trick, as often those of certain families experienced from time to time?

I had certainly experienced my share in the past, mostly from anonymous sorts who pretended to be potential suitors who admired *'my adventuresome spirit.'* Or perhaps it was the Montgomery family name.

Then more recently when my books were published and it was learned who the author truly was, I had attracted a different sort who thought that it was *'absolutely marvelous'* that a woman might succeed in that endeavor.

Such condescending drivel.

Was this a trick? Attracted by the family name? Or was there some sort of connection.

No stone unturned, I thought.

When Brodie returned, I did need to suggest that we learn more about C. Walmsley in Guildford, and I wanted to go to the newspaper archive and see what I might be able to learn about that ten-year-old murder.

While I waited for Brodie, something I was not yet used to but had agreed to be more conscientious about, I made additional notes on the chalkboard.

It was late afternoon when the bell sounded from the landing. It was fairly safe to say that Mr. Cavendish would not have rung the bell to announce Brodie's arrival. I went out onto the landing.

On the street below, my great-aunt stepped down from the automobile she had recently acquired, driving goggles in place that gave her the appearance of a bug. Granted, a very colorful bug in a vivid purple driving costume.

I had not previously seen this one. It seemed that she was acquiring quite a wardrobe for the roadway. However, this did raise the concern about her setting off during the day with all of the usual London traffic about.

There was a blast of sound, a horn, as Lily stepped down, along with what appeared to be some colorful language—I could only imagine, as a horse-drawn tram swept past quite close.

"Hello, dear," my great-aunt greeted me as she arrived on the landing, Lily following.

"The roadway is quite congested this time of day. I had never noticed," she commented as she removed the goggles.

"Mr. Munro was good enough to follow in the coach if there should be any difficulty." She leaned toward me as if sharing a secret.

"He can be quite protective of Lily."

Yes, of course, I thought.

"Not as if he didn't trust my driving skills," she added. "Mr. Hastings just happened to need to pick up a new harness from the leathermaker."

And they would no doubt be returning by way of the Strand.

"How are you, dear?" she thought to ask. "Lily was quite anxious to speak with you, and I thought... why not drive to the office?"

Why not? Although a call on the telephone might have worked just as well. I had learned not to ask such questions.

"I was not prepared for how rude some people can be," she added.

Considering the scene I had just witnessed, I could only imagine and managed a smile in greeting.

"Will your machine be safe parked on the street?" I inquired.

"Mr. Cavendish has promised to alert us if there is any difficulty," my great-aunt replied. "Kind man, he is most diligent. And Mr. Munro will be along shortly."

There it was, her escort. I had visions of several years from then with countless little old women let loose on the streets of London in automobiles. It was a rather frightening prospect.

"The office does appear remarkably improved, and the building as well. Don't you think, dear?"

I provided tea and coffee. It did seem that a bit of whisky might be dangerous if she was to return to Sussex Square in the automobile. Not that my great-aunt hadn't proven that she could hold her *spirits*, as she called them.

Lily had been unusually quiet. Even now as she moved about the office, then stopped to inspect the chalkboard with my latest notes.

"What did you wish to speak to me about?" I asked. The girl who turned to me then hardly seemed a girl, but a young woman and most serious.

"It was something I thought of after ye left," she said, crossing to Brodie's desk where she picked up a pen then set it back down, fidgeting as my great-aunt had frequently scolded me.

She looked up and it struck me again that the girl was no more, but had been replaced by a very striking, if serious, young woman.

"Ye said that very often in the inquiry cases that ye and Mr. Brodie investigate it's something someone says and is not even aware of that provides a clue."

I remembered the conversation. I exchanged a look with my great-aunt.

"Quite remarkable," she commented. "The coffee you made is most excellent."

"Please continue," I told Lily as I sat at the desk.

Lily took the chair that I usually occupied when Brodie and I were discussing some point about a case.

"It was the time that Miss Charlotte came to Sussex Square for my music lesson, before..." she stopped, emotions there in that blue gaze. She gathered herself.

"She was right sad. When I asked her about it, she didn't want to say at first. But after a while when I asked again, she said it was a difficulty between her and the man she was goin' to marry. She said it was probably just nervous feelings before the wedding."

Understandable, I thought, having experienced such things myself.

"Did she say what it was over?" I asked.

"It seems that someone came to her with some information about him, from a long time ago, and asked a lot of questions about something that happened before."

"Did she say who it was?"

"She said that he was from the newspaper and wrote for the dailies."

"Did he give a name?"

"She mentioned it..."

"Was the name Burke?" I asked.

She nodded. "That was the name. She said that he was serious, that he found some information about a case that her fiancé had handled and asked if he had ever mentioned it. It frightened her."

Theodolphus Burke, doing what Mr. Burke did, obviously looking for that next story. The man really was a snake.

"Did she say what that case was?"

"She was too upset, and then ended the lesson time. It was the last time I saw her."

That blue gaze filled with tears. "Do ye think it could be important?"

I reached across and squeezed her hand. "As I said, everything is important until the case is solved."

She nodded. "I just wish I thought of it before."

"But it may help now," I told her.

Blaming oneself was too easy, I knew for a fact.

"They ye'll tell Mr. Brodie when he returns."

I promised that I would.

The service bell rang on the landing. It did seem as though Munro and Mr. Hastings had returned from the leathermakers. And the weather had set in, rain hitting the street and sending clouds of mist into the air as I went out onto the landing.

I assured Lily that I would add what she had shared with me to the chalkboard, and attempt to learn what it might mean. I then watched as they departed, Lily with a strong arm looped through my great-aunt's arm as they descended the stairs.

I might have done the same once or twice while my sister and I were growing up.

It did seem that there was a deep affection between them.

Munro was there at the curb as they arrived. There were several moments of conversation and I caught the stubborn angle of my great-aunt's chin, when she finally accepted the point he was obviously determined to make.

He assisted her into the coach. Once the 'cargo' was secure, somewhat reluctantly, Mr. Hastings maneuvered the coach into traffic toward Sussex Square.

Mr. Munro glanced up at the landing as he assisted Lily into one side of the motor carriage. I nodded in acknowledgment.

I did so appreciate his care and protection when it came to my great-aunt, and now Lily. He then rounded the motor carriage and climbed inside.

That was something new, I thought and watched with some trepidation as he started the motor carriage, then set it in motion and maneuvered the chugging beast into the line of carts, cabs, and trams on the street.

I pitied anyone they encountered.

Brodie returned sometime later, 'dark as thunder' my great-aunt had once said of someone. It was a description that perfectly described him now. His attempt to meet with Judge Cameron had obviously not gone well.

I was learning how to navigate these moments with a bit of Old Lodge whisky and silence. Until that dark gaze found me along with the frown.

"I left several messages with the judge's clerk," he finally explained. "Without a response. Then, as the hour grew late, I was informed by the same scrawny clerk that the judge had left for the day." He looked past me to the chalkboard.

"Wot is it ye have there? More notes?"

What I had there was the information from my meeting with Mrs. Mallory and then the visit from Lily and my great-aunt.

I explained each of the notes that I'd made.

"Burke?" he commented. "Wot the devil would the man be bothering Charlotte Mallory about?"

That was what I intended to find out. And then I thought a trip to Guildford might be necessary. However, that was for the following day, after my visit to the newspaper archive. It did seem that there was much Mr. Burke had failed to mention about what he knew.

This wasn't a race. It was about finding and stopping a murderer. It did appear that Mr. Burke had not yet found that information.

"Aye, it could be useful, most particularly with that letter Charlotte Mallory intended to send."

He was thoughtful, in that way that I liked to watch—the frown surrounded by the beard, that dark gaze staring off with thoughts churning behind them, then finding me, and the way it softened.

"Mrs. Ryan will be waiting supper for us at the town house," I casually mentioned. Food to soothe the savage beast?

"Ye could tempt a dying man."

Fourteen

THE OLD BAILEY, LONDON

BRODIE LEFT the town house early for the ride across the city to that notorious prison, the Old Bailey, adjacent to the Criminal Courts.

It was a massive, monstrous series of buildings adjacent on Bailey Street, hence the name, and very near the old Roman Wall, as Mikaela had once explained.

The prison of that name had been built over three hundred years earlier in what she had described as an amalgam of massive cut-stone walls in the Gothic style.

She knew a lot about that sort of thing, although she dismissed it as meaningless flotsam. Still, he admired that about her, the education she'd acquired, while he had his education mostly from the streets.

He knew other things about the Old Bailey: The reputation for those poor souls incarcerated within those walls, no matter the path in life that had brought them there. The public hangings that had ended only a few years earlier. Then there was the walkway from one's cell to those gallows, the skeletons of those who had gone before buried beneath it.

He had seen it all, much different from her knowledge of the place, in an effort to save a man that had failed. And he might have once ended there as well.

She never held the difference between them over him, something else he admired in addition to her keen intelligence and that woman's sense that she claimed to have. Something that he had never experienced in the women he'd known.

There were other things too, and taken on the whole, there were times when he just wanted to watch her, watch that keen mind as it worked, then see that smile when she arrived at some answer.

Women were not supposed to be logical. She was that, and more. And in those moments, he felt both pride and something verra near surprise to have her in his life. Not that it was always easy. There was that stubbornness, and she would never hesitate to speak her mind.

Then there was the other part of it, of course, he thought on that long coach ride. The softness of her, the way she breathed in sleep at night beside him...

If he could just manage to tame that independent way about her, taking herself off on some matter or another, that had a way of terrifying him as if the devil was on his shoulder tormenting him.

Most likely a hopeless proposition as her great-aunt, Lady Montgomery, had pointed out in the beginning.

"She has always had that independent nature. I suppose it comes from the dreadful situation with her father. Trusting someone will not come easy for her. However, once she gives it..."

Forever, he thought now.

It was a word that had never existed for him before. His life had always been day to day, and survival, even after he joined the MET. But *forever* did have meaning now—if he could just protect her and keep her alive when she went off on some clue.

That was the other part of it. She had a particular temper about his protection of her, insisting that she could take care of herself. And she was quite accomplished in that. All well and good.

He just needed to find a way to protect her without her knowing it, he thought as the driver arrived at the entrance to the Criminal Courts.

He looked up at the driver and paid the fare. He could have sworn the man said something.

"Good luck to you on that."

Once the fare was in hand, the man touched the brim of his hat, then snapped the reins over the backs of the team and guided them back into the city.

As he had the day before, Brodie followed the signs from the entrance to the second floor, where the judges had their offices before attending court.

It was early, deliberately so, and the thin, pasty-faced clerk from yesterday had not yet arrived. He passed by the area where he had waited with no success the day before, the office for Judge Cameron just down the way, very near that additional stairway that led to the court.

Looking around, he saw the hallway was completely empty. According to the information board at the entrance, it appeared that none of the three judges who usually sat criminal cases and were expected that day had arrived yet. Nor had their staff.

However, the board had provided information that he needed. Judge Cameron was hearing a case beginning at ten o'clock in the morning in Courtroom One.

Brodie took the slender tool that he always carried along with his revolver from his inside coat pocket and opened it, much like that knife Munro had given him. Then, with one more look around he inserted the curved end of the pick into the lock on the door of Judge Cameron's chambers.

As Mikaela had commented more than once, one could take the man out of the streets, but not the street out of the man.

He supposed that was true. Old habits die hard, he thought,

as he carefully maneuvered the pick in the lock, then finally heard that last tumbler click open.

He smiled to himself. Instead of being shocked or outraged the first time he used that particular method of entering a flat or locked warehouse, Mikaela had surprised him.

"You must show me how it's done!"

He pushed the door open, stepped inside, and closed it behind him.

There were times that things learned on the street were verra useful. In particular when it came to avoiding a pasty-faced clerk who was full of himself. Or anyone else for that matter.

And it was there he waited for Judge Cameron to arrive, seated in a thick upholstered chair, before that massive desk where final trial documents were signed and sealed a man's fate. So that he might express his condolences, then ask the questions that might help find the one who had murdered the judge's daughter.

~

MIKAELA

I was familiar with the Times newspaper archive from past inquiry cases. It had provided a valuable source of information.

Actual copies of newspapers, dailies, and crime sheets had been kept for decades on racks on two floors of a moldy, foul-smelling building that the Times owned very near the Strand, and now more recently contained photographic archives on film rolls.

Those rolls were catalogued by date and year, in metal tins to protect the film, and available for viewing on one of the viewing machines on the second floor of the building.

I had spent days and often weeks, searching through old issues of newspapers looking for information regarding a case, only to leave after countless hours with ink-stained gloves that the attendant insisted upon, a dreadful headache, and then starting all over again the next day in search of a crumb of important information.

However, all those past issues on film had been catalogued so that all I had to do was request the film archive from a certain date, rather than looking through countless pages of entries. Modern inventions were quite marvelous.

Brodie had departed the town house early after informing me the previous evening that he was going to return to the Criminal Courts, determined to have his meeting with Judge Cameron, while I wanted very much to search for information regarding that five-year-old murder that seemed to have some importance for the case we were pursuing.

I had managed, however, to delay Brodie's departure for a short time, even though a determined Scot presented quite a challenge.

I wasn't certain now whether it was the warmth of the bed with icy rain pelting the windows of the bedroom, or 'my charms,' as he called them, that had finally persuaded him.

"I don't want to be late," he had grumbled, after which I informed him to quit complaining about it, and...

Hmmm. I did hope that he wasn't late.

As for my task for the morning, I wrote down the year my great-aunt had been fairly certain that earlier murder had occurred and submitted the call slip to the clerk. He returned with a tin of film for issues of the newspaper including the crime sheets for the entire year of 1886.

"Has Mr. Burke consulted any of the archives in the past two weeks?" I inquired with a thought of what Lily had shared from her last conversation with Charlotte Mallory. He checked his visitor log.

"I don't see that he requested anything from the archive, although I am not the only clerk. However, if he had checked out any of the film archives, it would be shown in here."

I thanked him, then took the tin with that film roll to the viewing machine. I then threaded the film from one spindle over the viewing plate with that light above, and onto another spindle, scrolled to the first crime sheet, and began my search.

In addition to the year of that murder, I had a name—Ormsby, fairly well-known, according to Aunt Antonia.

Failing that, I could always search the death notices, as she claimed the young man was killed in a riding accident only a few months after that tragic murder.

How difficult could it be?

That is, if my great-aunt was correct about when the murder took place. If not, I might be here most of the day searching, or possibly into the following day.

It was very near midday when I found it. The entry on the crime sheet covering the murder was brief, with scant details, but it was enough.

It made note of a young woman by the name of Amelia Harris of Abbington Lane, who was found dead after a late supper with friends. She had been found strangled to death after not returning to the family home.

The name Harris was familiar. Aunt Antonia had mentioned something about the family business, coffee imports.

Several persons were questioned, including a man, Mr. E. Walmsley, a bookkeeper returning from a late appointment.

Walmsley! The same name that was on that letter to Charlotte Mallory.

The report then went on to mention that several persons were questioned but no suspect was detained.

I now had a specific date and that report on the crime page of the Police Gazette. I then scrolled through the next few issues of the newspaper that followed that date.

I eventually found the funeral notice for Amelia Harris, then a subsequent article about the 'horrible crime and a devastated family' by Times writer, Walter Morrison. I made notes of everything including Morrison's name.

The next article I found was several days later, reporting that Mr. Gerald Ormsby of London, to whom Amelia Harris had been engaged to marry, was being questioned in the matter. There were additional articles, as the Harris and Ormsby families were well known.

Mr. Morrison was quite flamboyant in the additional articles he wrote, sensationalizing the details that followed. Mr. Ormsby was eventually 'detained,' and held on charges of murder.

There was one witness, a man by the name of Walmsley, and the evidence seemed quite incriminating even though Mr. Ormsby was to be defended by Sir Edward Mallory, considered to be one of the most successful barristers in London when it came to defending a client.

Apparently there had been a falling-out between Amelia Harris and Gerald Ormsby. He had been outspoken in that he refused to accept that the marriage would not take place. And there was that witness who was to give testimony at the trial.

I stared at the stunning headline of the next article as Mr. Morrison followed the trial. The prosecutor for the Crown was unable to produce the witness. He had disappeared!

Without the witness, the Crown's case against Mr. Ormsby collapsed and the judge was forced to dismiss the charges against him. The judge was Harold Cameron!

There were attempts by Mr. Morrison of the Times to meet with the Harris family in the aftermath however, Amelia's father refused to meet with him.

In following issues of the Times over the next two months, articles about the tragedy continued.

Amelia's mother was stricken with some sort of fever that was attributed to mourning the murder of her daughter. She died shortly afterward. Amelia's father, devastated by the double loss, was rarely seen except to take care of the affairs of his import business.

This was followed by an article about a devastating fire in the warehouse office at the docks. Caught in the inferno, Simon Harris perished. The only survivor was the long-time warehouse manager.

There was another article several months after the devastating tragedies. Gerald Ormsby was riding in Hyde Park and suffered a tragic accident when he was thrown from his horse, his neck broken.

I sat back in the chair before that reading machine, in an attempt to grasp the information I'd learned. So much tragedy, a murder unsolved that had devastated a family, and a witness that had gone missing.

But what did all of it mean all these years later in the deaths of two young women?

I made notes from the additional information I had found, then returned the roll of film to the clerk.

"Do you know of Mr. Morrison, a writer with the Times?" I inquired. It might be useful to speak with him about anything else he might remember from that earlier murder.

"Mr. Morrison?" he replied with some surprise. "He's been gone must be six or seven years now. Heard that he had a bit of a habit with the drink that finally got him."

There would be no information to be found there. I thanked him.

It was early afternoon but seemed much later with the weather. A thick rain had continued through the morning and into the afternoon, and I had neglected to bring my umbrella.

With the Times archive building very near the Strand, I had arranged to meet Brodie back at the office afterward.

He had returned as well, Mr. Cavendish informed me as I arrived.

The office was warm and inviting, a fire burning in the coal stove. Brodie sat at the desk, pipe in hand, as he studied the chalkboard. He looked up as I entered the office.

"I was startin' to think I might need to have Mr. Cavendish send the hound after ye with this weather."

He rose from the desk as I removed my coat. He took it from me and hung it to dry beside his.

"And I see that ye left without yer umbrella."

That might explain strands of my hair wet against my cheeks.

"It is a bit wet out," I replied as he went into the adjacent bedroom and returned with a towel.

"For an intelligent woman, it is surprising that ye go about without yer umbrella or a stout pair of boots."

"I was anxious to get started this morning."

The scolding, if it could be called that, continued as he took my bag and set it on the desk, then proceeded to dry my hair, me, and finally remove my shoes.

"Yer feet are wet as well!" He made one of those sounds, much like a parent scolding a child.

"That has been known to happen when crossing the street in a downpour," I pointed out. Yet, I had discovered that I liked these moments when this part of him—protective, caring, perhaps a little worried, escaped from behind that dark gaze.

"Come and stand by the fire and warm yerself."

"Is that a dram of Old Lodge you have there?" I inquired of the tumbler beside his pipe on the desk.

That dark gaze narrowed as he went to the sideboard, a new acquisition for the office, and retrieved another glass.

"Wot am I to do with ye?"

I had some thoughts about that as he returned and handed me the glass with whisky shimmering like gold. However, I supposed it would have to wait as I studied the chalkboard.

"You've made notes," I commented.

"Some."

"Your meeting with Judge Cameron was successful?" If not, I was fairly certain I would have already heard about it.

"More or less," he replied, taking a sip from his own glass with a thoughtful expression.

"And that would mean?"

"I did meet with the man. He was not particularly accommodatin'. He reminded me that I had no authority as I was no longer the MET, and threatened to have me arrested."

"For what?" I inquired.

"It might have been about enterin' his office before he arrived. It is most usually locked."

I could imagine how he had managed that.

He had left particularly early. It seemed that he wanted to make certain he was not turned away again.

"Arrested for picking the lock to his office." I concluded the obvious.

In typical Brodie response, he brushed it off.

"I don't suppose that put Judge Cameron in a particularly cooperative attitude."

"It was a most interesting conversation," Brodie replied.

"I expressed my condolences over the death of his daughter," he continued, "and explained that we were making inquiries on behalf of a *friend* of Charlotte Mallory."

"He claimed no knowledge of anything that might have upset her, and explained that she was anticipating her forthcoming marriage to Mr. Eddington."

I was not surprised, considering the secrecy that Mrs. Mallory had undertaken in meeting with me. Either he had spoken the truth that he had no knowledge of any upset, or chose not to acknowledge that there had been.

"Out of curiosity, I then inquired about that murder case that her ladyship recalled."

"What was he able to tell you?"

"That is the '*less*' part of the conversation. He claimed only a vague memory of it, an unfortunate situation, he called it. And he inquired who our client was. He was most insistent."

"What did you tell him?"

One corner of his mouth lifted in smile. "I told him what a lawyer might say, that it was confidential."

I could only imagine what Judge Cameron's reaction might have been to that.

"You sensed there was more that he wasn't saying," I concluded.

Brodie had that way about him, that sense of something from

working countless cases for the MET and then in his private inquiries. And as I had discovered, almost always correct.

I would have pointed out that it was very much like a woman's intuition about things—a frequent discussion between us, however I kept to the matter at hand.

"What *did* he tell you?"

"He remembered that Sir Mallory represented the suspect at the time. It seems that Daniel Eddington was a young law clerk and had presented the initial defense to the court that the accused had spent the day and evening at his club."

"What about a witness to the crime mentioned in the newspaper articles?" I inquired.

"He remembered that the witness disappeared and the court was forced to dismiss the charges, not something that usually happens."

A witness to the murder, a man by the name of Walmsley, by what I was able to find in the newspaper archive. And that same name on the letters sent to Charlotte Mallory!

"What were ye able to learn?" Brodie then asked.

I went over everything I had been able to find in the film archive of the newspaper.

"You have told me there is no such a thing as coincidence." I turned from the board where I had been adding my notes as I spoke.

There was more that I had learned, that I still struggled to understand.

"Wot is it?" Brodie asked. He did know me quite well.

"Mr. Morrison with the Times wrote a brief article after Amelia Harris was murdered. His style was somewhat theatrical." That was as close as I might describe it.

"It seems that a red rose was nearby when her body was found, and then several more arrived for the funeral. The color red is for passion," I reminded Brodie.

"There has to be a connection to the murders of Charlotte Mallory and Elizabeth Cameron," I concluded. "I'm certain of it."

And that name? The witness who disappeared—Walmsley? I was certain the name was the next piece to the puzzle.

"Aye, verra possible," he agreed. "A trip to Guildford might be useful, to find what the person might know who sent those letters."

Brodie poured us both another dram of whisky.

"I'll contact Mr. Dooley to see what he might be able to learn about that warehouse fire," he added. "It shouldna be too difficult to find information. Harris, ye said the name was? A coffee importer?"

With our plan made to go to Guildford the following morning, I realized that I hadn't eaten all day.

"I will buy supper at the Public House," I told him. My clothes had dried for the most part and I was suddenly quite hungry.

He took the glass from my hand.

"Aye, to the invitation, however *I* will pay. For now, I can still afford to feed ye, despite the fact that ye eat like a horse, and take inquiry cases where there is no fee," he added pointedly.

Spoken like a true Scot.

"Of course, dear," I replied as he held my coat for me.

Fifteen

GUILDFORD WAS a quaint village in Surrey south of London, surrounded by farm land.

It had changed very little over the last three hundred years, with cobbled lanes, white-washed houses, many with thatched roofs, a stream that meandered through the middle of the village, a church and a handful of other buildings built around a town square. One of those buildings was the Borough Hall that also contained the local postal office.

It was two hours travel from Paddington Station in London, that sprawling domed rail station with a dozen tracks spreading like fingers across various parts of London and beyond.

By comparison, Guildford station had two tracks, one incoming and one outgoing, and a single-story red brick station-house with a roof that extended out over the platform as a means of protecting passengers from the weather that had followed us from London.

I had remembered to bring an umbrella from the office and opened it as we departed the rail car upon our arrival.

We made inquiries and the station master directed us to the postal office at Borough Hall, a place where all, he claimed, who lived in Guildford were known.

"For collecting the taxes," the clerk said with a nod.

A driver appeared and took us to Borough Hall. We had arrived before midday from London. The mayor was off on some bit of business, and we were assisted by a clerk, an older man with sleeves rolled back and an apron, who appeared as if he managed the tavern we had passed on the ride from the rail station.

When Brodie introduced us, he replied with that rural accent that I had become familiar with on my travels in the past beyond London proper. "From London, are you now."

"I have a post sent from Guildford from a friend I haven't communicated with in years," I replied and ignored the bemused look Brodie gave me. It was, after all, a small lie and hardly the sort that would cause any harm. "If you know where I might find them?"

He gave me a long look, the sort that takes in head to foot. He apparently decided that I wasn't the criminal sort or one who would cause anyone harm.

"What might the name be?" he asked.

"Walmsley."

"It has been some time since you've visited then," he replied. "Johnathan passed on early this year after a long illness. His wife, Cora, lives in a small cottage just past the leathermakers."

"It's hard on a woman on her own with no family. Lost a child right after they came here. And I hear she's not well either." he added. "You might keep that in mind."

"How far?" Brodie inquired.

"Just down the way. "You might want Gilly, who brought you from the station, to take you there, what with the weather. He'll be back soon after returning with Mr. Soames from a meeting with the church council."

The rain had thickened and the roadway, mostly dirt, was awash and not the best for walking. It seemed we had no other choice but to wait.

"You're welcome to wait here, or across the way at the ale house. My wife makes excellent sandwiches with fresh meat."

And that answered the question about that apron. He obviously worked two positions, as clerk for the mayor and at the tavern.

"That will do verra well," Brodie replied and thanked him.

We set off for the ale house, Brodie's hand on my arm as if he thought I might wash away with the rain in the street.

The ale house was full for that time of the day, no doubt due to the weather. The customers appeared to be farmers, workers apparently from the local mill, a local leathermaker by the conversation at the bar, and Gilly, who had stopped by after delivering Mr. Soames to his meeting and was waiting to return to pick him up after.

Mr. Ross waived Gilly down and explained that we would need his services after the midday meal.

Gilly was a lanky, ruddy-faced lad with dark hair and dark eyes. I liked him immediately. It might have been those dark eyes, full of mischief and keen appraisal of myself.

Brodie put in an order for two sandwiches, that Mrs. Ross prepared.

"Are ye certain one will be enough?" Brodie teasingly inquired.

"Perhaps one for the return to London," I suggested which brought the intended response.

"The lady and gentleman have come calling on Cora Walmsley," Mr. Ross informed Gilly.

I caught Brodie's bemused expression at being called a gentleman.

"They will need a ride in your rig."

"I can take you as soon as you finish," Gilly replied. "The mayor said it was going to be a long meeting and there was no need for me to wait."

As boasted, the sandwiches were delicious. Afterward, Brodie signaled to Gilly, who had taken up a game of dice with one of the other customers while he waited.

He brought his rig around from across the street in front of the Borough Hall.

It was an old coach that carried passengers as well as cargo, evidenced by the small wood crates that filled the seat across as well as the boot.

"Deliveries I need to make," Gilly explained as he shifted the crates. "Eggs that I picked up on the way back. These will go to the grocer after I deliver you."

Eggs. I caught Brodie's amused expression.

In no time at all, even with the weather, we reached the small cottage Mr. Ross had spoken of.

There was electric in the village proper, however none here. A faint light glowed from the small window that faced out onto the road and smoke curled from the stone chimney.

"Mrs. Walmsley takes in mending," Gilly explained. "Poor lady lost her husband winter past. Doesn't seem to have any other family. Mostly keeps to herself.

"The vicar sees that she has food when she needs it," he continued. "I heard that she's not well."

An older woman who had lost her husband, apparently had no other family, and took in mending and sewing to support herself.

I didn't know what to expect when we set out. What did a woman who was forced to accept church charity in order to survive have to do with Charlotte Mallory? And for what reason had she sent those letters?

Brodie seemed to sense my hesitation. "It canna hurt to ask a few questions."

I knew that he was right. Yet, it was this part of our inquiry cases that could be difficult. Still, C. Walmsley had sent those letters.

As Brodie knocked on the door of the cottage, Gilly said that he would return in an hour in order for us to make the afternoon train back to London.

We waited several moments and began to think that Mrs.

Walmsley wasn't going to answer. Then, there was a sound from the latch and the door slowly opened.

"Yes?"

Everything that I might have expected—someone perhaps hoping to frighten a young woman for financial gain, or out of some other scheme—immediately disappeared.

Cora Walmsley was small and slightly stooped at the shoulders. She wore a simple gray gown that was much mended. Gray hair was pulled back into a bun, and the lines on her face spoke of pain and heartache, which I certainly had no intention of adding to.

"You are C. Walmsley who recently sent a letter to Charlotte Mallory in London?"

I saw the uneasiness that filled those eyes. "You are not Charlotte Mallory."

"No, but we're here on her behalf."

"Behalf?"

"There has been an incident," Brodie explained. "Miss Mallory is dead and your letter was found with her."

"Dead?" she replied, obviously quite surprised. "Are you the police?"

"No," Brodie assured her. "We are trying to find out what happened on behalf of a friend."

There was still that suspicion. I took the letter out of my bag and showed it to her.

"You sent her this letter, and she had written you back." I had that letter as well. Possible evidence, Brodie had called it.

"We are only trying to find some answers."

"Dead?" she repeated and shook her head. "I never meant no harm, not for her."

Not for her? What was that supposed to mean? Someone else perhaps?

She finally stepped back and opened the door.

"I meant no harm when I sent those letters," she repeated as we sat at the table to one side of the main room of the cottage.

"Why did you send them?"

She looked from me to Brodie, then finally said, "All I've got is tea to offer you."

"That is not necessary Mrs. Walmsley," Brodie assured her. "We do not want to impose."

She fixed tea, perhaps taking the time to try to decide what to tell us, if anything.

She set mismatched cups on the table.

"I read about you in the dailies," she said, returning to pour tea into the cup before of me.

"Lady Forsythe. You don't use the title?"

"I find it awkward at times, and I now use my husband's name as well," I explained with a look over at Brodie.

She set the teapot down.

"My husband passed this last winter," she explained. Her face softened. "He *was* a good man." And then as if to convince us of that, or perhaps herself, "He was!" Her voice trembled as she continued.

"We came here almost five years ago it is now." She looked from Brodie to me. "He said that the country air would be good for our son and he bought this cottage for us.

"He said the money for the cottage was an inheritance he didn't know about beforehand. I thought it was strange at the time, as both our families were simple people, and I never heard about any inheritance.

"Afterward he kept the books for the church and other places about the village to pay for food and medicine for our son.

"Our boy died that next winter. The doctor who makes calls in the village said that his lungs were 'gone' and his heart just gave out. My John was not the same afterward. He blamed himself for the loss of our boy.

"John got sick just about this time last year. The physician said that it was the influenza that so many got about that time. I took good care of him, but he only got worse. I never caught it. The doctor said that it happens that way sometimes."

She stared down at her hands wrapped around the chipped tea cup.

"It was near the end when he told me where the money for the cottage came from. It was as if he needed to ease his mind about it."

She reached across the table and picked up the envelope that contained the first letter with that cryptic message she had sent Charlotte Mallory. She stared down at it.

"He said that he was given the money for doing something important for the man he worked for, but it was necessary for us to leave London afterward. He did it for our son. I know that doesn't excuse what he did..."

Secrets and lies, I thought.

"Who was the man he worked for?" Brodie asked.

"Sir Mallory, the barrister, for several years," she replied. "It was a good position and paid well."

"And the reason he was paid to leave London?" I inquired.

Cora Walmsley looked up then, and I had never seen a more miserable expression on someone's face.

"Because of what he saw," she replied in a soft voice.

"Wot did he see?" Brodie asked.

"He had left work and he was on his way home. He wasn't able to find a driver so he walked that night. He passed by Rules, that fancy restaurant. Just beyond, he heard a boy, one of the newspaper boys finishing his shift, shout that a young woman had been found dead just beyond.

"The police had been summoned. That's when a young man ran into my husband as if he was running from a fire. He was finely dressed and had blood on the front of his shirt."

I sensed there was more.

"He didn't recognize the young man at first. The newspapers were filled with the story about the young woman who was murdered. Her father was a well-to-do merchant. Harris was the name.

"There were those who heard the young man and woman

arguing. He was taken in by the police. Johnathan said that the young man claimed to have been another place when the young woman was attacked and killed. His family hired the best lawyer for his defense against the charges."

"The young man's name?" Brodie inquired, although I already fairly certain what that was.

"Ormsby," she replied. "A very well-placed family it seems."

"And the lawyer hired to defend the young man?"

"Sir Mallory."

The finest lawyer that Ormsby money could buy, and John Walmsley's employer.

"John went to him and told him what he had seen that night. He was told that it wouldn't be necessary for him to speak in court."

"And it was shortly thereafter that it was suggested that he leave London," Brodie concluded.

Cora Walmsley nodded.

"And the letters?" I then inquired.

"I saw the announcement that Sir Mallory's daughter was engaged to be married to the man who came to my husband and persuaded him to leave."

"Who was the man?"

"He was a law clerk at the time, by the name of Eddington."

He had learned his skills well from one of the most powerful barristers in England.

"And you decided to contact Miss Mallory," Brodie replied.

"I thought she needed to know the sort of man she was going to marry, the kind that would do knowingly something like that."

People are not what they pretend to be.

And the second letter.

Secrets and lies are the devil's work.

Cora Walmsley had answered the question about the letters that Charlotte Mallory had received. Both letters were an attempt to right a horrible wrong that had obviously haunted John Walmsley all those years. And no doubt an attempt to warn Charlotte Mallory against marrying Andrew Eddington, who was complicit in the scheme, something that was quite illegal—the bribery of a witness for the sake of a client, Gerald Ormsby.

Ormsby was eventually released for lack of evidence, and then dead merely a matter of months later in a riding accident. Perhaps justice had been served.

All of it was tragic to be certain, and the Walmsleys had both suffered for it, along with the loss of their child.

Yet, there was still the question: why were two young women now dead?

"Wot are ye thinkin'?" Brodie asked as the train wound its way back toward London.

We had left Guildford just over an hour earlier with some answers. However, with other questions that still had no answer.

After leaving Cora Walmsley's cottage, we had stopped by the church at the edge of the village. There we had left funds specifically to help her with food and anything else she might need.

There undoubtedly were those who would have argued that while tragic, what she had done in sending those letters was cruel.

Yet, she had broken no law even though it would have undoubtedly been said that her husband had in the money he had taken to remain quiet about what he had seen and then disappearing.

A tragic choice made not out of greed, but with the best of intentions, yet he had carried the guilt from it to his grave.

"The two murders are somehow connected," I finally replied, then looked at the man beside me who had far more experience in such things.

"But how? And why?"

Brodie's hand covered mine. "Your woman's intuition?"

"It's there. I know it is. We just haven't found it yet."

He folded my hand in his, something that had become a habit.

"Aye," he agreed. "There is something more that we haven't yet found. Perhaps Mr. Dooley will have information about that warehouse fire when we return."

There was a note from Mr. Dooley tucked into the door frame of the office when we arrived.

He found 'one of the lads,' as he said, referring to his fellow police, a constable who remembered the fire well. He included the man's name. He had been on the watch at the docks the night of the fire, and we would do well to meet at the location and speak with him as well.

Perhaps there was something he could tell us about that night.

For myself, I wanted to go over everything we had learned with the hope that I might find something that could be helpful in solving those two murders.

In the meantime, I needed to contact my good friend, Templeton. She had an acquaintance with the manager of the opera house, and a new production was to begin the following evening.

Several weeks earlier I thought it might be a good experience for Lily.

Aunt Antonia had looked at me with disapproval when I spoke of it at the time.

"Opera? It is so very boring and everything is in Italian. It will be over the dear girl's head. She will never wish to attend another production."

"It's not opera," I explained. "It's a cabaret that will be performing at the Opera House."

"Oh, excellent. I've not been to one."

I had invited my sister as well; however, she was far into wedding planning and jitters as they call them, and there was no amount of coercion I could have used on Brodie.

"It is one of those things that women appreciate far more," he had made the excuse.

I suspected that he would rather have had someone poke him in the eye than accompany us. It did seem there would be four of us attending, which then included Munro, as he never let my great-aunt venture out alone and unprotected in the city. Although as I had pointed out more than once, pity the person who attempted to accost her in any way.

The cane she always carried was hardly to assist in walking. And I had overheard recently a comment Munro had made to Brodie, that she has specifically requested a revolver that she might keep in her handbag, much like the one I carried when out and about in different parts of the city.

He had asked what the devil a cabaret was. I explained what I remembered from my school forays in Paris.

"A burly que?" he then asked. It was close enough that I understood.

Not precisely, I thought. Supposedly there would be no removal of clothes.

"Ye may as well know that her ladyship has requested a firearm for when she's out and about," Munro confided in me at the time, and I was always willing to be supportive where my great-aunt was concerned.

"Robbers, and all sort of bad characters, I suppose," I replied at the time.

He shook his head at the time. *"I pity anyone of that sort she may encounter. They have no understanding what the woman is capable of."*

I did agree in that regard. I had witnessed her taking down a street thief who had the misguided ambition to relieve her of her handbag when she was leaving after dining with old friends. When the confrontation was over the young man needed several stitches at hospital before being take to the Yard.

A revolver in the hands of a determined eighty-six-year-old woman?

From that moment on, whenever my great-aunt was out and about, she was accompanied by a tall, fierce-looking Scot with that sharp blue gaze that was much like staring into a glacial abyss.

"*Entirely unnecessary,*" she had declared. "*However, he does have the ladies in quite a stir when he is about. Fascinating to see.*"

It was therefore arranged that Munro would accompany Lily, my great-aunt, and me to the cabaret the following evening.

Sixteen

CONSTABLE NOLAN AGREED to meet us at St. Katherine's Dock early the next morning before he began his shift for the day.

He had been with the MET for over fifteen years and had worked different areas of London including the London Docks.

I was familiar with St. Katherine's Dock from that first inquiry case in the matter of my sister's disappearance and the murder of her companion, Mary Ryan, the daughter of my housekeeper.

After all this time, my sister safely found and now planning her wedding to James Warren, the memory of that time swept back over me—the fear, anger, and then the hopelessness in not knowing who was behind it and if I would find her alive.

I had a habit, from my younger years and early experiences, of withdrawing into myself over such things, trying to make some sense of it all, then pushing back the unpleasant memories that were still there and very likely would be forever. That bit of wisdom from my great-aunt who had experienced some of her own difficulties.

As she had said in the past, it was just *life*.

"Get over it, my dear, and get on with it."

Now *there* was someone who knew that same sort of fear, anger, and those other emotions that had a way of raising their ugly heads. The one person I had ever known, other than my great-aunt, who knew exactly what those were about and didn't attempt to coddle me or convince me that 'it would soon pass' or it was just my imagination.

Someone who let me muddle about, stomp, and curse when I felt it necessary—yes, I have been known to curse from time to time, until I had worked my way through all of it once more.

And then he was there. That dark gaze filled with an understanding of past things that we each carried along with us, and then a hand reaching out for mine.

"What might we find at what is left of the warehouse after such a devastating fire?" I asked as our driver made his way through the early morning streets past the Tower and toward the East End.

"I have seen fires in the past, several of them here in London. A dangerous business to be certain," Brodie explained as he stared out the window at the incessant rain that had greeted us once more that morning upon rising.

"A captain with the fire brigade told me on one of the fires I was called to, that there is always somethin' that is left behind—a bottle of the drink, or some small piece of something that tells who might have been there. And for whatever reason, the remnants of the Harris warehouse might be able to tell us something, even after five years."

"Is there still business conducted there?" I asked. "Shipments that are still received?"

"For two years after, but not for a long time now, Mr. Dooley was able to learn."

The telephone call had come quite early at the office on the Strand. Mr. Dooley had found the former manager of the warehouse, who managed two other nearby warehouses, and oddly enough, still received a stipend from the Harris company to keep watch over the property, which was still owned by Harris Imports.

"That seems odd after all these years," I commented. "What could there be to keep watch over? Burnt ruins?"

We arrived quite early at the docks with that row of warehouses along the wharf, in order to meet with Constable Nolan before he needed to be off to make his shift.

There were only two steam ships moored there waiting, it appeared, to be unloaded. Captain Turner had once explained that often the ships arrived late in the day then waited until the next day for dockworkers to unload their cargos.

At this time of the morning, the tide had not fully turned, and in spite of those cargos still in their holds, the two ships rose quite high in the water at their moorings.

"The river is a fickle woman," he had told me. *"And a dangerous one, particularly with the rain that floods it. That is when most ship captains will make certain to wait out the storm in the channel before entering the river so as not to find themselves at high tide next to Buckingham Palace. It would not go well with the Queen."*

Constable Nolan was heavyset, more of the muscular sort, in full police uniform, with a nod for Brodie as the rain thickened and I opened my umbrella.

He greeted us with a tip of his hat as Brodie introduced me as his 'associate,' rather than introducing me as his wife.

I had suggested it as it seemed to be more credible when most women were simply looked past, particularly in professional positions.

"This way then," Constable Nolan indicated the row of warehouses and the darkened hulk of the one on the end.

"I did speak with the former manager for Harris Imports. According to what he told me, he has stayed on as a sort of watchman since there is still a storeroom that survived the fire.

"Quite an effort that was," he continued. "Saving the rest of the warehouses when it went up. And tragic that the owner died in the fire. You'll need to be careful where you step, miss. A great deal of it has been cleaned up and then picked through in the years since. But there are still some roof timbers and the loading dock still there."

And in that way of disasters there were the creatures that had set up residence in the ruins—at least two cats that skittered into the shadows as we arrived, along with a host of pigeons that filled the rafters over that storeroom at the back of the site where the main part of the warehouse had once stood.

I had some experience exploring ruins, though admittedly not usually charred ruins. Still, I took care where I stepped as Constable Nolan led us through what remained of the Harris Imports warehouse.

According to my great-aunt, the company was once quite prosperous, with coffee imported from Brazil and sugar from the West Indies. All of that apparently changed when Amelia Harris was murdered by Gerald Ormsby.

The tragedy was the first of a series of events that destroyed the Harris family and the lucrative import business Simon Harris had built.

I picked my way through the remnants of charred and crumbled walls that still smelled of smoke after all this time, as rain soaked everything.

What, I thought, might these ruins tell us, if anything, about the recent murders of two young women?

Brodie and Constable Nolan had slowly moved ahead, Brodie taking everything in with that dark gaze, occasionally shifting something out of the way or poking with the tip of his umbrella. He picked up something from amidst the rubble.

Then, he continued on with Constable Nolan. As they reached the storeroom that had survived the fire, someone called out from wharf-side where the warehouse stood before the fire.

"Mr. Martins, the former manager," Constable Nolan explained and introduced him as he joined us.

Brodie explained that we were investigating a connection to

the Harris fire for a client and asked if it was possible to unlock the storeroom.

Mr. Martins was hesitant, and no doubt suspicious.

"There's naught inside but a few tools," he replied dismissively. "Nothing of value."

"Yet it is locked," Brodie pointed out.

"Been that way since before the fire."

"You receive a stipend to watch over the site, after all these years?" Brodie asked him.

"It's not much, but the least I can do for all the years I worked for Mr. Harris."

"How does that work?" Brodie then asked

Mr. Martins shook his head. "I don't know anythin' about that. The attorney takes care of it."

"Mr. Harris's attorney?" I inquired, knowing something about that sort of thing.

"By the name of Winslow. He came to me after the fire and said that it was somethin' Mr. Harris put in place to take care of those who worked for him."

It appeared that was all Mr. Martins knew, or was going to tell us. And he certainly wasn't about to provide access to that storeroom. Loyal to the end, even after death.

Constable Nolan needed to set off for his shift in another part of London, and it was clearly obvious that Mr. Martins was not about to allow us to continue any sort of inspection of the charred remains of the warehouse.

Brodie, polite as ever, merely a disguise for other things that stirred in his thoughts, bid the man good day, and we departed.

The tide had lowered substantially, dock workers now offloading the two cargo ships we had seen upon our arrival even in the pouring rain. Out beyond, the wharf water swirled and churned murky gray with white caps that appeared, then disappeared as if hiding.

I had experienced ship travel on my adventures and encountered different waters in the Mediterranean. It was said that nowhere else was the water as unpredictable as in the River Thames. In the past it had flooded the city several times.

"What are you thinking?" I asked as we left the wharf and found a driver.

He was thoughtful.

"How might it be possible that Mr. Martins continues to receive payments all these years after the fire and the death of the owner?"

"Perhaps through a trust," I replied as he gave me a hand up into the coach.

"A trust?"

"It's a legal arrangement with documents that places one's properties—jewelry, funds, a residence or perhaps a business—into a status that can continue on even after their death, with others appointed to handle certain matters."

It was something I knew a little about.

"Our mother placed certain things in a trust for Linnie and me. There weren't many things—an heirloom ring and a few other pieces of jewelry that she inherited from her mother." I smiled at the memory.

"A doll with a porcelain head that one of us might pass on if we had a daughter. Along with a portrait of her as a child with her father that was important to her.

"Certainly not our family home," I added, "as it never belonged to her, and the bankers claimed it after... our father's death."

He knew the details of that sordid affair from my great-aunt, one of those things I preferred not to think about but raised its ugly head from time to time.

"Our mother did what she thought best. The trust she set up still pays a few pounds every month. And the jewelry is there for Linnie, along with the doll for her daughter, if she should have one."

"Where are those things now?" Brodie inquired.

"The portrait is at Sussex Square in one of the upstairs rooms so that Linnie and I could see it from time to time as children. Particularly Linnie, as she was so very young when our mother passed and barely remembered her. It's a way for her to at least see what she looked like. The doll is there as well."

"Aye, I don't imagine ye were one to play with dolls. What of the other things?"

"They are kept at the bank for safe keeping. The bank sends the funds to Mr. Laughton each month, and he sends them on to each of us."

"I have married a woman of means," Brodie said with a faint smile.

He had of course. Our great-aunt had made it understood that my sister and I, as her only heirs, were to inherit her properties when she passed on, which I hoped she would put off for a least a few more decades.

There were also the funds she had distributed to us each month, which I had objected to, particularly after the success of my books.

She had insisted at the time. *"It is my money, dear. I will do as I wish."*

That had settled the matter.

"If I should pass on first, you will be a very wealthy man. But do remember the Viking send-off," I reminded Brodie.

He made that particular scoffing sound that I was certain was invented by a Scot.

"A portrait, a doll, and a few odd pieces of jewelry?" he replied. "I would prefer to keep you around for a while. That is, most of the time."

Such endearing sentiments. And then a different expression appeared in that dark gaze.

"At least ye have the portrait of yer mother to remember her by."

We returned to the office on the Strand after leaving the warehouse area at St. Katherine's Docks.

It was still early in the morning, and I updated information on the chalkboard that included my notes about what I observed at the site where the warehouse once stood, including the storeroom.

I finished and dusted off my hands, attempting to find something in all of it that made sense—a connection that might explain two murders.

Brodie was at his desk, an object before him laid out on a piece of butcher paper left from one of our suppers from the Public House. The man refused to throw anything out. A habit no doubt a left-over from his days on the street when he had nothing.

If I had heard it once, I had heard it dozens of times since we first worked together.

"*It could be useful*," he had declared of the latest bit or piece he had picked up; a bit of wire, a piece of leather, or something else that one might consider rubbish. And somehow women were the subject of frequent humor about trinkets they acquired.

I give him credit for the wire, however. It had come in most useful when picking a lock. A cabinet that currently stood in the bedroom now contained those other bits and pieces.

"What have you there?" I asked as I approached the desk. It looked very much like a piece of charred wood.

"A souvenir?"

"In a manner of speaking. I found it under some of the other debris." He picked up the odd piece and handed it to me.

"Tell me what you see."

The object I had seen him inspecting closely at the warehouse site was a piece of charred wood. I picked it up.

"Something for your collection perhaps," I cheekily replied. "A paperweight perhaps?" I suggested.

"What else?"

"Black, charred wood, and somewhat oily."

"What do ye smell?"

"Something... sharp." I looked up at him.

Brodie nodded. "I smelled it as well."

"After all this time?" I set it back on the desk and rubbed my fingers, covered with soot.

"I suppose it is possible," he replied. "There is a man I know, a captain with the fire brigade. He might be able to tell us something about it."

Most curious, I thought. Particularly after all this time. Of course, it was possible that it was simply old residue from something that had been inside the warehouse.

I checked the time on my watch.

"I want to speak with Sir Laughton regarding the possibility of a trust that Simon Harris had set up, with the manager still paid after all these years."

It was possible that my great-aunt's attorney knew the man and might be able to explain how such a thing as a trust might work. It could explain a great deal. But there again, what did it mean if he had set up a trust?

"Ye have that theater performance tonight?" Brodie asked.

"We're to leave from Sussex Square at eight o'clock for the nine o'clock performance."

He nodded as he came around the desk

"It will give ye the chance to dress in yer finery for a change."

My finery?

"I prefer my walking skirts and boots. They are far more practical."

"A lady who prefers woolens and leather to silks and satins." He slipped his arms about me.

"Yes, please," I replied.

"Do ye miss fancy *soirees*, as her ladyship describes them, supper parties with champagne, and the companionship ye find there?"

He had become most serious.

"I have never been one for fancy soirees or supper parties with all of that gossip and pretentiousness. And you know well enough that I prefer my great-aunt's whisky to champagne." I wrapped my arms around his neck.

"As for companionship," I teased.

A dark brow angled sharply.

"I prefer the intrigue of an adventure."

"Adventure?"

I smiled. "Always, Mr. Brodie."

Seventeen

WE SHARED the midday meal at the Public House, then Brodie was off to find the fire brigade captain he had spoken of in the hope that the man might be able to tell him something about that charred 'paper weight,' as I referred to it.

I put through a call to Sir Laughton's office. He was able to meet with me later in the day, which would give me enough time afterward to return to the town house, change clothes, and then meet Lily and my great-aunt, along with Munro, for the cabaret that evening.

Sir Laughton's offices were on Fleet Street, very near the Chancery House and the Royal Courts of Justice.

Highly experienced in matters of law, he had overseen my great-aunt's legal affairs for as long as I could remember, and had guided her through the somewhat chaotic process of formally adopting both me and my sister to protect us from our father's losses and ruin.

If she held any animosity toward our father—he was after all quite dead by that time—she had kept it to herself until we were much older, and then only to myself.

"*One's deeds do catch up on one.*"

And then her somewhat infamous 'get on with it' speech. "*I never liked him. He had a weak chin. However, your mother, poor lamb, was quite taken with him. Or I should say, taken in."*

I was of much the same opinion, and for several years while gaining my maturity, I found myself constantly checking my chin, much to Aunt Antonia's bemusement.

"No weak chin there, my dear. You must simply refuse to have it."

As it turned out, neither Linnie nor I had that character aspect.

I arrived now at Sir Laughton's offices with my well-developed chin, and gave my name to Mrs. Abernathy, the woman who managed the front of his office, including his appointments.

"Good afternoon, Lady Forsythe. It is so very good to see you again. How is her ladyship?"

Mrs. Abernathy had been in service to Sir Laughton almost as long as he had been my great-aunt's lawyer, and knew our family well.

We exchanged greetings, then she pressed a button on a small panel at her desk and announced that I had arrived. She then showed me to his office.

"My dear, Mikaela," he said, coming round his desk. "It is good to see you. I was quite surprised when Mrs. Abernathy said that you called for an appointment. You know that you need not be so formal." He then added, "I do hope it is nothing serious."

"I have questions," I replied, setting aside my umbrella. He assisted with my long coat, then hung it on the coat rack near the door.

"It is in the matter of an investigation that Mr. Brodie and I have undertaken."

He nodded as he returned to his chair behind the desk. "And Mr. Brodie is well also?"

I assured him that Brodie was quite well.

"How may I assist you?"

I explained the basics of the two murders, and then specifically asked about the possibility that Simon Harris might have established a trust to see to his affairs after his death.

"Simon Harris, Harris Imports. I remember that tragic situation. And to answer your question, yes, it is possible. Her ladyship has such a provision in her own trust that will provide for you and your sister for years to come, as well as her various properties. Carrying out specific duties for someone after one is gone, with a Trustee appointed to carry out those duties."

Then, that would explain the regular payments that had been made to Mr. Martins all these years since, and still...

"Is it possible to find out if there is in fact a trust for either Simon Harris or Harris holdings?" I then asked.

"There is no public record of trusts. The trustee named in the trust would hold the document on behalf of the person who had it created. Their responsibility would be to manage and administer the trust according to the terms set out in the trust."

"Would anyone else have a copy of it?"

"The lawyer who drew it up would have a copy. Perhaps a bank, if funds are to be distributed, or the title registrar if the trust calls for the transfer of property. I assume this pertains to the inquiry case you and Mr. Brodie are pursuing."

I acknowledged that it was.

"How else might we learn what is in the trust?"

Sir Laughton sat behind his desk, chin resting on steepled fingers as he considered the question.

"It might be possible to obtain a copy of the trust, as far as specific instructions are concerned, if you were a party to the trust, or perhaps a claimant."

"Claimant? What sort of claimant?"

"If, perhaps, you believed that you had an interest in the estate held by the trust and had not been properly represented."

"How would one go about that?"

"You would need to be represented by someone with knowledge of such matters," he explained.

"An official letter of intent would be drawn up and sent to the office of the holder of the trust."

"How long might that take?"

"It could take several days to establish the need for the disclosure of the trust."

"Could take?" I replied.

It seemed that it was possible to expedite the matter based on the particular wording in the letter of intent.

"For the sake of argument, how quickly might it be done?"

That gaze sharpened above those steepled fingers.

"I am reminded that you are remarkably like her ladyship."

I smiled at that. "Then, you are able draw up such a letter on my behalf, as a claimant and as expeditiously as possible, so that I might learn what the provisions of the trust are." I concluded the obvious.

"Plainly speaking, you are asking me to determine if there is a trust, who holds it, and then to tell you what is in it."

"That is precisely what I am asking."

He shook his head. "Very much like her ladyship. Very well. I will have my clerk search the archive of legal documents filed by most of us about London, and have the letter for the Harris representative awaiting that information. Where may I reach you when it is done?"

I asked him to contact me at Sussex Square the moment he had sent the letter and when he might have a response.

He promised to have some word for me by end of day. I told myself that it was the best I could have hoped for.

As I left, navigating my way to the corner through the swirls of rain that had accumulated on the sidewalk, I thought of Brodie and wondered if he had been able to find the man he hoped to speak with regarding his 'paper weight.'

I briefly returned to the office, even though it was late of the afternoon. I made notes on the board from my meeting with Sir Laughton. I was hopeful that I would have word soon from Sir

Laughton and had drawn a line under the description of a trust that I hoped he would be able to find.

I then left a note for Brodie as we had agreed we would do when going about in separate directions.

I suppose I should have objected having to account for my whereabouts, as in the past with others, but didn't. That surprised me somewhat, but in addition to our growing personal relationship, I found that I liked Brodie very much and understood his concerns that came from his work with the MET.

It was a bit flattering and oddly comforting that someone cared for my safety, even if he could be a bit high-handed about it from time to time.

Mr. Cavendish and Rupert were nowhere to be seen when I had arrived. Given the nasty weather and with both Brodie and me gone, they were undoubtedly down at the Public House where it was warm, dry, and there was food.

I called for a cab, then waited until the driver arrived below. I locked the office and set the bolt, then descended the stairs.

I recognized the driver from previous calls. He stepped down from atop the hansom.

"Good day, miss," he said with a lopsided smile. "Nice weather out, this afternoon. Where be your destination?"

He held open the gate and assisted me into the cab.

"Sussex Square," I replied.

As he reached to close the upper gate across the opening against the rain, I glimpsed a man in front of the haberdashers across the roadway.

It might have been the scarcity of those about on such a dreadful afternoon, the fact that the shop was closed, or the way he suddenly pulled up his collar as he seemed to stare across the way.

He had no umbrella as he stepped out from under the canopy in front of the shop, then pulled the brim of his hat low.

He was dressed in a dark suit with long coat over as he

continued to stare, then slowly disappeared down the opposite sidewalk.

Brodie would have laughed and then teased me. But it was there, that certainty despite his being hardly visible through the pouring rain. I had seen the man before.

~

BRODIE

Bethnal Green Fire Station was in the East End.

The red brick four-story building was little more than two years old with two large bays, a tall tower at one end of the building for hanging hoses to dry after a fire, and a stable yard in the foreyard for horses that pulled those wagons.

Captain Kearney was with the brigade at Bethnal Green, having transferred from Holborn the year before.

Brodie knew him from his time with the MET, when both had found themselves called to the fires in the East End where families were crowded into flats and cook-fires were often the cause of blazes that spread throughout a building.

Kearney was a good man, more than twenty years in with the brigade that had grown from district fire brigades to the consolidated Metropolitan Fire Brigade, which had formed several years before in an effort to provide better fire service to the greater London area.

He was a burly figure of a man who stood head and shoulders with the younger firemen, with that long handlebar mustache, and a face with deep lines, no doubt from squinting into the heat of a burning building.

"You are a long way from the Strand," he greeted Brodie as he came out of the office beside that first bay.

"Is there a fire that brings you here, my friend?"

"In a manner of speaking," Brodie replied. He gestured to the gleaming fire wagon that stood in the bay with an enormous boiler mid-wagon.

"Steam power?"

The captain nodded as two of his men carried a coiled hose from the adjacent tower, and proceeded to mount it on the wagon.

"It was just brought over from city maintenance. It is supposed to pump water faster than a two-man team. We will see." He dried his hands.

"Things are quiet today, so far. Come inside," he told Brodie. "I will buy you a cup of coffee and you can tell me what brings you to the Green."

"We have shared some adventures, eh Brodie," he said after he had poured them both a cup of coffee and sat back in his chair, in the large open area just beyond an arched opening. It was lined with cots end-to-end along one wall, a large dining table with benches in the middle, and a half-dozen wardrobe closets against the other wall with helmets above.

"That last fire at a tavern before you took yourself off in private business was a nasty one," he recalled.

Brodie nodded. "A difficult fire, that one. And started by a disgruntled customer."

Kearney nodded. "You chased the man down in quick time."

"Aye, but not soon enough to save that poor girl who worked there."

"That is the problem with a city that is over a thousand years old, with buildings on top of buildings cheek by jowl, and many of them built of wood over the centuries. A fire starts and it has its way with others before we can get to it.

"But it's better now since bringing all the districts together and organizing them, along with building the new fire stations." He made a sweeping gesture indicating the building where they now shared coffee.

"It gives the ability for all to respond to a fire if necessary." He took a long sip of coffee.

"Now, what is it that brings you here. It cannot be that you've missed me. My wife might object."

Brodie smiled. "I miss many of the lads I worked with, good men, and there are others..." He would have let that go. As far as he was concerned, it was old business, best left in the past.

Kearney nodded. "Word gets around among the lads and those with the Metropolitan Police—what Abberline did. Not right by my book." He poured more coffee for the both of them.

"Now, my friend. How may I be of assistance?"

Brodie pulled out the piece of charred wood wrapped in butcher paper that he'd brought from the site of the warehouse that had once been Harris Coffee Imports.

"Wot can ye tell me about this?" he said, laying it out on the desk.

The captain picked it up and turned it over in his fingers.

"Wood, badly charred," he commented as he rubbed his fingers down the length of the piece, then rubbed them together.

"Oily residue on the underside of the piece that obviously was protected all these years. Tell me what you know about it."

"A warehouse fire some years back at St. Katherine's Docks. It was owned by a coffee importer, by the name of Harris. I pried this from a timber that had once been part of the side wall near a back storeroom that survived."

"St. Katherine's Docks, you say," Kearney commented. "And you're investigating the fire after all this time?"

"In a manner of speaking, as it might pertain to another crime," Brodie replied.

Captain Kearney then smelled the piece of wood.

"There is a bit of a smell left. Wood always soaks it up, but usually it dries out either with the fire, or over time. You said that you pried it out where the timber at the side joined the wall of the storeroom?" he shrugged. "This still has the smell of coal oil."

Brodie's gaze narrowed. "Ye smell it as well then."

Kearney nodded. "One can't work the fires all these years in all sorts of places and not know it—coal oil, usually used to start a stove fire that gets away and you have a nasty situation."

"How fast would such a fire spread?" Brodie asked.

"It would depend on the amount of coal oil used, which seems a bit odd for a warehouse where coffee was stored. And then, what set it off? A small amount spilt by accident might not have been the cause."

"Supposedly it started late at night, an oil lamp that was left burning after a shipment arrived, and the fire got away and took most of the building."

"I remember the news articles about it at the time. Tragic situation for Harris, and he supposedly tried to put it out before the brigade arrived."

"Aye, *supposedly*," Brodie commented.

"You believe the fire was deliberately set? For the insurance money?"

"No claim was every made according to articles that were published afterward. And that smell of coal oil would seem to contradict the story of simple lamp oil. And coal oil spread about, at least on that wall?" Brodie added. "There is a manager still there who keeps watch over the place."

"Have you spoken with him? He might be able to tell you something."

"He was... less than cooperative, "Brodie replied. "It seems that he receives a stipend each month to watch over the site."

"You know as well that a warehouse fire is not unusual, particularly when the owner is perhaps deeply in debt. And that piece of wood would seem suspicious."

"Aye. I thank ye for confirming what I thought."

"I hear your inquiry business has done well."

"Well enough, although we may be forced to leave the building. There is a new owner and the rents always go up."

"I hear other things as well," Captain Kearney added. "One of the lads picked up word that you have someone working for you now. A woman, he said."

Brodie thought about that before replying.

"In a manner of speaking. She is an associate for some of the inquiry cases, and my wife."

It was not often that he needed to explain, but he was finding that it came more easily now.

Kearney's eyes widened above that handlebar mustache.

"Wife, is it?" he exclaimed. "My Molly said it would never happen. The woman must be special."

"Aye," Brodie replied. "That she is."

He had what he wanted, confirmation of his own suspicions, yet was not certain what it meant to their current investigation.

If Harris had set fire to his own warehouse and was then caught in it, it wouldn't be the first time someone found himself in financial difficulties and then took such drastic measures.

"I thank ye kindly for yer thoughts in the matter, and the coffee."

"Ha! Married!" Captain Kearney slapped his knee and broke out in laughter as he left.

It was after midday when he returned to the office on the Strand.

He didn't expect Mikaela to be there. After meeting with Sir Laughton that afternoon, she would go to Sussex Square to join Lady Montgomery and Lily before setting off for the cabaret.

He understood the responsibility she felt to find answers for the murders after bringing Lily from Edinburgh, and he agreed with her that they must find those answers.

"Miss Forsythe was here earlier," Mr. Cavendish informed him as he stepped down from the cab.

"Only a short while before leaving again. Said if I saw you, that she left you a note."

Brodie nodded as he stepped under the overhang above the alcove. The Mudger, né Cavendish, joined him.

"I've seen it like this before out at sea. A big one is comin'. Could be like the one a few years back that flooded up to the Strand."

"I need to find someone," Brodie told him. "You might best know where he can be found—Mr. Brown."

"Brown?" Mr. Cavendish spat out. "He's a bad sort. You know as well as any that the man can't be trusted. What might you want with that filthy, lyin' bugger?"

It seemed the Mudger, known to commit crimes in the past, had no respect for the man.

"Does he still control the docks and the workers there?" Brodie asked.

Cavendish nodded. "As far as I know."

"Ye know where to find the man?"

"I can put the word out... Is this about the two murders?" the Mudger asked, then, "I know, don't ask. What I don't know can't hurt me. But still, there is Miss Forsythe. You know how she can be, no disrespect meant."

None taken, Brodie thought. He knew exactly how she 'could be.'

"She is off with her ladyship this evening. And if you work quickly, there is no need for her to know that I've sent ye off to see what ye can learn."

"Right yer are," Cavendish replied as he whistled for the hound who suddenly appeared from under the alcove.

"Me hat," he told the hound, who disappeared once more into the alcove then reappeared with a battered bowler hat in his teeth.

Cavendish grinned as he firmly set the hat on his head, then wrapped the woolen scarf more securely about his neck.

"I've been teaching him to fetch. I hear the beasts are right smart that way."

Brodie could imagine who might have told him that.

"Ye have yer blade?" he asked.

The Mudger patted his jacket. "Where I can get it right quick if I need it. And I have the hound."

Not the defense Brodie would have preferred that he have where he was sending him.

"Brown will want to know what's in it for him," the Mudger reminded him.

"There will be a fee paid once I meet with him, and the information proves out. Not before."

Brodie glanced overhead the sky.

"If ye canna find the man, get back before nightfall. No one will be about once the new storm sets in."

"As you would say, Mr. Brodie, it's a fine soft rain."

The Mudger grinned that gap-toothed smile as he paddled off on his platform, the hound running alongside and then disappeared through the pouring rain.

There was no one on the streets he trusted more than the Mudger. The man had an uncanny ability to change himself from '*helpless beggar*' to fierce enemy that few would want to encounter.

It was a lesson he'd learned a long time ago. The outcome, a draw if it was to be called anything, was a friendship of respect and care. And then there was the immediate bond between the cripple and Mikaela.

Not out of sympathy, because in the way of hers, that sense she claimed to have, she understood from the beginning that Mr. Cavendish would never have accepted it.

And that was another thing, Brodie thought as he put in a call to Mr. Dooley for any information he might have on Brown.

He had always known the Mudger by his street name. Mikaela had quickly learned that his name was Cavendish and called him by it.

He suspected that the man had taken a bit of a fancy to her. For whatever reason, Mr. Cavendish had taken to washing somewhat regularly, pulling his overlong hair back in more acceptable fashion, and now wore clothes that in the very least didna smell like the hound.

Mikaela insisted that it was due to an affection that he had grown for Miss Effie at the Public House. Be that as it may, the man still had a habit of defending Mikaela in an argument.

"*She is probably right, you know,*" he had told him recently. "*The ladies often are. It's that other sense they seem to have. It's hopeless to argue with them.*"

Hopeless. Aye, Brodie was finding that out. It called for different measures, such as tonight, and his hope of contacting a man he knew from the streets.

He finally reached Dooley.

The streets had been quiet of late as far as any reports of assault against business owners. Brown's people guaranteed protection from other known gangs about London.

But Dooley and his men hadn't picked up rumors of any plans in that regard. It might have been the weather.

He changed out of the suit of clothes he usually wore when making appointments with clients, and pulled on rough woolen trousers and a woolen jumper that looked as if it might have been something the Mudger had pulled from a rubbish bin on the street.

When planning a visit to the streets of the East End and a man like Brown, it was best to dress the part, a part he was all too familiar with.

Eighteen

MIKAELA

I ARRIVED SOMEWHAT LATE at the Theater Royal where the cabaret was to be held for that one-night performance.

My friend, Templeton, no stranger to theatrical performances, was to join us, for hopefully a performance that was to be as the playbills about the district had advertised—an evening of music, with the ladies and gentlemen of the cabaret troupe providing an exciting and oftentimes bawdy entertainment.

Aunt Antonia had dressed the part.

"I have attended such performances in the past, in Paris," she had explained when we first made plans to attend. "Of course, that was some time ago. Quite entertaining and risqué."

The evening promised to be quite remarkable for more than the sort of entertainment that it provided the people of London, including several well-known members of polite society. And also, for a reunion, if it could be called that, between my very good friend and Mr. Munro.

They had shared a somewhat fiery relationship in the past— that *was* the only word for it.

Any doubts in that regard disappeared completely at the

discovery of a particular piece of furniture at Templeton's country home quite by accident.

It was in the matter of a previous inquiry case, and the circumstances had taken Brodie and me to Surrey. It was in the course of that case that we discovered the rather bold painting on the headboard of her bed.

There was no mistaking the images of the two persons painted there. The artist, whoever it was, could have rivaled DaVinci.

As I was saying...

I heard someone call out and was immediately seized about the shoulders and pulled into a heavily perfumed embrace.

"He assured me that you would be here, tonight," Templeton exclaimed. "It has been too long with you and Mr. Brodie off and about on the Continent."

Considering that greeting, *he* could only be Sir William, William Shakespeare that is, her muse.

"And he has shared the most amazing rumor!"

I could only imagine what that might be.

"Her ladyship and a young woman arrived some time ago..." she continued, looping her arm through mine and drawing me to the line of attendees who were eager to enter the theater.

"You could have told me that Mr. Munro would be accompanying them," she said in a somewhat peevish tone.

"I would have thought that Sir William would have provided that information," I replied.

She gave me a sideways look. "There was not a word before. I have discovered that he can be quite mischievous at times. I have come to the conclusion that he likes to play tricks on me."

"Oh my," I commented. "A bit of discord from the spirit world?"

"You know it's true. He has been helpful from time to time in your inquiry cases."

That was open to question. However, the timing of those two particular incidents did make me wonder about the truth of it.

"Has he been well?" Templeton then asked.

I assumed it was not Sir William she was inquiring about.

"You might ask him yourself," I suggested as we joined my great-aunt, Lily, and Mr. Munro.

"This is verra exciting," Lily exclaimed as she grabbed me by the hand.

I thought that rather an understatement as I saw the looks that passed between Mr. Munro and my friend.

Explosive might have been a word to describe it, or possibly *cataclysmic*, as there was a violent crash of thunder overhead. The sky opened at that exact moment, and what had been a steady drizzle turned into a downpour just as we entered the theater.

The cabaret performance was an enormous success, if response from the audience was any indication, including Lily.

There was music, a troupe of dancers, short theatrical performances played for humor, and a bit of scandalous teasing among the characters of a pantomime, along with a bit of magic performed, and a daring burlesque that I thought might set proper London society on its ear.

Throughout, my great-aunt hooted with laughter and exchanged looks with me, and Lily was rarely in her seat as she clapped and cheered the performers along with a good many in the audience.

I thought of Brodie. I do believe that he would have enjoyed it, quite different from opera or the usual stage performances in London theaters.

More than once, I caught the stolen glances between Templeton and Munro, along with bits and pieces of conversation impossible to hear over the music and singing.

I had thought everything quite finished between them some months earlier over some matter that might have had to do with Ziggy, her iguana.

Yet, apparently not by the heated glances that passed between them. By *heated*, it was by no means angry, but more of the smoldering sort that I had written about in one of my novels.

I suppose it did one good to smolder from time to time. I

thought of Brodie again, and wondered if it ever went away, that feeling that was almost like a longing.

I wished that for my friend, who in the time I had known her, had entertained the *company* of others, including the Prince of Wales, if rumors were to be believed. And then simply left, never looking back, according to what she had once told me. Tonight she had looked back, several times.

I returned to Sussex Square with Lily and my great-aunt. Upon arriving, Mr. Symons informed me that a courier had brought round a message.

I opened the note from Sir Laughton.

> *Through my clerk's efforts I have learned that John Mortimer Esq. was the attorney for Simon Harris, and still is for the Harris estate, including the Harris Trust.*
>
> *Through somewhat creative negotiations, I have acquired the trust late this evening. I look forward to you calling on the office in the morning.*

Somewhat creative negotiations? I could only imagine what that might mean.

Still, it was good news, and I was hopeful the details of the trust might reveal something important to our inquiry case.

I looked up from my aunt's desk in the library of Sussex Square at a sound and discovered Lily peering tentatively around the edge of the door.

It was late when we returned and my great-aunt had immediately gone up to her rooms.

"So much excitement this evening!" she had exclaimed. "I do wonder if we might have such a performance for Linnie and James's reception after the wedding."

Oh, my. That could be most exciting.

My sister had declined to attend the evening with the excuse there were too many details of the forthcoming wedding to see to. I had my own suspicions, of course.

What details, I was tempted to inquire, could be handled of an evening and not left to the morning?

No doubt, one of those details that needed 'attending' was James Warren, her fiancé, who just happened to also be my publisher. But who was I to remind her of proper pre-wedding behavior, when Brodie and I...

As I was saying, Lily now looked at me with a most serious expression, quite the opposite of her excitement through the evening.

I invited her into the library. I did hope this was not one of those serious conversations that girls who are rapidly becoming young women are curious about. With the memory of my own curiosities at very near her age, I was not prepared for those conversations quite yet.

Still, I reminded myself that Lily had far different experiences than I had by the age she was at now. Being raised in a brothel could give one a particular view of things.

"I've been meanin' to ask ye somethin', and I wanted to speak with ye before ye left this evenin'."

She sat on the chair at the end of the desk.

"It's about Miss Lenore's wedding."

I could have sworn I heard a sigh of relief from 'someone' in the room.

"What would you like to know?"

"I heard from one of the house maids that it's most usual for people to give gifts to the bride and groom at the wedding."

I continued to listen.

"I have money from my work at The Church before I came to London. I want to buy a gift for Miss Lenore and Mister Warren. Problem is I don't know what might be right, or where I might purchase somethin'."

Dear girl, I thought. She had come from nothing, living on the streets as a small child, taken in by the madam at a converted church in Edinburgh, where she worked as a maid with the usual prospect of working in a brothel when she was old enough.

Only the fact that The Church had burned down had changed that prospect, after which I invited her to come to London.

Still, when she arrived, she had only the dress she wore and another one that was already too small, along with those few coins that she had earned from the *ladies,* doing their laundry and helping with other maid services.

I knew what those few coins meant to her, and yet she sat before me quite serious about purchasing a wedding gift. It was unlikely those few coins would be enough for the usual sort of gift.

"I see," I replied, and I did.

The girl was proud and spirited. Not the sort to be coddled or lied to. Still, I saw the look on her face and in her eyes. This was obviously something that was very important to her. And something that Brodie had reminded me of even as he agreed to bringing her from Edinburgh.

"I know ye and I know yer not the sort to take on something without thought. But ye need to understand that her life has not been easy. It will be up to ye and meself to help her find her way in this new life, much like havin' a child.

"And for all her boldness and spirit, there's a fear underneath it all that she might be thrown away again. Be certain that this is for her and not for yerself."

I was certain then, and now. I suppose it might have come from my own early experience, that feeling that my sister and I had been thrown away. Whatever it was, I wanted Lily to have an opportunity for a different life than the one she'd been handed.

I gathered my thoughts. There seemed to be only one thing to do under the circumstances.

"Then we should go shopping for a gift."

"Where?"

She had been to the dressmakers and the shoemakers with my great-aunt; however, those things were necessities, and quite boring truth be told.

"We shall go to Harrods," I told her. I then described the department store that offered everything from exotic food to perfume, jewelry, furniture, and included a lady's salon.

"The ladies at The Church wore a lot of perfume when they were entertainin'."

I could only imagine.

"We will go after Mr. Brodie and I have completed the inquiry case," I told her then. That was most important now, and I was hopeful that we might be able to conclude it. She understood.

"Then we will make a day of it," I promised her. "We will have lunch in the restaurant and see what we may find for a gift." I was confident there would be no difficulty there.

She nodded. "Will Mr. Brodie come as well?"

I could almost hear his response, something very colorful about ladies shopping.

"Probably not. Now, you must tell me how you are coming along with your reading lessons." My great-aunt had mentioned that Lily attempted to claim the book in question, a rather cumbersome historical volume, had somehow been misplaced and she had no idea where it was.

"Your tutor will be returning tomorrow and will expect a progress report."

Even as I said it, I couldn't believe the words that came out of my mouth. By the expression on her face, Lily obviously felt the same as I had, reading stuffy old books written by stuffy old men, when I preferred Jane Austen and Mr. Dickens.

"I'm reading another book that her ladyship assured me would be all right," she added, avoiding a direct question about the 'missing' book. At the excited expression on her face, I was almost afraid to ask.

"It's an adventure story written by a lady by the name of Emma Fortescue. It's real excitin'."

Well... that was most interesting.

"Which book?" I inquired. "I hear that *she* has written several," I did hope that it was not the one with the adventure in the Greek Isles.

"It's the one about a long train trip across Europe and the dangerous people she meets in a place called..." She tried to pronounce it.

"Istanbul?" I suggested.

"That is the one, right enough. Have ye read it?"

"I have heard of it."

That particular novel was one of the less 'adventuresome' sort. At least as far as handsome strangers were concerned.

"I suppose that will be all right," I added, knowing full well from my own reading experiences that it would do no good to ban her reading other books. She would undoubtedly find a way to read them anyway.

I sighed. We were no blood relation, yet as both Brodie and my great-aunt had pointed out, we were very much alike. It did seem that now the shoe was very much on the other foot.

Brodie went out onto the landing of the office.

It was late, verra late, and still no word from the Mudger. He had told the man to return no later than nightfall, as the chances of finding Thomas Brown or any of his people would run afoul of the weather. And now it was well into the night.

He cursed as he returned to the office. Wot was keeping the Mudger? Had he encountered Brown and several of his men?

He could handle himself well enough with one or two. Brodie had seen it himself. Or had there been an accident of some sort?

With the weather anything was possible, the man navigating that bloody platform about as if he had a death wish. And wot of the hound? That bloody, smelly, vagrant.

Did the beast know enough to return to the Strand if there was a difficulty?

He had before, but then it was possible that something had

happened to him as well, given Brown's reputation... if the Mudger was able to find the man.

He heard both sounds almost at the same time—a frantic scratching at the door of the office and the bell clamoring out from the landing. When he opened the door, the hound charged past and shook himself off in a puddle of water on the floor of the office.

He could have sworn the beast grinned up at him. Mikaela had taught him to do that, he was convinced of it. She had a bond with the beast from the beginning, feeding him biscuits and sponge cake.

He went out on the landing and then down the stairs where the Mudger waited on the sidewalk.

"I told ye to take care not to be out late o' the night. Was there trouble?"

"You also asked me to find someone," the Mudger pointed out.

"Ye found him, then."

"One of his men first, on the street, then the man himself, holed up in an old tenement like the king himself—beg pardon to Queen Vic."

The Mudger grinned up at him and Brodie could have sworn there was a resemblance to the hound.

"Had to persuade his man. Between me and the hound we got the message across just who we wanted to speak with, and not one of Brown's other men."

"He agreed to meet?"

He nodded. "It seems the two of you have had some dealings before. He said you were to come alone. For some reason he doesn't trust you."

That worked both ways.

"Where?"

The Mudger gave him the information. If he failed to show within the next two hours, there wouldn't be another opportunity.

Not the best of situations, Brodie thought. Still, a man like Brown with his fingers in several different pies, might have information about the fire and the man whose business had once rivaled the other trade companies.

"Aye."

He returned to the office and grabbed his coat, a patched and worn piece that looked as if it might have been pulled from the charity bin, then pulled his cap low. He checked the revolver in his pocket and the knife sheathed down the side of his boot. When he reached the bottom of the stairs, the Mudger was waiting. He looked up from under the brim of the derby hat.

"I'm goin' with you."

Brodie shook his head. "He told ye that I was to come alone."

The Mudger squinted up through the driving rain that created halos around the street lamps and filled the gutters.

"There's some that say I'm only half a man, with me legs gone."

"No," Brodie was firm in his decision. "Ye've done well enough for the night, just findin' the man. If there's trouble, I'll handle it."

"Alone?"

"I was raised on the streets," he reminded the Mudger. "There isn't anything the man can try that I havena seen, or done myself."

"That may be so, but I wouldn't want to have to answer to Miss Mikaela if anything was to go wrong. The woman has a temper."

That she did, Brodie thought with a faint smile as he waited for a cab or possibly a drayman still out in spite of the weather.

"He didn't say nothin' about the hound," the Mudger pointed out with a sly expression.

Brodie looked down at the hound. The beast had followed him back down the stairs and then dragged something long dead out of the alcove. He knew the animal was good in a fight, and he had found Mikaela in the course of a previous inquiry. Still...

"That one?"

"He'd serve you well, Mr. Brodie. With just a word or two."

"A word or two?"

The Mudger hooked a thumb over his shoulder in the direction of the hound.

"He knows three words that Miss Forsythe taught him. The first is '*stay*,' the second one is '*come*,' and the third one is '*kill*.'"

Some men's wives kept docile cats to take care of mice. His taught the beast commands that rivaled what a man might use. And then there was that whole argument about his ability to find someone.

He had insisted that it was an accident or luck. She had proceeded to prove him wrong with an example of the hound's fine hunting skills.

"He mostly ignores the first command," the Mudger continued. "But he's sharp on the second one."

"And the third?" Brodie asked.

"Ah, well, He gets a bit excited with that one. You only have to say it but once, then don't get in his way."

He caught the sound of the horse-drawn wagon, then sight of the coal man retuning from his last stop.

"The hound will do you well, sir," the Mudger continued. "And knows his way through most of the East End if there should be trouble."

"Come along, then," Brodie told the hound as he waved down the coal man and asked for a ride to the end of the Strand, where he would be able to find a cab. He climbed aboard the seat and the hound clamored after, tail wagging.

It took the better part of an hour to get from the Strand to the location where Brown had told the Mudger he would meet with him.

More than once, he was certain the man lied. Payback, perhaps, for that previous encounter, and then Brown's men would remind him of it in their own well-known way when he arrived.

Brodie had looked the other way once before when he was

with the MET, a decision at the time to save what mattered most —more than fifty barrels of wine that had escaped the tax man, or the life of a young boy badly injured in Brown's scheme. Verra likely he would have died if Brodie hadn't gotten him to Mr. Brimley.

Afterward, Brown kept his contraband barrels of wine for a hefty profit, the tax man lost out on substantial revenue, and the boy recovered. And Brodie knew that he'd made the right choice.

The way he figured it now, Brown owed him. However, the man's memory might be short in that regard.

He left the wagon after they crossed into Holborn and continued afoot, the hound loping along beside him. More than once, he considered it a fool's errand to bring the animal.

He'd grown up on streets like this, lights from single lanterns burning dim in most windows, the sudden scurrying among the shadows, both man and beast. And he'd learned what it took to survive.

It hardened one, forced them to close off things that might have mattered, and search out those things that could ease the pain for a few hours, a night, and then back out on the street. And he had learned those lessons well—stay, come, kill.

They served him well when he was with the MET because, unlike many of those who patrolled the streets, he knew what was out there, what waited, what mattered and what didn't.

Until a woman, who wasn't like the others out there, wasn't afraid of the dirt and filth, and didn't turn away from the hard reality of the streets... didn't turn away from a man like him...

He found the street the Mudger told him to look for, then that tenement with the light that glowed in the third window from the right on the second story window.

He checked the revolver, then moved the knife from his boot to the back waist of his trousers.

"Stay," he ordered the hound, then crossed the street.

He avoided the main entrance of the tenement and instead circled around to the back. There, he caught a movement in the shadows, waited until the man moved and circled round to the front, then climbed the stairs to the service entry and slipped into the building.

Brodie glanced both directions in the dimly lit hallway, then at the stairs. The sound of voices guided him to the flat with that third window that he'd seen from the street below.

He didn't knock then wait for permission to enter. Instead, he opened the door, catching those inside by surprise. Two men nearby scrambled and would have drawn weapons, while the man he had come to see slowly recovered his surprise, then grinned.

"Mr. Brodie, we meet again."

They exchanged careful greetings, much like two men in an arena circling one another, taking each man's measure, and attempting to decide when to land the first blow.

"The Mudger tells me that you are looking for information." Brown smiled. "I am flattered that you would think of me."

Brodie kept a watchful eye on the other two men, as well as the one in front of him.

"Keep both hands where I can see them," Brodie told him.

Brown slammed both hands down on the table and let out a roar of laughter.

"What is it that brings you here, Brodie?"

"A favor that ye owe *me* in the matter of fifty-odd barrels of verra high priced wine that ye saw a good profit from," he reminded him.

There was a slow nod. "Perhaps. That depends on the favor."

"Information about a fire some years ago at a warehouse at St. Katherine's Docks."

Brown nodded. "Harris Imports. A large loss that would have made a nice profit if I had been in charge."

"The story is it was an accident, a horrible tragedy, with Harris dyin' in it that night."

"That is the story."

"And his man, Mr. Carney, who worked for him then, and still does, all these years later."

Brodie saw the change in Brown's expression, the way his eyes narrowed and sharpened, even as he casually asked. "And what might your interest be?"

Brodie took the piece of burnt wood from his pocket and laid it on the table. Brown picked it up, rubbing his fingers along the wood then smelling it, much as Brodie had. He shrugged.

"That piece of wood tells a different story," Brodie commented.

Brown motioned both of his men out of the flat. But undoubtedly no farther than a shout away. It was what he would have done.

"Harris Imports," Brown commented. "I heard about it at the time. A pity to be certain, all that cargo up in smoke. And now you have this piece of wood.

"You ask yourself why would a successful and wealthy man set fire to his own warehouse, and then die in it as well, his daughter murdered and then the death of his wife shortly after. I suppose grief can be a powerful thing."

For some, Brodie thought. But the man before him? That was highly questionable.

"And now your suspicions about that fire, and the two murders of those young women."

Brodie's gaze narrowed. The idea that there might be a connection had been there from the beginning, that single rose left behind connected them. However, both he and Mikaela felt like they were stumbling about in the dark with nothing that made any sense.

Yet, as he had learned in his work for the MET, there was always something, even seemingly random, that connected things. It was just a matter of digging deep enough and learning what that flower left behind meant.

Brown nodded as he continued to inspect that piece of wood. "There is a smell about it, even after all this time. A bad smell I would say, particularly when Carney has built up a sizeable side business."

"What sort of side business?" Brodie inquired.

"The sort that avoids the larger docks and the tax man, and brings a right smart profit."

"For whom, with Harris dead these long years?"

"That would be the question." Brown replied. "I encountered the man on a trip regarding interests of my own. Seems it is a regular occurrence at Queen's Dock, and he's made an arrangement with the owner of the warehouse next to the those burnt ruins to store the goods when he moves them.

"The man is not what you would consider honest, nor intelligent, but he is loyal to a point, and greedy, and therefore dangerous," he added.

"It's hard to find a trustworthy man, one who can think for himself when the situation requires it," he continued while Brodie put together the pieces of what he was telling him.

"I wouldn't trust the two I sent out into the hallway farther than I could throw either one," Brown admitted. "Or the one you obviously made it past downstairs. Then there is yourself." He smiled.

"You're just the sort I need. You have worked both sides. You know how the system works, the sort of people I deal with. You have the reputation for being straight up and not afraid of anything or anyone."

Brodie watched him, the way the man stretched his legs out, hands still on the top of his desk, and that smile.

"Yer offering me employment?" he asked simply because it seemed ridiculous.

"I would call it a partnership," Brown replied. "I want to expand my business interests, and it occurs to me that it could be profitable for both of us. And it's not as if you are still with the MET. Barrels of wine would be considered only the beginning."

A man with ambitions. He wanted to laugh, but didn't.

"I have my own business, and it suits me well enough."

"You haven't asked me what I might know about the two murders—the Rose Murders, that fool at the Times called them."

Brodie didn't care to be indebted to the man. He preferred it the other way around. But if there was something the man knew about the murders...

"What do ye know?"

"I know that one was the daughter of the barrister, Sir Mallory, and the other the daughter of Judge Cameron. And then the flower that was left on each body. No common street criminal would waste time on such a thing. A reasonable man might ask himself what do they have in common?" He smiled.

"You have what you wanted now?"

Brodie nodded. That and more, he thought, the meeting obviously at an end.

"It now seems that you owe *me* a favor," Brown casually mentioned as he sat back in his chair.

There was that smile, but not the sort that anyone who knew him would want to see across a table.

"There is a man, Carstairs, who has worked for me in the past. He got caught by a young constable eager to make marks for himself and unaware who he was dealing with."

"Go on," Brodie told him.

"He's in the Old Bailey under a sentence of five years. I hear that you know people in certain places who can assist with a word or two from you."

He was speaking of Sir Avery with the Agency—the man did know things. A favor then, for the information he'd just learned.

"I will see what can be done."

It was as far as he was willing to agree, with the certainty that it would require another arrangement with Sir Avery, something he had hoped to avoid.

Brown nodded. "I'm curious," he then added. "Do you still carry the knife yer partner in crime gave you?"

Brodie didn't bother to respond.

"I thought as much," Brown answered his own question. "I warned my men and while I am fairly certain they could eventually take you down, not before losing a leg or an arm. You have the reputation, Brodie."

He stood then, a tall, broad-shouldered man, with tattoos down the length of both arms, and cold, hard gaze.

"You know where to find me when you have word about Carstairs." He held out a hand.

It was like shaking hands with the devil.

Brown nodded. "And that offer for work stands."

Brodie was cautious as he left the building the same way he had entered, with revolver in hand. The only surprise was that the man at the back entrance was no longer there.

He crossed the street. The hound was still there and looked up at him expectantly.

"There'll be no fight tonight," he told him.

The hound whimpered. He could have sworn the beast was disappointed.

It was well after midnight as he left Holborn, the hound beside him, and found a driver on his way back to the service yard. He climbed aboard and the hound followed.

He nodded to the Mudger as they returned to the Strand and the hound leapt down from the coach. Then he climbed the stairs, still carrying the damp and cold from the past hours on the back streets and a past that he had left behind, but not far enough.

He didn't expect her to be there. She had left a note and then gone to Sussex Square. Still, there she was, stirring now under the covers of the bed as he set the bolt on the door, then hung his coat.

"Are you all right?" she sleepily asked, then he saw the faint glow of the bedside lamp as she turned up the flame.

A simple enough question that they'd each asked each other before when out and about on an inquiry case.

He didn't immediately reply as he returned the revolver to the drawer in the desk, then pulled the knife from the waist of his trousers and placed it there as well.

Then he went into the bedroom with its bare floor, simple

furnishings, and the shade pulled low on the window with the sound of icy rain upon the glass.

He took off his boots, laid his trousers over the back of the chair beside the bed, turned the flame down on the lantern, then slipped into bed and pulled her to him.

Her warmth drove back that cold, empty feeling deep inside that had been a part of him for so long, and was there tonight as if he couldn't escape it.

"Aye," he whispered against her hair.

Now, everything was all right.

Nineteen

#204 ON THE STRAND

BRODIE and I had returned to the office after taking breakfast at the Public House.

I had updated my notes on the chalkboard the night before, after returning to find that he had been to the office, and had then left again. Mr. Cavendish had been present, minus the hound that had been sent along with Brodie.

I had now added what he had learned from his meeting with a man by the name of Brown.

Brodie knew a great many people from his time with the MET and before. Mr. Brown apparently operated a very lucrative business in smuggling, extortion, and everyday street crime, with a network of associates, as Brodie put it.

Just your everyday successful businessman. And exceedingly dangerous, according to what the Mudger had shared with me.

"Yet, you went to meet with him," I pointed out, and left that open for a response. That dark gaze met mine.

"Old business," he replied. As if that was an explanation.

"Did you consider that it might be dangerous?" Even as I said it, I thought that I might have sounded a bit like a nagging wife.

"What I mean is..." I started to explain. There was an amused smile behind that dark gaze.

"I know wot ye mean. The most dangerous part of it might have been the hound mistaking me afterward for one of Brown's men."

He then asked, "Wot time are ye to meet with Sir Laughton regarding the information he was able to obtain?"

"Ten o'clock."

He nodded. "I'll just go with ye. I may have some questions for him." He had grabbed a towel from the bedroom and went to the door with soap and towel in hand.

"I have a need to wash off the street," he explained as he left the office and went down the landing to the accommodation that had been added some time before and included a boiler for hot water, wash stand, and marvel upon marvels, a flush commode!

When he returned, he shook water from his hair, and smelled delightfully of soap.

"Can ye be ready by quarter past?" he inquired as he towel-dried his hair. It fell into waves about his neck. "That should leave enough time to reach his office."

"I am quite ready now," I replied.

I had already dressed for the day and my notebook was in my bag, while he stood there in trousers, bare of foot, without a shirt in spite of the cold and the rain—he was after all a Scot and they were quite used to such things. However, I was still not used to the sight of a half-dressed Scot with that light dusting of dark hair across his belly and...

I quickly went to the bedroom and retrieved a clean shirt and tie, then returned.

He handed me the dark-blue muslin shirt he'd worn the night before, then slipped his arms through the white shirt, which was far more presentable, and buttoned it.

When he would have tied the tie himself—always a frustrating endeavor that usually brought on several curses—I brushed his hands aside.

I felt that dark gaze on me.

"I never had anything that was truly my own."

I looked up. Everything I might have expected—some comment that I was taking too long, and I was, deliberately so. To his simply deciding not to wear the 'bloody thing,' nothing could have surprised me.

For once, I couldn't think of anything to say.

"On the streets, wot ye find is wot has been cast off, that no one wants any more. In my time with the MET... we were always looked at with suspicion, even hatred, by those we came across in a crime.

"Here," he glanced around at the office before continuing. "There are things that are just... things. Pieces of furniture, the desk, yer chalkboard. Oh, there is the Mudger—Mr. Cavendish and that bloody hound. But they dinnae belong to anyone. At least not the hound."

"What about Munro?" I reminded him.

"Aye, and like a brother to me. But he doesna belong to me either." He reached up and wrapped the hair that fell over my shoulder around his fingers.

"For the first time, there is something that is truly mine." He pulled me closer and lightly kissed me.

I might have pointed out that I didn't *belong* to him either, although I suppose that was splitting hairs over it all as we were married, and that had meant making a commitment to each other. I understood what he meant. More importantly, I knew where it came from.

"We don't want to be late for our meeting with Sir Laughton," I reminded him. "We do have a case to solve."

We arrived on time for our meeting, and were immediately shown into Sir Laughton's private office.

"The legal community is actually quite small," he explained after his clerk left and closed the door.

"We know who the barristers are as well as other lawyers, the major firms in London, and very often most of their clerks as we often work together on cases, or across from each other in court.

"Through someone I know, I was able to learn the name of the firm that represented Harris Imports as well as Simon Harris, the owner of the import company. As you will see at the top of the copy of the trust document, his lawyer was Sir Elliott Mainwaring, Esquire, both in matters regarding the business and personally as well. And still is, according to provisions in the trust document, which he had one of his people copy and certified it to be exact," he added.

"Even though Simon Harris is dead?" I asked.

"As you will note as you read through the copy of the trust, it is what is called a *living document*, in that with certain provisions, the terms of the trust continue on even after the death of the person it was created for.

"I am certain that you are aware of the provisions of the trust that her ladyship has created for yourself and Lady Lenore. It is much the same here, with the particular provision that Mr. Carney, employed as manager of Harris Imports, is to continue certain responsibilities as outlined."

"We have learned that he is compensated," Brodie commented. "How might that happen?"

"Through a bank account established at Lloyd's Bank. They would have a copy of the trust agreement as well, for such purposes."

Somewhat familiar with the language of such documents after my great-aunt created her trust, I noted several similar provisions, one in particular made for the upkeep of the family burial sites at Hampstead, along with the provision that had established Lloyd's Bank as recipient for any additional funds through "Mr. Harris's business," and compensation for Mr. Carney to be distributed by the bank, with a record of account kept.

There were, of course, other legal provisions. There was the family home in Knightsbridge, which was to be sold, along with other holdings, and Harris Import ownership in four cargo ships.

Simon Harris had obviously been a very successful business-man. There was one other piece of information that drew my attention. The date of the trust was September 12, 1881, barely three months after the death of his wife, and only days before that tragic warehouse fire where he died.

"Might it be possible to obtain information from the bank regarding Harris Shipping?" I asked.

I wondered what Mr. Carney was paid the past years for 'over-seeing' what was left of the warehouse, along with possible other transactions with the information Brodie had learned about Mr. Carney's other enterprise downriver of the docks.

Sir Laughton handed Brodie a letter with a wax seal on it.

"I anticipated that you might ask," he said. "That letter is a legal notification instructing the manager at Lloyd's Bank to accommodate your request for that information. If there is any difficulty, I could provide a special warrant for the information, although that is most unusual."

I wasn't at all certain what we might learn as we left Sir Laughton's office and gave the driver instructions to take us to the bank.

We already knew from the information Brodie had learned that Mr. Carney was paid a small stipend to watch over the ware-house site at St. Katherine's Docks. The only part of what he'd learned from his meeting the night before with Mr. Brown was that Carney also had a smuggling operation, it was said, farther down river, south of the main London docks.

The manager of Lloyd's Bank was quite hesitant at first.

"This is most irregular. Our customers' information is private and held in strictest confidence," he first objected.

"We understand, sir," Brodie politely replied. "However, this is in the matter of a private inquiry of great importance. Yer assistance might very well aid in the resolution of a serious crime, which I am certain ye would not want to obstruct."

I knew he could be very persuasive and had seen and heard it before. I called it his *polite forcefulness*, which usually brought results from whoever was on the other end of the conversation.

Admittedly there had been that same forcefulness in that conversation in Scotland when he had proposed to me. Of course, there were various methods of persuasion. I listened to that now, along with the look Brodie gave the manager. I would not have refused if I had been on the other end of it. But then...

"Perhaps there is someone else we might speak with in the matter," Brodie continued. "The president of the bank, perhaps. And we are prepared to provide an official warrant for the information."

That decided the matter, as the manager very quickly withdrew his concerns and objections.

"That will not be necessary," he assured us. "I will have the information provided immediately, if you will wait in the private office we have for our customers."

He promptly showed us to that office, then quickly excused himself to retrieve the information we had requested.

"Very persuasive," I complimented Brodie. "You would have convinced me to cooperate."

That dark gaze was still quite serious.

"I can be, when I want something."

Were we still speaking of those account records?

The manager returned promptly with a bank clerk and two ledgers.

"These should provide the information you are looking for." He had the clerk deposit the ledgers on the desk.

"If there should be anything else, you have only to let this young man know and he will provide it." There was a stern look that passed between them.

I caught the frown on Brodie's face. Volumes of records, entries in ledgers, a stack of papers, receipts, and letters, were usually met with that same reaction. I rounded the desk in the office that had been provided, sat in the chair and opened the first ledger for Harris Imports.

"How did you ever manage to file reports when you were with the MET?" I inquired as I started through the entries that went back more than twenty years.

"I usually persuaded someone to make them for me," he confessed. "With me telling them the details, of course."

"Of course," I replied.

There were others who used dictation for their notes, particularly in the courts, where clerks recorded the details of a trial or hearing in official records.

My publisher, Mr. Warren, had recently explained a new invention used by another author, that recorded his voice onto a cylinder, which could be then be played back and transcribed by a clerk typist. It was very similar to the phonograph invented by Mr. Edison some years before.

I quickly scanned through the earlier entries. Harris Imports had been a very lucrative enterprise, with receipt of cargoes noted, bills received and paid with substantial profit. The entries notably changed at the time of the horrible tragedies for the Harris family.

There were entries for invoices paid and entered by a clerk for a funeral, then for a second funeral. There was a brief pause with only entries for payments received, which seemed reasonable, given Harris business.

The entries changed as I found those payments that were made to Carney. They were made regularly and in the same amount each time, no doubt for watching over the warehouse site, as he had explained to us. Then, there was a significant change in the dates and the amounts of transactions in the year following the tragedy.

"Ye found something?" Brodie asked.

He had been pacing the office, then took a seat in the other chair, but had begun to pace again.

"Just over a year after the death of his daughter and wife, and the fire at the warehouse, there were substantial withdrawals from the account."

He rounded the desk to see what I had found. I had written

down several entries on one page alone and quickly added them up.

"These alone come to almost four hundred pounds." I showed him the list. "And there are more on the next several pages. There must be several thousand pounds that were withdrawn from the account just with the ones I've found, and there are more, including those made just the week past."

"The question is, who made them?" Brodie commented on the obvious.

"This says they were made by Carney, but for what purpose?" I added.

"I don't know anything about that," the bank clerk who had brought the ledgers and stood guard as if we might steal something replied.

At least one of our questions was answered.

"The cash withdrawals were made to a man by the name of Carney, according to the document the bank has for Harris Imports. It's been in place for some time."

According to a copy of the same trust document we now had.

"The first transactions were quite small, and then increased substantially," Brodie pointed out.

"Yes, it does appear so. I handled some of those myself. You can see my initials in the last column."

"And you didn't question them?"

"We have the document authorizing the withdrawals. There didn't seem to be any reason to question them."

"Why was the amount increased?" I asked.

"It was explained that it was necessary for maintenance of the estate properties. Our manager, Mr. McDaniels, approved the change, and it continued thereafter."

Brodie and I looked at each other. Maintenance of the estate properties?

"And these other transactions to M. Stevens each month?" I asked.

That most certainly couldn't be the warehouse site, as all that remained was the storeroom. Admittedly there had been cleaning of the site after the fire, but that was several years in the past.

"Mr. McDaniel approved those as well."

"And it seems that Mr. Carney continued to receive his usual stipend of one thousand pounds per year."

"That is correct," the young man replied.

It made no sense, I thought, as we left with the new information we now had. But what did it mean?

"M. Stevens?" Brodie commented as we found a coach and climbed inside. "Ye know of it.?"

"Moyses Stevens Florist, in Belgravia," I replied. "One can order floral arrangements for special occasions. Aunt Antonia has used them for years. They make deliveries and decorate as well. I would imagine she will have them provide flowers for the wedding."

It was not all that unusual, particularly in the case of a death. However, it did raise the question, who ordered the flowers? And whom were they for?

Mr. Carney had been authorized to make certain banking transactions based on the trust document. I suppose it was possible that he had ordered the flowers, however it hardly seemed something he would be concerned with. And then there was the information Brodie had learned from Mr. Brown.

And what of that very generous stipend he continued to receive? Through my great-aunt's various business interests that Munro handled for her—apparently similar to Mr. Carney's position with Harris Imports—I was aware that substantial amounts of money often exchanged hands with trusted employees.

"A large enterprise such as Harris Imports wouldn't have been able to cease operation overnight," I pointed out as we left the bank. "I imagine it would have taken some time to end operations, with cargos still arriving and bills to be paid for those.

"Perhaps," Brodie replied.

He sat across from me in the coach, arm braced on the open

window in spite of the rain, chin propped on his fingers in that way when he was deep in thought.

"Or perhaps not," he commented. "Most transactions could have been handled with a draft to the bank, much the same as Munro makes for payment of her ladyship's bills.

"I have heard him complain over the number of drafts he is forced to write each month." There was a faint smile. "No easy task for someone who learned to count on his fingers."

He was thoughtful once more. "There would be no reason for cash to pay transactions, unless..."

I finished the thought. "Unless, it was something illegal? Mr. Carney's business enterprise downriver, perhaps?" I suggested.

"Aye, it would not be the first instance of an employee to take advantage of his employer."

"Even so," I pointed out. "What does that possibly have to do with the murders of Charlotte Mallory and Elizabeth Cameron?"

We returned to the office on the Strand. I added the information we had learned that morning at the bank, then stood back and stared at the board.

"What are ye thinking now?" Brodie asked.

"We need a new list."

"Yer almost out of room. We may need to acquire another board."

I ignored his sarcasm as I began a new list of the names of those we had spoken to and each one's connection to either Charlotte Mallory or Elizabeth Cameron.

It was late afternoon when I finally stood back from the board. I had a headache that was beginning to throb quite seriously, my back hurt from bending over as I made the last part of that long list, and I hadn't eaten since a pastry early that morning as we left for our meeting with Sir Laughton.

I had made the list in the order we had met with each person we'd spoken with, including Sir Mallory and his wife, Judge Cameron, and Daniel Eddington.

What did that list tell us? Something? Anything?

"Come along," Brodie said as he rose from the desk. "Ye have that look on yer face."

I turned from the chalkboard "What look is that?"

"That look as though ye might take the next man's head off. I've seen yer temper, and dinna want to be that man."

"I have no idea what you are talking about," I replied, more than a little put off that he thought he knew me that well.

"It's that look," he pointed out. "The one ye get when ye've gone too long without food. Ye have the look of the hound."

I didn't know whether to be flattered or insulted. I had a soft spot for the hound, to be certain. He was very intelligent, but he was also an independent sort who might take himself off at any moment. Admittedly, he did have an enormous appetite, mostly sponge cakes and biscuits with an animal carcass thrown in for good measure.

"You are mistaken," I told him and summoned my most indignant expression. "I am nothing like Rupert. I am far cleaner in my personal habits and not given to biting one's leg off just for sport."

"Both which I am grateful for."

We locked the office, then set off across the Strand toward the Public House. Mr. Cavendish was not about, and I fully expected to see him there with the hound.

The smell of food reached us as Brodie held the door for me, not wanting to make me wait further for food as he explained it.

The fare of the night was stew with an assortment of vegetables, and fresh baked bread.

"It's good you are here early," Miss Effie commented as we took a table very near the bow windows that looked out onto the Strand.

"With the dockers' strike and their meetings, we were out of food last night by half past six in the evening. I heard they're back at it tonight as well. If they don't settle their grievances, we won't have any food to serve.

"If you need Mr. Cavendish," she continued, "I convinced

him and the hound to take the room at the back with the weather out."

"Not at all," Brodie assured her.

The stew was hot, just the sort of food that warmed one through on a cold evening. However, Brodie barely touched his.

It was often like that when a case was most perplexing. I recognized it now in the expression on his face, the way those dark brows sharply angled together and his frown showed, surrounded by that dark beard.

"What is it?" I asked as Miss Effie returned and refilled our coffee cups.

"There's more to this, something we are missing," he replied.

I set down my cup. I felt the frustration as well, along with a growing uneasiness. I had made certain that I included everything we had learned since taking the case.

Yet, I had learned from Brodie's experience from his time with the MET that some cases went unsolved, like the Whitechapel murders.

He had warned me about it from that very first case we undertook to find my sister. I had refused to accept it then, and refused now. I was not of a mind to tell Lily that we had failed to find Charlotte Mallory's murderer.

We returned to the office.

The coal fire had burned low and it had grown cold with that sharpness that usually came before snow.

Brodie put on more coal as I removed my coat, then went to the board.

"Motive, means, opportunity." Chalk in hand, I repeated what I had learned early on in our investigations.

According to Brodie it was always there, it was simply a matter of discovering each one and that would reveal who had committed the crime. And in trying to find each of those during an inquiry case, we were able to solve the case. Usually.

"Yer talking to yerself, lass," he pointed out as he came up beside me and studied the board.

"There are times when it is helpful. It helps me think. It has to be there," I replied. "It's just a matter of going back over everything. We already know what *means* were used to kill both Charlotte Mallory and Elizabeth Cameron.

"The *opportunity* was quite obvious, when each was alone, returning from an appointment or having met earlier with friends. Not robbery, nor assault," I continued.

"What then was the *motive*? Who would want to kill two young women, and why? And a red rose, like a bloody calling card! What does that mean?"

We then went back over everything we had learned about the murders:

Two young women encountered alone and then murdered.

Two families devastated by those murders; Daniel Eddington left to mourn the loss of the woman he hoped to wed.

The letter Charlotte Mallory had received from Cora Walmsley.

The discovery that Johnathan Walmsley had been paid a substantial amount of money to leave London years before.

The fact that the Harris warehouse manager, Mr. Carney, had been paid a stipend each year since the tragic death of Amelia Harris.

Rumors from a man Brodie knew that Carney had built a smuggling operation at Queen's Dock on the tidal basin not used by the larger cargo ships.

That bank ledger with those entries for transactions, current as of the last month.

"It's here. I know it is," I insisted with growing frustration as I stared at the board.

The question was, what was it?

The dram of whisky Brodie had poured for each of us when we returned to the office, along with the heat from the fireplace, had begun to have its way with me. He took the tumbler from my hand.

"Ye'll not find it tonight. Yer tired. Go to bed," he told me.

He was right, of course. I had never been able to solve a problem by chasing it down. It was often necessary to leave it, then come back at it.

"And yourself?" I asked as I gave in to the fact that I wouldn't find the answer that night and that Brodie knew me so well.

"I'll be along straight away," he replied.

'Straight away' turned out to be several hours, as I wakened and discovered the bed quite cold beside me.

A light glowed under the door to the adjoining office. I pulled the comforter around me and left the bed.

Brodie was at his desk, a thoughtful expression on his face as he stared at the chalkboard.

The fire in the coal stove had burned low and the room was quite cold. I glanced at the clock on the wall next to the desk. It was well after three o'clock in the morning.

"Have you found something?"

"There is no such thing as a coincidence," he replied.

Twenty

HE ROSE from the desk and went to the chalkboard.

"It's here, in yer list of names." He picked up a piece of chalk, and began to connect each name to information we had learned as he explained.

"In that previous case of Amelia Harris's murder, Gerald Ormsby never went to trial after the one witness, Mr. Walmsley, disappeared.

"Within a matter of weeks after the charges were dismissed, Gerald Ormsby was dead, in what was described in the new articles ye found as a riding accident.

"We learned that Simon Harris established a trust very near the same time that the trial was dismissed, before he died in that fire," he continued.

"We also learned that substantial payments have been made from the trust in the care of Mr. Carney, as well as regular payments to the florist. And 'coincidentally,' a rose was left at the site of both murders?

"Also, according to details of that trust, Mr. Carney, the former manager of Harris Imports, has been receiving a substantial annual stipend to manage the properties of the estate that include that warehouse site at St. Katherine's Docks.

"In addition, from what I was able to learn from Mr. Brown, Carney has been dealing in certain 'shipping' operations."

He finished by circling Carney's name.

Coincidence? No coincidence.

Was it possible, I thought, that Gerald Ormsby's accident was no accident at all?

I studied the information in my first list.

Gerald Ormsby died after his trial was dismissed. That was followed by that tragic fire at the warehouse where Simon Harris had died.

"How is that connected to the murders of Charlotte Mallory and Elizbeth Cameron?" Even as I asked the question, the possibility was there.

"Ye said it yerself, lass, the rose in each case—like a calling card."

"What would be the motive?"

"The daughters of the two people directly involved in setting Gerald Ormsby free all those years ago."

If that was true..."And you're saying that Carney is responsible? But why now? What reason?"

"That is what I intend to find out. I'll be at the docks when Carney arrives for the day, for the work he supposedly does at the warehouse next to the Harris Import site. And ye need to pay a visit to the florist to see wot ye can learn about that payment made to them each month."

I knew precisely what he was doing, sending me off to question the florist. However, before I could protest...

"It's important," he explained. "It could tell us where the flowers are sent. That could tie Carney to the murders."

He was right of course. "And it keeps me out of the way if there should be any trouble from Carney."

There was that smile. "I wouldna want ye to hurt the man before I can question him further in the matter."

We'd had the conversation before, in fact several times, about that overbearing Scot habit of attempting to protect me. It could be important to learn what information the florist had. I would concede that much.

"I know the florist shop quite well. They are not open until nine o'clock. I have time to return to Mayfair for a change of clothes before calling on them."

He had already returned to the bedroom for clothes suitable for calling on a potential criminal, the coarse woolen trousers and jumper that he preferred to white dress shirts and a fine woolen suit.

I had learned that one could take the man out of the streets, but not the streets out of the man. And I had to admit that he cut quite a stirring figure with that dark beard and overlong dark hair under the cap he seized from the coat stand. Very much like a brigand or the smuggler he was going to see.

"I will see ye back here afterward," he said with a nod and a rather brief kiss.

"You will be careful..." But he was already gone, the sound of his boots on the stairs fading as he reached the street.

I made coffee, then dressed, as there was still sufficient time to return to Mayfair before setting off for Belgravia, where the florist shop was located. I sipped coffee as I studied the chalkboard and the information Brodie had added.

I trusted his experience, and it did seem that Mr. Carney might very well be the connection we were looking for.

By the time I was ready to leave, the rain had let up, and Mr. Cavendish appeared on the sidewalk.

"Do you want to take the hound along, miss?" he inquired.

I glanced past him to where Rupert lay in the alcove, head resting on the stones at the entrance, the rest of him still inside.

"He obviously needs the rest," I replied.

"He was out late last night in spite of the weather. Didn't show up until daybreak. Out causing a ruckus no doubt."

Mr. Cavendish managed to wave down a driver and I climbed aboard.

"No need to rouse him," I replied. "I believe it's called *beauty sleep*," I added and gave the driver the location of the townhouse in Mayfair.

"Well, then, he won't be up and about until late in the day."

At the townhouse, I washed and dressed for my visit to the florist shop. Mrs. Ryan appeared in the parlor, carrying a tray with coffee and biscuits. There were a substantial number of the biscuits.

"Mr. Brodie is not with you," she commented.

"He's off and about on an inquiry," I replied as I entered notes into my notebook about that last conversation with him before he left the office.

"And you will be off as well?"

I had dressed for the weather in a long, split skirt, sturdy walking boots, and a warm jumper over my shirtwaist.

"A call I need to make this morning."

"The mail is on the hall table, and you might take the extra biscuits with you for the hound."

I smiled. In spite of her complaints when the hound had stayed over at the townhouse, she had a definite fondness for him. Though she would never admit it.

I waited for her parting comment. And there it was.

"They'll only grow stale, and no sense wasting the food."

Rupert would very definitely appreciate the thought.

I finished the biscuits and coffee, and placed a telephone call for a driver. I had just finished making my notes when Mrs. Ryan announced that he had arrived.

"There will be more rain," she said as she met me at the entrance. "Best wear your long coat and don't forget your umbrella. It's good that you have several, with the ones you leave at the Strand."

"It looked like it might clear for a while earlier," I commented. She shook her head.

"It will be a downpour most of the day. I have it on good authority."

We were obviously speaking of an Irish saint. She did believe in them.

"And you will be careful?"

She was much like an over-protective mother. Yet, I knew where it came from.

"Careful as church mice."

She made a scoffing sound very much like Brodie. "And you can protect yourself? There are dreadful people the places you go, and don't try to tell me different. Mr. Brodie should be with you."

I thought a flower shop hardly measured up to 'the places' she referred to. I patted the bag I always carried.

Moyses Stevens's shop on Victoria Street in Belgravia might have looked like any other shop front on the street, with those narrow, bowfront windows, dwarfed on either side by establishments with far more imposing entrances. Except for the royal warrant displayed in one of those windows.

The shop and the creative, extravagant displays they provided were well known across London. My great-aunt always called on them for her special occasions, holidays, and my sister's upcoming wedding.

The shop bell rang overhead as I entered. I was always fascinated by the fact that the narrow entrance led to a narrow hall with a reception desk, the rest of the shop opening up beyond. And always a fresh, extraordinary arrangement on display at the desk, no matter if it was raining or snowing outside.

I was greeted by the woman at the desk and asked to speak with the owner. I assured her that it was not over some disappointment with their service. She proceeded to make Mrs. Stevens aware that I wanted to see her.

"Lady Forsythe," she greeted me when she arrived. "It is a pleasure to have you in our shop again."

We exchanged the usual greetings.

"Is there something I can assist with for yourself or possibly Lady Montgomery?"

"There is a matter of grave importance that I hope you can help with."

"In whatever way I can," she assured me.

We sat at the client desk.

"You have an account for Harris Trust, or possibly Simon Harris?"

She nodded. "Yes. It's an old account, paid regularly each month by the trust."

"Can you tell me what it is for?"

She sat back, somewhat surprised. "I am not in the habit of divulging client information. You do understand that I have a responsibility to maintain discretion for my clients."

I assured her that I did.

"I suppose there is no harm. The account is for flowers to be prepared on the eighth day of each month, and specifically made of white and pink lilies. Those were the instructions put in place after the deaths of Mr. Harris's wife and his daughter."

I assumed that meant delivered to a cemetery. I was not a regular visitor to them. It was something I hoped to put off for some time. And my send-off most certainly was not going to be in a gloomy, overcrowded piece of land with others moldering in their graves beside me.

I was quite certain that some London property developer would come along and seize the land for a new rail station or a cluster of residences. Someone would be given the responsibility of moving the graves, and I had visions of attendants losing their hold on my casket, dropping it, and my bones rolling out onto the ground. Not for me.

I was determined that my send-off would be very much like what my great-aunt had planned, in a Viking long boat, set afire, then put adrift out to sea where no one could drop me.

Of course, I did need to convince Brodie of my plan in the event that I went first.

"Where are they delivered?"

"The bouquets are not delivered; a man picks them up promptly at ten o'clock in the morning."

Carney, perhaps?

"He's never given his name. He simply provides the same note, signed by Mr. Harris when he first requested the bouquets."

I described Carney.

"That is the gentleman."

I would hardly have called him a gentleman.

"Has there ever been a request for other flowers? Perhaps red roses?" I inquired.

"Yes, quite recently. When he arrived to pick up the bouquets, he requested two red roses to be added to the order."

Two red roses, like a calling card left behind by the murderer.

"And he returned just yesterday. Quite unusual, I thought, as it was not the usual day of the month."

"Returned? For what?"

"For another red rose," she replied. "When my assistant commented on it, as it was unusual that someone would return for just one flower, he replied that it was for someone very special."

A third rose? For someone special? His next victim?

I thanked Mrs. Stevens for the information, then quickly left the shop.

On the ride back to the Strand, I kept thinking about what I had learned.

A third rose—for the next victim?

Carney had been the one to pick up the bouquets each month, that I assumed were meant for the graves of Harris's wife and daughter. But what did the roses have to do with it?

Red roses—symbolic for passion.

What did it mean? What was Carney's part in all of this? Was he the murderer?

According to the information Brodie had learned from Mr. Brown, the man had been operating a shipping enterprise downriver, unknown to the port authorities but well known to those who operated smuggling operations and other illegal activities.

He had worked previously for Simon Harris, as manager of the warehouse at St. Katherine's Dock, and then as a sort of care-taker, as it were, put in place to carry out certain tasks after Simon Harris died.

But for what reason?

We knew the *'opportunity'* in each of the murders as well as the *'means,'* the bodies left mostly untouched with a red rose left on each one, like a calling card, a message left at each body.

But what was the motive?

Was it as Brodie had surmised, that it was related to the tragic murder of Amelia Harris years before?

Why now? And who was doing it?

I signaled the driver with my umbrella to quicken the return across the city.

Brodie cursed. It was well past ten o'clock in the morning and the man still hadn't shown.

He had reached the docks in good time and waited in the shelter of the adjacent warehouse where he could keep watch when Carney arrived.

Workers had eventually arrived, not the same as the ones he'd seen earlier, but a scraggly lot from the streets. It seemed the dock-workers had chosen not to return to work, as those meetings Effie had spoken of apparently continued.

The warehouse manager looked up as Brodie approached.

"If you lookin' for work, there's enough to go round," the man told him. "I have a ship coming in today and I need to move all of this to make room. The bloody strike is costing me every day, and now a new cargo. But you look as if you can handle the work."

Brodie explained that he wasn't there for work, he was looking for Carney.

"The filthy bugger," the man spat out. "He knew we had cargo comin' in, but it's like him to disappear when you need him. He was here before first light, said he had to take care of something downriver." The man gestured across the loading bay of the warehouse.

"Took off out of here like it was somethin' urgent, and he ain't been back. If I wasn't so hard-up for workers, I'd send him on his way for good. Now I have to get these men working meself to make room for that cargo that's due in."

Brodie thanked him for the information. He had an uneasy feeling about what the man told him. Something urgent downriver that had Carney at the dock before first light?

Instead of going to the high street to find a driver and return to the office, Brodie returned to site that had once belonged to Harris Imports.

He shook his head at the thought, from that instinct acquired on the streets. She would have laughed at the notion, considerin' the number of times that he had teased her about her woman's intuition, and that little voice. But it was there, and if he was honest with himself, she was right more often than not.

She called it 'that voice' that had cautioned her more than once. Call it whatever she liked—intuition or experience, it was there now taking him toward that locked storage room that had survived the fire years before.

With the warehouse reduced to burnt-out timbers and ash, what was the reason to lock the storage room after the fire?

Tools perhaps? Or possibly items that Carney used for that downriver enterprise Mr. Brown had spoken of?

Only now, as he approached, the padlock was open and the latch pushed aside. He slipped his hand into his coat and retrieved the revolver as he slowly pushed the door open to the storeroom.

Daylight slanted in through the opening and revealed no one

was inside. He returned the revolver to the waist of his trousers and took out the hand-held light he had brought with him.

He quickly swept the light across the storeroom, the walls where the usual tools a dock worker might use hung—spars and grappling hooks. A cot for sleeping stood to one side, along with a handful of a man's clothes, the room apparently where Carney slept of a night. Not what Brodie would have expected with those large sums of money withdrawn according to that bank ledger.

There were bottles on a shelf. Two empty, one half full.

It seemed the man was inclined to the drink with a preference for gin, along with a wet spot where he had no doubt spilled the drink before leaving.

Intuition or experience, Brodie brushed his fingers across that wet spot. More gin? It was a wonder the man was in any condition to leave on that 'urgent matter,' he thought as he went to smell the residue fully expecting a bit of those familiar fumes. He suddenly stopped.

Not gin, nor any other soothing spirits that might be found in the local tavern but something else—something he knew well enough from past experience—chloroform.

It was faint, but the sharpness of it was still there. Now the question was, what need did a man like Carney have for chloroform?

He left the storeroom as he found it, then quickly made his way to the high street behind the docks, found a driver, and gave him the address of the office on the Strand.

Bloody rain, Mikaela thought, as she arrived back at the office and stepped down in the flood of water that washed over the curb onto the sidewalk.

With the rain, the flooded streets, and the usual London traffic, it had taken very nearly an hour to return. It was now close to midday, and Mr. Cavendish was there, squinting up at her from under the bill of his hat through the pouring rain.

"It's good to see you, miss." There was an urgency in the greeting. "Mr. Brodie returned earlier. He's up there now with a visitor."

A visitor? And that unmistakable urgency? Had Brodie discovered something after he left to find Carney?

I quickened my steps, mindful of the wet stairs, as Mr. Cavendish saw the need for some reason to announce my arrival and rang the service bell on the end of that rope at the top landing.

The door opened before I reached it. That same urgency was there in Brodie's expression, and on Munro's face as well.

I could tell that something had happened.

"What is it?" I asked.

Brodie was there as I entered the office, his hand on mine. I glanced about the office, past Munro to the desk, and saw it. A single red rose lay on the desk.

Twenty-One

I LOOKED AT BRODIE. There was something in that dark gaze, something he needed to tell me. I then looked at Munro. He shook his head.

"Something's happened."

"I took the girl to the dressmaker's this morning," Munro explained. "For the dress she's to wear to the wedding. I then had Hastings take me to see to other errands for her ladyship. When I returned..." He shook his head again.

"She was taken from the shop when the woman went to make changes."

Taken?

"By whom?" I demanded and barely recognized my own voice...the confusion, then the fear that followed.

Impossible, I wanted to tell them both. It could not have happened that way. Lily was strong and resourceful. She would never have been taken. She would scream, curse, and fight, and very likely the other person would be the worse for it. After all, she had that knife that Munro had given her.

"There must be some mistake," I insisted. "Perhaps she left on her own."

"The seamstress saw the man take her, but was unable to stop him," Munro explained.

"She would have fought back," I insisted.

"I found something in that storeroom at St. Katherine's Docks earlier."

There was something in Brodie's voice that sound ominous. "The man verra likely used chloroform. There was a stain from a bottle on a shelf."

I tried to grasp everything he was saying.

"There was a note left along with that rose," Brodie added, his voice oddly calm.

I had not seen it at first among the papers that usually covered his desk. I stared at it.

"What is in it?"

I caught the look that passed between Brodie and Munro.

"Tell me!" I demanded.

Munro looked away, and the fear inside me was like a fist that closed around my throat. Brodie's hand tightened around mine, the other gently took me by the arm.

"It says we should not have interfered."

A warning? A threat?

"No!" I protested.

Brodie took me into his arms. If there was more to the note, I didn't hear it, my face buried in the front of his jacket as he held onto me.

I tried to push him away. Far stronger, he held on.

"Not Lily!" I was angry, terrified, then angry all over again. Old feelings from when my sister disappeared returned, painful. I wanted to scream and curse. I did both.

And when I had worn myself down as Brodie held me and stroked my back, "We have to find her."

"Aye."

I wanted answers. I wanted to know who had done this. Why?

"We will find her," he assured me as he brushed the hair back from my cheek.

Munro had taken himself out of the office and onto the landing. He stood with his back against the outside wall of the office, his head bowed.

"He blames himself," Brodie explained. "If he had not gone off to see to those errands...it might have been different."

That slowly sank in. Perhaps. But the truth was that he couldn't have known.

I went out onto the landing. It was cold, and wet, and miserable. I laid a hand on Munro's arm. He looked up, and I saw everything I felt in the expression on his face.

"I would cut off me arm to protect the girl."

As dreadful as that sounded, I knew it was true, that unshakable Scot loyalty to their own, very much like Brodie.

I shook my head. "And what good would that be? You will need both arms to help us find her."

Horrible as the situation was, I caught the faint ghost of a smile on his mouth.

"We will find her," he said. "And make no mistake, those that done this will pay."

Time was precious, and difficult as it was, we needed to think what was to be done to find Lily.

"According to Mr. Brown, Queen's Dock is where Carney set up his 'business' operation." Brodie told Munro. "The man at St. Katherine's this mornin' told me that Carney was there early and said that he had business down river. It is verra likely he took the girl there."

"Ye trust Brown?" Munro asked.

"He wants a favor. I trust him that far." He looked over at me, "And the entries in the bank ledger are proof of his little enterprise. Apparently, goods are smuggled in, as the coast guard no longer patrol that area, then sold for a keen profit."

It made sense, still it was a terrifying possibility that they might be wrong.

"The man will know by now that we're aware the girl is gone," Munro pointed out.

Brodie nodded. "But he doesna know wot we have learned from Brown or what I learned this mornin'."

"Aye, that could be an advantage. We will go to the docks," Munro replied.

There was more. However, he chose to speak with Brodie in that language they shared that I knew little of.

"While I don't understand what is being said," I protested, "I will not be spoken over as if I am not here."

A look passed between them. Munro nodded.

"I will make the arrangements and return here."

There was a brief look in my direction as Munro left.

"What arrangements? How are we to do this?" I asked.

"It will be dangerous, for Lily and anyone attempting to find her," he replied.

I heard the unspoken, and I was not having it.

"I understand that very well."

"Mikaela..."

I heard it coming. It was that old argument and I knew where it came from—his need to protect me.

"I am an excellent marksman and I can help," I pointed out. "I will not be set aside in this. If..." I started to say, then changed what I would have said.

"*When* we find Lily, she may need me. I am going with you."

"Aye. But ye will do as I say, and there is no argument in it."

Munro returned in little more than an hour. He had changed clothes and now wore a black turtleneck jumper, trousers, and a black jacket, with a billed cap against the rain.

"Ye have everything we might need?" Brodie asked. A looked passed between them.

I could only imagine what that might include.

"Aye, in the alley behind the smoke shop." Then he added, "It will take a good hour to reach the docks."

Brodie nodded and went to the chalkboard. He drew a diagram.

"We'll go by way of Cannon to Victoria Steet. Is the livery stable still there?"

He seemed to know that part of London well.

"It is," Munro replied.

"From there," Brodie continued, "we make our way to the river and the docks."

"There are only two buildings still standing," Munro added. "If the man has taken the girl there, she will be in one or the other."

And if she wasn't there? I chose not to think about that.

Munro was obviously familiar with the area as well. As I listened, I reminded myself that there was a time before Brodie was with the MET...two young men surviving on the streets of London as best they could, and whatever that might have included.

Brodie had spoken of it, dismissing it out of hand. Yet, that experience was there. I had long suspected there was far more behind that almost stoic demeanor and that intense dark gaze. It came as no shock that I had married a man with somewhat of a dark past.

I would take that against others I had known, I thought. A man I had learned that I could trust.

"We go in together as far as the back of the warehouse," Brodie was saying, then came away from the chalkboard.

"Then I will take one and ye the other."

Munro nodded. "There is a watchman who keeps an eye on the warehouses from a shanty at the docks. I will see to him," he added with a look over at me.

"And another inside, I've seen." He retrieved the rather ominous-looking knife in a leather sheath that he always carried and I had seen before. He tucked it into the back of his trousers.

"What about Carney?" I inquired.

Munro looked over at Brodie. "If he's there, he will most likely be inside the one warehouse where ye said he was doing a bit of business."

"Aye, "Brodie nodded. "Still, we have no way of knowing where he's taken Lily. We need to keep him alive long enough to find out where the girl is."

I knew what he was saying and pushed back any misgivings or feelings of guilt over what they intended.

"We should go while there is still light," Munro said.

The weather had not eased. His coat was dark in places as he had not bothered with an umbrella. Brodie was dressed much the same, in worn clothes, as he had been earlier that morning.

Anyone who saw them would assume they were nothing more than common workers, perhaps like those Miss Effie had spoken of, hoping to find work.

I went into the adjoining bedroom. My worst fear was that we might be too late, that Lily might have come to harm, or worse.

"The thought will do her no good," Brodie had told me when I voiced my fear.

I knew he was right, but it was still there.

I had worn a walking skirt for my travel to Knightsbridge earlier in the day. With a jacket over, hardly the sort of costume that would disguise me. Still, I had my stout walking boots, wool neck scarf, and long coat.

It would have to do. Time was critical and I would not delay long enough to return to Mayfair for something more appropriate. And there was always the possibility that Brodie and Munro would take the opportunity to leave without me.

There had been that brief conversation when I had no idea what was said. I would not have put it past either one of them.

"I am ready," I announced as I returned to the outer office.

I had already checked the revolver that Brodie insisted I carry when on an inquiry case, and I had slipped the knife Munro had given me down the inside of my boot.

Brodie had set the time to leave for ten o'clock that night, as that would give anyone at the warehouse where we hoped to find Lily time enough to be well 'into the drink,' as he described it.

I ignored both of them as I put on my long coat, and pulled on a brimmed hat against the rain. I didn't wait for either acknowledgement as I pulled on my gloves, then left the office.

I found the wagon at the back of the smoke shop and found Mr. Cavendish with the team of horses.

"You'd best take the hound for what you need to do."

Rupert sat on the pavement beside Mr. Cavendish's platform.

"I would go with you meself, but someone needs to watch the office."

Brodie shook his head as he and Munro arrived in the alley and climbed atop the wagon.

"Not this time," Brodie commented with a look at the hound.

"As you say," Mr. Cavendish said as he moved to one side of the team.

Munro picked up the reins and the horses set off down to the far end of the alley.

Brodie was probably right about the hound. We had no way of knowing exactly what we were going to find when we reached Queen's Docks, and it was a good distance from the Strand. It was probably best that he remain.

Still, there was no way of knowing what Rupert might do on his own. He was, after all, a creature of the streets. Not unlike the two who sat in the front of the wagon, I thought as I caught sight of Rupert trotting behind the wagon.

Then, as we reached the end of the alley and Munro turned the team toward the main thoroughfare that would take us along the river to Queen's Docks, Rupert leapt into the back of the wagon.

"Good boy." I scratched his ears and then ordered him to lie down under the wagon seat, out of sight.

It took almost two hours to reach Victoria Street, then very near another hour on a street filled with wagons and carts in spite of the rain. After that, we headed down an adjacent roadway toward the river.

The rain had not let up the entire way, and I had soon joined Rupert under the wagon seat with the edge of the canvas pulled up.

The wagon eventually slowed, and there was the faint nicker from the team in that way of horses greeting other horses.

We had reached the livery Munro had spoken of, and he guided the team behind the small corral and shed where it might not be noticed.

I pushed back the canvas as Rupert jumped down, circled the wagon, then returned, waiting expectantly.

"What is that bloody animal doing here?" Brodie demanded as Munro circled round the other side of the wagon to the back and threw back the canvas.

"He jumped into the back of the wagon," I explained. "There was no stopping him, and I was certain we could not delay to return him to the office."

"No stopping him? Did it occur to ye that it might be dangerous for him?"

"He has proven himself most capable in the past," I pointed out.

Munro had retrieved an ax from the back of the wagon. He handed it to Brodie.

"If Lily is here, there are things that will have to be done tonight," Munro said as he looped a second ax through his belt.

I understood.

"I'm going with you." And before Brodie could make his usual objections, I continued. "If something has happened..." I didn't want to think about it; however, two young women had been murdered. "If she is here," I continued, "and has been injured, I can help. I'm going. And that's the end of it."

The objections were there, then his expression softened.

"Aye. But yer to do exactly as I tell ye."

Munro had already set off, keeping to what remained of the

shadows as he moved toward the first warehouse. Brodie and I followed.

Dozens of thoughts ran through my head. If Lily was there, what if she was injured? How would we find her? The answer to that particular question brushed against my leg as we stopped where we had last seen Munro. Rupert looked up at me expectantly.

We followed as Munro moved around the side of the warehouse to the front of the wharf and boat landing, then eased one of the large doors open. He glanced back and held up two fingers.

"There's two inside," Brodie whispered. "Stay here."

He joined Munro and they slipped through the doors.

Several moments passed, then there were sounds of a struggle. There was a shout, followed by a curse, then silence. In spite of Brodie's instructions, I ran to the entrance of the warehouse.

Rupert bolted inside and I followed, then stopped.

Two men lay on the floor of the warehouse, one at the back where it looked like he might have attempted to leave, the other only a few feet away from where I stood.

Munro stood up from over the nearest body and wiped the blade of his knife. He looked at me, then called out to Brodie in a low voice.

He came from the back of the warehouse where I had glimpsed that other body.

"The hound seems to think that she's here somewhere," he said, taking my arm and turning me back toward the entrance and away from that body.

I forced myself past the sick feeling at what I had just seen inside the warehouse. It wasn't as if I was not aware what both were capable of, and I had seen dead bodies before. Still, it was the possibility that we might not find Lily alive.

"Is one of them Carney?"

"He's not here," was all he said.

That meant that he was still out there, somewhere, as well as

Lily. And with that warning shout I'd heard, he would know that we were here.

Munro quickly joined us, his tall frame discernible in the fading light. He inclined his head toward the second warehouse, then moved in that direction.

Brodie hesitated, his hand on my arm. I knew what he would have said. I moved past him to follow Munro.

The second warehouse was nearer the water, with a landing at the edge of the river. Munro moved along the near side. Brodie stepped past me and followed him.

There had been no sign of Lily at the first warehouse. Was she inside this one?

And with it again came the thought that she might be injured. What would happen when Brodie and Munro entered the warehouse? Another scene like the first, only worse?

I was about to go after them when Brodie returned. He shook his head. They had not found her.

Anger was followed by tears that stung my eyes. She was here, somewhere.

"We have to find her!"

He nodded.

"There are several shanties along the wharf," Munro said. "She could be in any one of them."

And it would take time to search them. Time we might not have.

Rupert grew restless beside me. He had gone with Brodie and Munro into both warehouses and had found nothing.

He knew Lily. In fact, the two had struck up a strong friendship when he had accompanied me to Sussex Square. He had tracked me, more than once. Yet I knew it was from his sense of scent.

I whispered to Brodie, my hand resting on top of Rupert's head.

"He might be able to find her."

I knelt down beside Rupert.

"Find Lily," I told him. "You must find Lily. Go."

Rupert looked at me expectantly and I began to think it wouldn't work. My heart sank. Then he was off, as I had seen him before, nose to the ground, tail sticking up straight as an arrow. I went after him.

Brodie and Munro followed, searching the first shanty at the wharf as Rupert circled then ran to the next one. And the next one, as my thoughts raced.

As it grew darker with the fading light, we ran along the waterfront, Rupert racing before us. And all I could think of was Carney.

Was he in one of those huts? Where was Lily? Was she still alive?

A baying sound came from just ahead at the wharf. Had Rupert found her?

The blow almost took me to the ground. Then I was dragged back to my feet, a fist wrapped around my hair, and a too-familiar smell of drink, sweat, and traces of chloroform.

I fought, but the long coat tangled about my legs as I was hauled back against a thick male body.

"What have we here?" Carney spat as I struggled to reach the revolver in my coat pocket.

Carney was taller and stronger, the beard on his face scraping my cheek, the smell of him choking me. Unable to reach the revolver, let alone the knife in my boot, I thrust my elbow back hard into his midsection and tried to spin away from him.

There was a sound of surprise as the blow took the air from his lungs. I would have escaped except for that meaty paw of a hand on the front of my coat. He hauled me back against him, his hand around my throat.

A shout, his name, and Carney spun back around, taking me with him.

Then Brodie was there.

"Let her go!"

Carney shook his head, his breath hot and foul against my

cheek as his hand tightened around my throat. I could hardly breathe.

"Let her go," Brodie repeated, a hand-held lamp in one hand, his revolver in the other pointed at Carney. "I'll not say it again."

I thought for a moment that Carney might release me, then his hand tightened and his other hand came wrapped around the hilt of a knife. If I could have said something past that strangle hold Carney had on me, I would have told Brodie to shoot.

I knew the risk, but I trusted him.

I looked at Brodie as Carney dragged me back with him. I saw something in the expression on his face, the bleak, dark look in his eyes, and knew what he was about to do.

Gunfire exploded in the dark, the sound echoing off nearby huts and the crumbling buildings that lined the quay.

Carney staggered as he continued to pull me with him. Brodie fired again and Carney went down, taking me with him.

I fought my way out from under that wretched body. And Brodie was there.

"Is he dead?" I whispered past my bruised throat.

He knelt down beside Carney's body.

"Aye."

"Good." It came out as little more than rasping sound, yet horrible as some might think it, I was glad that he was. But what did it mean for Lily?

"The bloody hound has found the girl," Munro announced as he reached us.

"She's alive."

Carney was forgotten. Brodie took my arm and we followed Munro past the hut to the wharf that ran along the riverfront. He swept the beam of a hand-held lamp across the heavy timbers of the wharf. The light found Rupert and an iron grate that he excitedly circled.

A thin voice called out from below that grate. Lily!

"Are you all right?" I asked as I knelt beside the grate.

Her face was pale in the light of the hand-held lamp, her eyes wide and dark. A slender hand was wrapped around one of the bars of the grate.

"It's cold and there's a lot of water. It's getting deeper."

"The tide is comin' in." Munro said in a low voice. "Ye can see just beyond, on the building along the way—high water mark. It floods during high tide, and it's already up to her knees."

"Aye, we have to get her out."

"It would take too long to go back to the wagon for rope," Munro added.

Brodie nodded and unbuckled his belt. "Take off yer belt."

After they both removed their belts, they looped them through the bars of the grate and then tied them off.

"The water is higher," Lily called out.

Brave girl, yet I heard the fear in her voice.

"Stand away," Munro told her. "The timbers are rotted. If we can move this, they may give way.

And she could either be crushed or swept away by that rising tide.

"Miss?" She reached through the grate with a thin hand. "I thank ye."

Farewell? Not bloody likely.

I took her hand in mine. "It *will* work."

I refused to accept that it would not.

She nodded then pushed herself as far from the opening as possible as Brodie and Munro both pulled on those leather straps they'd made at the edge of that iron grate.

It creaked and groaned, then slowly lifted, an inch, then two. As it did, the thick timbers that surrounded it buckled and then fractured, jagged ends protruding up from the deck as water swirled just below.

"More," I told them. "Just a bit more."

Another inch, and another. I thrust my hand down into that gaping hole. A cold, slender hand took hold.

Another timber gave way as they pulled again at the grate, and that opening widened.

I grabbed Lily by the back of her gown with both hands. She pushed her way up through the opening as water surged around her. We fell back, a tangled mass of arms and legs, very much like two fish flung onto the deck. But she was alive. I hugged her fiercely.

"Are you all right?"

"I knew ye and Mr. Brodie would find me. And Munro." Her smile was a bit wobbly through the tangled mass of wet hair and some obvious bruises on her cheek and neck. And my first thought was if Carney wasn't already dead, I would have gone back and killed him myself.

Munro had gone quiet, relief obvious on his face. Then he looked up.

"The hound."

It was Rupert, but hardly the baying sound when he found Lily. The sounds were vicious, frantic barking and snarls.

Munro had warned there might be others, part of Carney's smuggling business. He and Brodie had already found two others.

A man loomed up out of the darkness beyond the circle of Brodie's hand-held lantern. He staggered and lunged, a knife clutched in his hand.

He was dressed in a frayed, dark-blue wool suit, white hair wild about his head, a crazed look in his eyes, and his face, his expression amid the vivid burn scars twisted as he threw himself toward us.

"You should not have interfered!"

His voice was thin, hardly more than a whisper, but the words were the same as in that note. He was almost upon us.

There was no time to retrieve the revolver. I pushed Lily behind me.

There was a different sound, then a dull thud as an axe embedded in the man's chest.

He remained standing for a moment as though suspended by strings like a puppet as blood spread from the wound and soaked the front of his shirt. He tried to say something, but no sound came out as he fell back, just beyond that circle of light.

Munro stepped past me and went down on one knee beside the body as he swept the light of his hand-held over the man who had tried to attack us.

He was thin beneath the blue wool suit of clothes that any man of society might have worn, except for the stains and the frayed cuffs. Now, it sagged in loose hollows, the once-white shirt covered with blood as he stared sightlessly past Munro.

It wasn't the clothes, so obviously out of place here, but his features, the scars and marled flesh on his face, a mask I thought at first, and scars on his hands, a knife clutched in one.

And yet...there was something familiar, as I remembered the stooped figure of a man on the street days before, there watching.

I looked over at Brodie. "I don't understand. Who?"

"Simon Harris."

It took me a moment, everything we had learned, the lies, the murder of another young woman years before.

It made sense in a strange way as we returned to the wagon with Lily and the hound, then made the long ride back to the office on the Strand at the edge of the theater district, the lights and sounds in stark contrast to what we had left behind.

Upon our arrival at the office, Rupert had jumped down from the wagon quite pleased with himself, and then set off with Mr. Cavendish for a very late supper at the Public House. He deserved it, and more.

I provided soap and a towel for Lily, and she bathed in the accommodation down the way from the office, then crawled into bed in the room that adjoined the office. She took my hand as I tucked her in.

"That man...with the scars. He said he was sorry when that other man put me down in that room. Why would he say that?"

There were no easy answers. An apology perhaps? Madness at what he had set out to do, revenge against those he held responsible for his daughter's death all those years before? Perhaps to ease his own guilt? We would never know.

"Try to sleep," I told her and tucked the blankets in around her. She nodded.

"I don't think I can."

There was a yawn, then she turned onto her side, her eyes drifting closed.

I had telephoned my great-aunt to let her know that Lily was safe with us and would return to Sussex Square in the morning.

There was time enough to sort everything else out tomorrow, and contact both Sir Mallory and Judge Cameron, as well as Mr. Dooley to have the police retrieve the bodies from Queen's Docks.

Munro left for Sussex Square. He would return in the morning for Lily. I was exhausted as well, with my own bruises.

I made use of the accommodations with a fresh cloth and some soap, ignored my own bruises from my encounter with Carney, and returned to the office to find cartons of food on the desk.

"The Mudger sent a boy over. He thought ye might be wanting supper," Brodie explained.

Dear man, I thought.

Along with supper, were two glasses each with a dram of Old Lodge whisky. I needed that, and I needed food. In spite of the gruesome events of the evening, I was starving.

I have no idea what time it was when I suddenly looked up and realized that I had nodded off, and Brodie was there.

He took the empty glass from my hand and set it on the desktop, then proceeded to untie my boots and remove them. He pulled me up from the chair then over to blankets and a comforter spread on the floor.

"It's time fer bed, unless ye want to sleep with the girl."

"This will do quite nicely," I replied.

He added more coal to the stove, checked the bolt on the door, and returned the revolver to the desk drawer. He then joined me on the floor, pulling me against him, then drawing the comforter up over us both.

"Why?" I asked, thinking of the clues on that chalkboard that had taken us to Queen's Docks that night.

"Ye asked what the motive was," Brodie replied, his voice low amidst the hiss of the fire in the coal stove.

And then, "Revenge, for his daughter's death, against the man who killed her, and those who set him free."

I shivered and curled closer against his warmth.

"Will there be any justice?"

"Go to sleep, lass."

Epilogue

I HAD ASKED Brodie if there would be any justice in the murders of Charlotte Mallory and Elizabeth Cameron.

He knew better than most that the answer to that depended on several things, and in the end, it was difficult to know whether justice would be served at all, with those responsible now dead.

The Metropolitan Police was contacted the morning after we returned from Queen's Dock, with a full report provided by Brodie on the events of that evening.

The bodies were retrieved, including those of Simon Harris and the man who had carried out his scheme all these years later, Edward Carney.

Lily had recovered from her ordeal, as she had from other things in her young life. Having lived on the streets as a child, she accepted that she had been in the wrong place at the wrong time when she was abducted, and merely a tool for Harris's revenge scheme.

Taking her had been the means to send Brodie and me a very strong message, that *'we should not have interfered.'* However, we had. If not, Charlotte Mallory and Elizabeth Cameron's murderer might never have been known. Lily felt that she had done the right thing in 'hiring' Brodie and me to find Charlotte's murderer.

It provided some sort of closure for her. Yet, it was small consolation for the loss of a friend.

The web of lies and deceptions spread wider, all the way back to the murder of Amelia Harris five years earlier.

A lover's quarrel to be certain, that had ended badly, when she was killed in a fit of rage by Gerald Ormsby, well-placed in society to be certain. He had counted on his family position to escape prison, possibly even a sentence of death.

Sir Mallory most certainly played his part in the lie. He arranged for the sole witness to the murder to conveniently disappear with a very lucrative payment for the man's silence. Without a witness, Judge Cameron was persuaded to drop the charges against him and Gerald Ormsby escaped the hangman. For a little while.

In the weeks that followed that horrific murder, Simon Harris's wife passed on from a weak heart, weakened further by the death of their only child.

The loss of both set in motion a plan for Simon Harris's revenge against those he held responsible for his daughter's murder, and then the failure of the law to bring Gerald Ormsby to justice.

Only days after he buried his wife, a mysterious fire reduced a good portion of the vast Harris Import warehouse to burnt timbers and ash. The rumor began almost immediately, aided by Mr. Carney, that Simon Harris had perished in the fire.

Whether it was intentional or the result of a man stricken with grief, the story persisted and Simon Harris, badly injured and disfigured in the fire, used it for his own purpose.

The timbers in the warehouse had barely cooled when Gerald Ormsby was killed in what was described at the time as a riding accident in Hyde Park. There were rumors that someone might have caused the accident by startling Ormsby's horse. No one was ever named.

Simon Harris then set up a new enterprise with funds withdrawn from the bank by Carney. The trust had been set up the day after his wife's death, and made it possible for Carney to make purchases from smugglers, then turn around and sell at a profit from Queen's Dock with the coastal guard none the wiser.

A very lucrative enterprise indeed.

Yet, Harris had only just begun. It was discovered in papers found in a small flat very near Queen's Dock, that he had Carney follow both Charlotte Mallory and Elizabeth Cameron for weeks.

He learned their habits, their daily routines, their circle of friends. And then he set his plan in motion—to take from Sir Mallory and Judge Cameron what had been taken from him—their daughters, in an insane need for revenge for the death of his daughter.

But that was only the beginning. The wider circle of his web of lies was meant to also include those who had played a direct part in setting Gerald Ormsby free—Sir Mallory, Judge Cameron, and a man who was a young law clerk at the time, Charlotte's fiancé, Daniel Eddington.

It was impossible to know for certain if Charlotte was aware of Daniel's part in that earlier scheme. She knew about the payment that had been made to Johnathan Walmsley, but had chosen not to believe it, according to the note intended for Mrs. Walmsley that was found in her handbag.

That was something Daniel Eddington would have to live with, as would her father and Judge Cameron.

As for legal consequences, Brodie admitted that it would be difficult to bring charges against any of them, with the victims and both Harris and Carney now dead.

"Perhaps it is enough that they have to live with the consequences of their actions, knowing that brought about their daughters' deaths," he had suggested.

I was most careful in how I explained all of this to Lily. Charlotte had been her friend and she felt that loss deeply, although she tried to pretend otherwise.

With bruises fading, hers and mine, it seemed that we would be able to attend my sister's wedding without causing too much of a stir.

It was to be a small, intimate affair at Sussex Square just before Christmas, a double celebration that included the holiday, with only a hundred guests after my sister put her foot down.

Our great-aunt had originally planned for over twice that number. She was already making plans for a New Year celebration the week after for the hundred or so who would not be attending the wedding.

As the day drew closer, Lily had her final fitting for that new gown. I accompanied her for my own fitting.

Afterward we invaded Harrod's. I called it an invasion, as it took hours, with time spent in each department before Lily decided on a wedding gift for my sister and James Warren

"What do ye think?" she asked. "Will they like it?"

'It' was a glass table ornament, a foot-tall, remarkable glass elephant, reminiscent of our safari in Africa months earlier.

I thought it was magnificent.

"Absolutely," I announced. My sister had wanted to accompany us on safari; however, she was in the throes of pre-wedding planning after Mr. Warren proposed.

I tried to convince her that the *'pre'* part of the wedding planning fell far short of the *'after'* wedding part of all of it.

"Good heavens, Mikaela. Surely you are not talking about...that."

That was precisely what I was talking about. From what I heard about that first go-round of marriage, as Brodie would call it, *that* part of it had been disappointing for her to say the least.

"Not to worry," she assured me. "*That* is quite marvelous."

She did have the ability to surprise me from time to time.

Rupert had settled into his after-inquiry status in the alcove with a new bed. I thought he deserved it. Although Mr. Cavendish was in doubt.

"You'll spoil him, you will. It's bad enough that he goes lookin' for Mrs. Ryan's cakes every time you come to the office."

As for Brodie and the approaching wedding, I accompanied him to the tailor's shop for his final fitting of a new suit. To say it had taken some persuasion was a mild understatement. He preferred his serviceable black coat and trousers or the costume he wore when out on the street, both quite unacceptable for a formal wedding.

"I canna see spending money for something I will only wear once," he had grumbled, with a narrow eye on the establishment as we arrived.

"And I willna wear a man's corset!"

Corset? I could personally attest to the fact that he did not need one.

While it was not customary for a wife or other woman to accompany a man to his tailor, it was the only way I could persuade Brodie. I waited in the salon while he was being fitted for the final time before the wedding, which was then three days away.

As we had no inquiry cases at present, I was making notes for my next book when he appeared in the private salon. To say that he was quite an admirable figure of a man was an understatement.

The suit was black with stripes on the grey wool pants, a gray satin vest, and white silk shirt, with a gray cravat. And the man in it glowered at me.

"I willna wear the bloody cravat. It's a nuisance."

At moments like this I had learned to ignore the glower as if nothing was amiss. I did have to admit though, that he cut a stirring figure. And I couldn't resist.

"Oh, my," I said, as I set aside my notebook.

"That is all ye have to say in the matter? The bloody thing is too tight."

"Let me loosen it for you."

That dark gaze met mine.

"The cravat," he reminded me.

I smiled. Of course.

It was quite remarkable that the wedding occurred three days later without a hiccup. The bride was radiant, the groom was quite handsome, and the celebration went into the evening.

Afterward, I thought I heard the strains of the piano in the small salon. I found Lily there.

"Chopin?" I commented as I sat beside her on the piano bench.

"Miss Charlotte said that if I practiced every day, I might be as good as she was. But I dinna think so."

"I was never very good either," I said with considerable empathy.

"Ye dinna need to be. Yer an author, and a good one, Mr. Warren says. I canna imagine writing a book, or playing a full..."

"Concerto?" I reminded her of the word.

"That's what Miss Charlotte called it."

"I believe it's important to do what you are good at," I told her. "And not worry about the rest of it."

"I ken that one song that I learnt at The Church," she had replied. "But it's probably not right for a wedding."

I remembered it well and couldn't resist.

"Oh, I think it would be perfect."

She hardly needed encouragement and immediately plunged into a tune that was best described as bawdy.

As I joined her, I caught sight of Brodie standing in the doorway of the salon in his Saville Row suit, quite dashing in spite of earlier complaints. That dark gaze met mine as Lily and I sang together.

"There was a girl from Halifax who went about in her garters;
She charged six pence for just a look, and more to share her quarters!"

Author Note

Moyses Stevens Florist shop was established in 1868 in London, and is now the oldest flower shop, with several shops across the greater London area.

Rotten Row was a real horseback riding trail at Hyde Park during the 19th century and still exists, although rarely used today.

It was very possible during the time of the story for someone to disappear from society, as Simon Harris had after that horrific fire.

Discoveries and methods used in this latest inquiry case with Brodie and Mikaela include benzidine to test for traces of blood. Another element was the presence of coal oil after five years.

Impossible, you say? Not so. Under certain conditions it is possible that traces would remain, rare though it might be, which I chose to use for the benefit of the story and the reveal that Simon Harris torched his own warehouse to fake his death.

The dictation machine for sound recording, very much like the later Dictaphones used in the early to mid-20th century, was invented by a Frenchman in 1857, and then later improved upon with a new invention in 1878 by Thomas Edison using a wax cylinder. From there, records (yes, I did say records) and the phonograph were developed. And now we have streaming music.

Anyone who has been to London, particularly in the winter, knows that it can rain quite heavily, which has caused severe flooding of parts of the city in the past. There is now a solution in place.

The Thames Barrier is a steel retractable wall made of gates that can be raised into position across the river to protect from exceptionally high tides and storm surges, then lowered when the danger has passed. It was put into service in 1982.

Of course, it didn't exist in 1891, which resulted in dangerous flooding during heavy rain and tidal surges, and included the threat at the end of the story with the flooding of that underground chamber.

Queen's Dock still exists, modern, and new. However, at the time of the story, due to the accumulation of centuries of silt at that part of the Thames, the river had become quite shallow, and larger commercial cargo ships required deep water ports at the London Docks.

On a personal note: I had to put Brodie in a tailored suit from Saville Row at the end. Who could resist? Certainly not Mikaela Forsythe.

And next:

Danger, murder, and that growing relationship between two very different people continues with Book 11 – DEADLY CURSE.

Also by Carla Simpson

Angus Brodie and Mikaela Forsythe Murder Mystery

A Deadly Affair

Deadly Secrets

A Deadly Game

Deadly Illusion

A Deadly Vow

Deadly Obsession

A Deadly Deception

A Deadly Betrayal

A Deadly Scandal

Deadly Lies

Merlin Series

Daughter of Fire

Daughter of the Mist

Daughter of the Light

Shadows of Camelot

Dawn of Camelot

Daughter of Camelot

The Young Dragons, Blood Moon

Clan Fraser

Betrayed

Revenge

Outlaws, Scoundrels & Lawmen

Desperado's Caress

Passion's Splendor

Silver Mistress

Memory and Desire

Desire's Flame

Silken Surrender

Angels, Devils, Rebels & Rogues

Ravished

Always My Love

Seductive Caress

Seduced

Deceived

About the Author

"I want to write a book..." she said.

"Then do it," he said.

And she did, and received two offers for that first book proposal.

A dozen historical romances later, and a prophecy from a gifted psychic and the Legacy Series was created, expanding to seven additional titles.

Along the way, two film options, and numerous book awards.

But wait, there's more a voice whispered, after a trip to Scotland and a visit to the standing stones in the far north, and as old as Stonehenge, sign posts the voice told her, and the Clan Fraser books that have followed that told the beginnings of the clan and the family she was part of...

And now... murder and mystery set against the backdrop of Victorian London in the new Angus Brodie and Mikaela Forsythe series, with an assortment of conspirators and murderers in the brave new world after the Industrial Revolution where terrorists threaten and the world spins closer to war.

When she is not exploring the Darkness of the fantasy world, or pursuing ancestors in ancient Scotland, she lives in the mountains near Yosemite National Park with bears and mountain lions, and plots murder and revenge.

And did I mention fierce, beautiful women and dangerous, handsome men?

They're there, waiting...

Join Carla's Newsletter

Printed in the USA
CPSIA information can be obtained
at www.ICGtesting.com
LVHW040254301124
797932LV00005B/1158

* 9 7 8 1 6 4 8 3 9 7 5 4 7 *